Praise for LATE DAWN

"*Michelle Tanmizi dedicates her life to Creating Consciousness. Late Dawn is an insightfully-woven tale that is destined to create considerable consciousness about the future of the environment and our interaction with Mother Nature. It's a must read for anyone who cares about saving Planet Earth.*"

— **Todd Miller**, CEO, Celestial Tiger Entertainment

"*Beautifully crafted and inventive, Late Dawn comes to us at a critical time for our planet and our species. Michelle Tanmizi shares her passion for the environment and for animal rights on the pages of this thought-provoking book.*"

— **Jolinde den Haas**, Independent Film Producer &
Film Festival Programmer

"*In a very creative and inspiring way, Michelle managed to combine fiction with reality, as a reminder to us all that time is running out and we must start to take the earth and all inhabitants seriously and everyone can act!*"

— **Femke den Haas**, Animal Activist and Founder,
Jakarta Animal Aid Network

"*Ms. Tanmizi introduces us to a world at once alien to 21st century humans, yet of our own making. Despite this, our narrator, Marra, has a loving upbringing, yet some recollections suggest hidden truths. Late Dawn may be SF, but are we on a path that makes it prescient? An interesting read for all those concerned by how we are treating our planet. A 'thumbs up' for this debut novel from Michelle Tanmizi.*"

— **Andy Griffiths**, Scuba Instructor, Hong Kong.

"*Michelle has written an incredible book that is both compelling and provoking. It invites us to think beyond our time and to consider what history will have to say about us as a generation.*"

— **Denica and Bertram Flesch**, Founders of SukkhaCitta,
a sustainable fashion company. Denica Flesch is a
2019 Forbes 30 Under Honouree

"*Despite years editing various novels across genres, Tanmizi has managed to surprise me with a highly engaging science fiction story that eerily parallels current scientific trends, especially related to genetic engineering. This is one of those stories that forces you to invest in the protagonist and feel her highs and lows as she experiences them, resulting in a narrative that is difficult to put down. I applaud the efforts Tanmizi has put forth to create a believable world that both pushes the bounds of imagination and inserts a subconscious awareness of a possible dystopian future, and look forward to her future endeavors in this competitive genre.*"

– **Sam Strozzo**, International Editor and
Candidate for PhD in Media and Communications

"*Intense and thought-provoking, **Late Dawn** is an eye opener for the fact that 'actions create results'. It shows the importance of finding harmonious ways of co-existing on this planet we call home.*"

– **Danielle Martins**, International Best-selling Author of *Rising up from Mental Slavery—How to Unleash your Infinite Potential*

"*Michelle Tanmizi has combined many of her passions in her thought-provoking fiction novel **Late Dawn**. This exciting story focuses on conservation, animals and human behaviour. Her book may be prophetic and reminds us that we need to make changes today to safeguard the environment or we may face peril in the future. **Late Dawn** will entertain and fascinate you, whilst making you think about ways you can ensure the future of our planet in your daily life.*"

– **Jules Hannaford**, Author of *Fool Me Twice* and
host of Hong Kong Confidential podcast.

LATE DAWN

What happens when Mother Nature turns on us…

Michelle Tanmizi

Permission should be addressed in writing to Michelle Tanmizi at MichelleTanmizi.Author@gmail.com

Editors:
The Online Author's Office: Samuel Strozzo, Max Poloris, Zara Hannaford
Henry Holt & Co.: Libby Burton

Cover Design: Michelle Tanmizi

Book Layout: Anne Karklins

ISBN 13: 978-1-989161-86-9
ISBN 10: 1989161863

To Mother Earth
A kiss for you
From children all around

May angels wipe
Your furrowed brow
So sleep be calm and sound

May Man revere
And choose to hear
Your laughter and your pain

May creatures rest
In kind respect
May balance reign again

ACKNOWLEDGEMENTS

Writing a novel is challenging, frustrating, mind-boggling, and also one of the most rewarding things I have done. This journey would not have started if not for the Online Author's Office, namely Pashmina Reis De Souza. I am grateful for her unfailing optimism and encouragement.

Behind every book is a tireless editor. I want to give special recognition and thanks to the editors, Max Poloris, Zara Hannaford and Samuel Strozzo for their infinite patience and inspiring wisdom in helping me mould my literary work into a novel fit for bookstores. My gratitude also to Libby Burton for sharpening my work further and for the final name of my book, *Late Dawn*. Her confidence in the novel and the story made me giddy with joy and dance like a child high on sugar.

I have dreamed for a long time of holding a book with my name on the front cover and for this, I have to thank Judy O'Beirn and her team at Hasmark Publishing for making this dream a reality!

Thank you also to the team at HopVation Singapore who enthusiastically and with great commitment and care produced the book trailer for *Late Dawn*, making it look like a trailer to a future film!

To all my friends who encourage me on this journey, I am grateful for believing in me; to my family who put up with my typing until the wee hours of the morning, an apology and my relief and thanks for not making me pay the electricity bill; to the reviewers and endorsers of my novel, my most humble and sincere gratitude — your words are the wings which allow my novel to fly; and, to cafes and libraries for providing me a comfortable place to work and caffeine to keep me awake, what would I do without you?

And finally, to all readers and dreamers out there; you are a reason I write. Without you, bookstores are empty, books lie with cobwebs, orphaned and alone, and authors sit dispassionate and lost, wondering where their zest for life went. So thank you; for your love of books and for letting us ignite your imagination!

PROLOGUE

April 4793

Aarav is late for school and running as fast as his legs can take him. If he runs fast enough, he can make it just in time. If he doesn't make it, he will have to stand in the courtyard, in the morning sun, for which his classmates will tease him about later. Worse, it means that he will miss fifteen minutes of the first lesson that day — his favourite class, mathematics.

The journey from home to school is at least four kilometres. Aarav is angry at himself for having lost track of time while he was in the fields with his father. Being the eldest son, he will inherit his father's rice fields and be expected to work in the village, but he secretly wants to be a mathematician and work in an office. He dreams of carrying a briefcase and wearing a clean shirt everyday.

The road between his home and the school passes through rice fields. The land was all forest once but the villagers claimed it and now they grow rice there. The village is growing each year and more land is always needed for more home and more crops.

While Aarav is running, he notices that the trees at the far end of the fields are shaking, but there is no wind. He slows down to look. The little voice inside his head that usually tells him the good from the bad is telling him that something is not right, but he is late for school. He ignores the voice and decides to keep going.

As he starts off again, he realises that the bushes on the other side of the road are also swaying wildly. In fact, all the leaves in the surrounding woods are vibrating, every so slightly. Aarav stops running, and a feeling falls on him.

He looks left and right and again. Then, as if in slow motion, he sees dozens of elephants emerging, but they look out of proportion. They are too big. Aarav looks left and right again. The animals are bigger than any that he has ever seen, as tall as the two-storey house of the headman of his village. They are all waving their ears ferociously and shaking their gigantic heads in what he knows are signs of anger.

He wonders if he needs to return home to tell his father, who is still working the fields as do most of the men in the village. Even his mother and the women will be there helping the men this morning. It is harvesting season and all hands are needed to cut the rice stalks.

The giant elephants fully emerge from the forest, and he can see how massive their bodies are. Then he knows. Aarav turns and runs back towards his home.

But as he arrives at the entrance to his village, he knows that he is too late. He hears screaming voices amidst the trumpeting and growling. The ground trembles with vibrations almost like an earthquake. He runs straight to his house. But it's no longer a house; it's a pile of broken wood, mud and straw. He calls out for his mother, his little sister and his father. There is no response. People are running everywhere. Mr Gupta, his neighbour, is shouting at him to leave.

But Aarav won't go until he has found his parents and his sister, who is only five. The giant elephants in his village are knocking down the mud houses everywhere they go. As Aarav continues his search, he sees his uncle Krishna, running barefoot towards him, a terrified look on his dark face. Just as quickly, a giant elephant trunk curls itself around his uncle's waist, carries him up screaming and throws him against a tree. There is blood splattered everywhere and Aarav's panic gives way to tears. Bodies are everywhere, and the ground is scarlet with blood. The elephants are indiscriminate in their route of destruction. They appear bent on destroying the whole village.

He somehow makes his way to the edge of the village undetected and hides behind a large rock. He cries as quietly as he can. He knows that his family is gone. He sees people running on the road where he was previously, only to be picked up and flung into the fields. The screams are the worst sounds he has ever heard in his young life and Aarav covers his ears with the palms of his hands.

It is dusk when he finally dares to move. It has taken time, but there is silence now, thick and heavy. No more screams, no more trumpeting, no more shaking ground. He can see where his village once stood. The elephants have left. But Aarav does not want to stay there all night; they may return. The closest town, Ajjipura, is four kilometres away.

Finally he walks warily towards the only road that leads out of the village. There are bodies stretched out all along it,. Aarav keeps his head up, not wanting to see who they are, or were. He knows that he will recognise them all. He is afraid that he may see his best friend, Ali or Mr Gupta, or worse, maybe his mother, father or sister. It is one thing to know that they did not survive but it is another to have to see their bodies. He is not prepared for that; he is not strong enough. Tears are again welling in his eyes. He starts running. He does not care if an elephant will see him, he just runs as fast as he can towards the town.

It is dark when he reaches the outskirts. The silence tells him that there too, the elephants have attacked. He walks towards the only building he knows, his school. The gates are broken. The school is nothing more than rubble with half a wall still standing. Aarav can see that the classrooms no longer exist. Still, it is the only place he knows. He picks his way through the debris and makes his way further inside. It is still and silent, the only sound coming from his movements. There are bodies underneath stones and broken walls. He sees small legs and arms. His breaths come in short bursts and his heart feels like it is about to explode out of his chest. Despite this, he continues until he finds an area that is relatively clear. Then he goes to a corner and sits.

News of the giant elephant attack isn't reported until the next day. The World Peace Organisation sends in Peacekeepers to search for survivors. They discover a traumatised nine-year-old boy hiding among the rubble of a devastated school, in the small town of Ajjipura. He is among the few remaining survivors who are evacuated to the north of Old India in a WPO camp.

In a country with a population close to fifteen billion people, the Peacekeepers find only 90,465 alive. The giant elephants did exactly what they set out to do. They took back the territory that was once theirs.

Immediately after the description on the Indian subcontinent, reports start coming in about other animal attacks worldwide; giant wildebeests destroying Neo-Afrika; monstrous sharks, as large as the ancient megalodons, sinking ships; colossal snakes devouring inhabitants of Brasilia; gargantuan, poisonous spiders invading Neo-Australia.

One by one, cities and countries begin to fall.

CHAPTER 1

*"A true conservationist is a man who knows that the world is
not given by his fathers, but borrowed from his children."*
– John James Audubon

15 September 4848

I am sitting on my porch, listening to nature's symphony and
watching nature prepare for the night. It is my favourite time of the
day. The dusk sky is a magical orange-red with improbable tinges
of deep purple and pink. I am mesmerised by the sounds of the
wilderness as the day fades, by the occasional deep howls of the
Primes, three-metre tall gorilla hybrids with an arm span of five
metres and a very bad temper; the roars of the Liogers, stunning
Lion-Tiger hybrids, as large as a High Mobility Personal Tank at
five metres body length and a shoulder height of two with eyes of
liquid gold. These hybrids exist uniquely here in the Federation
States of America or the FSA as we call it, where I live.

Mostly, however, the sounds are those of birds singing. The
giant Mynas are my favourite because hundreds chirp in unison
like a choir holding on to a single note. They drown out all other
sounds. The Mynas normally sing for an hour or so before the
quietness of night time takes over. Then the giant cicadas, frogs,
and owls start their own serenades.

The symphony is brought to me via monitors placed in a
survey zone at least one hundred and eighty kilometres away,
within the vast wilderness that surrounds my habitation on all sides.
That is the area where the dangerous hybrids live. I am placed far

from them for my own protection. The speakers are on my porch so that when I close my eyes, I am transported by the sounds deep into where they are.

It is another typical mid-September evening in another year, seemingly not much different from the last, but a feeling of urgency is growing inside me. I feel that something big is going to happen. I don't know what it will be but not knowing might be the thing that frightens me most. This is why I've decided to record my thoughts whenever I can on my pad, as a journal. Should my feelings of foreboding become reality, maybe this journal will help future generations understand the events that lead to it.

I am a Sympathiser. That is what they call us, people who work for the CAEP, or the Coalition for Animal and Environmental Protection, people who believe in preserving the animals in our growing wilderness, in the forests and jungles around the world. We are based in several places around the globe, but I work for the FSA branch.

Nature has decided to give the animals the upper hand after hundreds of years of being hunted, persecuted and abused. I, for one, am not unhappy that this is happening. In recent decades, thousands of species of animals have become extinct because we decided to steal their territory and make it ours.

The Sixth Mass Extinction of the twenty-first century wiped out about sixty percent of the planet's animal species in five hundred years. The Seventh Mass Extinction started another half a century later, and before the attacks began, we estimated that the planet had already lost fifty percent of the remaining species that survived the last annihilation. Are the Animal Wars part of the Eighth Extinction cycle? If they are, then humans may well be part of that equation. Isn't that ironic? We have orchestrated our own destruction.

Before the animal attacks, Earth or Neo-Earth as we call it today, was a highly developed planet and cities were growing larger with sky-towers, immense buildings, multi-habitations and super-highways. The world population had finally started to increase again year after year since the fallout following the Nuclear World War of 2522 and the ensuing Ocean Surge the year after. Wilderness, forests and jungles around the globe were razed for human occupation and crop fields. Animals that used to live in them were forced into areas unsuited to their species — and those that did not move, we killed.

About fifty years before I was born the situation was calm. Wild animals had hardly been seen for decades. They did not come out into the open except for the occasional intrusion into a human habitat to look for food. Even in Neo-Afrika, animals kept themselves out of sight as much as possible, to the disappointment of tourists and the travel agencies, who have built an industry around attempting to catch glimpses of them.

Almost twenty years later, the former country of India was invaded by a previously unseen pack of beasts that were much larger than normal sized animals. The quiet years had bred bigger creatures and by the time they stormed the Indian cities, they were enormous. There had been sightings, of course, of the giant beasts for years before the attacks, but they were ignored or delegitimised as video manipulations or exaggerations.

The attacks on the Indian subcontinent marked the beginning of the animal invasions, which we now know as Year One of the Animal Wars. India was the first country to fall and now the whole territory is home to one massive, bountiful tropical rainforest. Today, no one except scientists and the WPO military visit India. It is too dangerous as the animals have dominion there.

There have been attempts to kill the newly evolved animals with firepower, but their unusually thick hides are impenetrable to small weaponry. Bombs have been used as well, which were effective in the beginning until the animals learnt to detect drones and scatter, making them difficult to target. In fact, our attacks serve only to provoke and infuriate them further and they retaliate by violent incursions into human zones, killing everything in their path. Evolution has given these new breeds of animals better defences with which to counter human attacks — superior size, increased intelligence and impenetrable skins. There was talk of using nuclear bombs to eradicate them completely, but in the disastrous aftermath of the Nuclear World War, all countries were denuclearised.

The WPO has established themselves a base in a large area to the north of the country, in the foothills of the Himalayas, with the sole purpose of studying the animals. Although country-specific decisions still reside with individual rulers, the WPO has ultimate authority over all decisions that affect the total world population and Neo-Earth.

Thick and high carphite walls and gates have been constructed at the border of the entire Old India to keep the animals in. Once the humans were out of the country, the animals were content to stay within the perimeter.

Carphite is a steel alloy combining titanium, tungsten, chromium, carbon and nickel. It was created in response to the urgent need of a material to build walls to contain the animals. It is lightweight and almost indestructible. Carphite has proven to be one of Man's greatest inventions and has improved our defence systems beyond any invention in the previous few centuries. Vehicles, homes, weapons, combat suits, federal buildings and towers are now all made of carphite and its many derivatives. Its versatility comes from its lightweight nature, its pliability, and its resistance to force. As it is man-made, there is no shortage. All other metals have been replaced by carphite. While plant and tree products have become extremely rare because it is dangerous to venture into forests, plantations, and jungles, mining for ores is still possible.

Old India has been the focal point for biologists, geneticists and the special military forces for decades now. It is Ground Zero. As it is near impossible to kill the animals, the primary mission has become to contain them.

What we did not know then was that Old India was only the beginning. After it fell, the island nation of Neo-Afrika turned. Tribes and villages had to be urgently evacuated as giant animals descended on towns and cities, indiscriminately killing humans;

not just predatory species like lions, but also normally docile herd animals like the zebras, deer and wildebeests went on stampedes and crushed everything in their paths.

Soon after, other animal invasions began all over the globe. It was as if the animals worldwide had organised a synchronised assault on the human population, after the catalytic moment of the fall of Old India. Imagine suddenly having giant animals stampeding through cities, killing everything in their path; it was so unexpected that millions of people were unprepared and lost their lives. Even zoo animals that were previously docile became agitated. The situation in the animal enclosures grew increasingly dangerous and eventually, all of the animals were killed.

While farm animals did not appear to have been affected, most of them started dying of an unknown virus and stopped reproducing. Overnight, farmers found carcasses of their livestock strewn in their fields, coops and pens. The scientists determined that it was an airborne virus that affected domestic animals and to safeguard the population from eating tainted meat, all farm animals were slaughtered and burned.

The wild animals multiply faster than in the previous decades and with each reproduction cycle comes another gargantuan generation. Scientists are unable to find the cause of the animals' sudden spurts of growth, even when some have been captured and dissected for study. What they can conclude from these studies is that the hybrids have highly developed cognitive functions and better defences against physical attacks — thick, impenetrable hides, longer claws, better senses of smell and hearing. With their enhanced intellect, these new animals have the uncanny ability to know when they are being stalked and turn the tables on the hunters, who unwittingly end up as food or simply murdered.

While predators become larger, so do their prey. The only mammal species that remains unchanged are humans. There are theories, of course, on why we have stayed the same. My favourite comes from the Spiritualists; they believe that "humans are perfect the way we are," since our evolution was completed millennia ago.

I take a slightly more pessimistic viewpoint. It seems to me that after too long at the top of the food chain, we are no longer nature's favourite children and so we are now at a disadvantage in terms of size. It is easier to kill us this way.

I've often wondered about the animals here in the FSA. Many are interesting and unique to this country because in addition to changes to their size, strength and cognitive abilities, many creatures here have become hybrids. I read that these genetic anomalies came from laboratory manipulations or tests. They escaped during the Animal Wars and then multiplied and reproduced in the wild. The Liogers and Primes are two such examples.

My parents, and especially my father, told me many tales of how our planet used to be millennia before and how animals were over half a century ago. My mother would laughingly call him a hobbyist zoologist. He studied the ancient animals and together, we would watch the video logs. He often told me that our new FSA hybrids were not so different from their ancient cousins and were not all that complicated to understand. Like humans, they require a safe territory to live with ample food sources. They kill only if threatened and pushed to the limits of their tolerance.

My mother was born in the Democratic States of Asia as Eva Mei and then became Eva Mei Stollen when she married my father, Rolf; she was a small woman with a large personality. She was a geneticist, wildlife behaviourist and medical doctor. She did extensive research into animal behaviour and mutations, trying to find a solution for humans and animals alike.

My father, from the Coalition of Europe, was a wildlife biologist and research scientist, a tree-like man with broad shoulders and kind eyes the colour of forest leaves. That was how they met, in a laboratory — hardly a romantic story, but the way they would tell it, it sounded like the most magical encounter in history.

They were polar opposites in terms of personality — the quiet, absent-minded scientist and his loud, confident wife — but the combination worked well and they complimented each other, like salted caramel. They were in love with each other until their last day.

I have inherited my mother's small stature but not her strong spirit. That part of me comes from my father. I am mild-mannered, shy and awkward like he was. My golden, curly hair straightened itself out when I reached ten years of age, and grew dark brown. My eyebrows are the same colour and are long and arched, giving me a look of perpetual surprise. I have been called pretty when I was fifteen, which made me very happy then, but I am not sure if that description still holds true today, at least from my own viewpoint; confidence is not an adjective I use often to describe myself. You could say that I look neither Asian nor European.

I am named after an ancient region of Neo-Afrika called the Masai Mara. I have only seen it in Old Earth video logs. Its majestic grassy plains and rolling hills are stunning. It is a place my parents had cherished dreams of living in to study wildlife but couldn't, since it is now off-limits to all human occupation.

My father told me stories about how the animals in the old world were much smaller and some were even adorable. After his death, I discovered several short, grainy video logs of how some humans kept animals of their own, and let them live in their houses. They even named them, as one would a child! In one of the video logs, a woman had a cat — a tiny little thing — and called her Molly. I had an academy friend by the same name, and found this amusing. I wonder why these animals were given human names. Was it done to render them more appealing? Less intimidating? Were they treated as children? All this intrigues me. I wish I could ask my parents about them.

I remember my father mentioning 'home' animals, but he never fully explained their function nor told me how and why humans were so attached to them. They called them dogs, cats and hamsters, the last looked a little like the giant rodents we have today. I have never seen a living dog or cat. I only know of Jaguards and Liogers, which look quite similar to the small, harmless-looking, now extinct felines. Dogs, on the other hand, resemble nothing we have today. I would have liked to have met a dog. I imagine it would be a perfect companion for the cold months.

According to my father, these 'home' animals all mysteriously died of the same airborne virus that killed the farm animals. Those that were not killed by the virus were systematically exterminated because humans were afraid that they too would turn against us. Eventually, the WPO sent out a decree that all these animals must be destroyed for safety reasons and this marked the extinction of their species. It must have been difficult, even heart breaking, to kill an animal that had shared your home and been given a human name. I wonder if it would feel similar to sacrificing a child. I don't know what I would do if I was faced with that choice.

Here in the FSA, I work alone in Sector Five, which is in the western side of the country. I am a field agent and have been posted to this Sector for over a year now. It is a large zone, entirely over-taken by wilderness. The CAEP cleared a nine square kilometre area of all bushes and trees and my habitation is right in the centre. Land on a slight elevation was chosen; that way, it is easy to see from the air and allows hovercrafts to land in the event of an emergency evacuation. Being on higher ground also gives me a vantage point to detect animal invasions. Due to global warming, all forests and wilderness even this far north of the equator resemble jungles with dense undergrowth and trees reaching high into the sky, competing for sunlight.

Since the start of the Animal Wars, the north and south of the FSA has been claimed by wilderness and forests. The remaining population who survived the animal attacks now live in three sectors: Fifteen to the west, Nineteen to the south, and the largest, Sector Nine, to the east. Needless to say, these sectors are now protected on all sides by thick carphite walls.

The population has reduced dramatically, but even so, putting the whole country's people in three sectors has caused severe overcrowding. Each occupied zone is crammed with habitation buildings, at least eighty levels high, because they are the most efficient way to put thousands of people in a small space. I am lucky to be living in a habitation and sector all by myself.

In our world, we live completely enclosed, in 'creature-free' environments. These are called lock-down habitations, and they are where all humans must live, by Federation decree. These habitations, whether single like mine or multi-levelled, are computer-monitored and protected by a force field that automatically disintegrates any living creature other than those that contain human DNA. No insects or animals of any kind remain. If we open our windows for outside air, nothing can crawl, slither or fly in. I once saw a giant butterfly turn to ash at the threshold of my porch. Butterflies, although the size of large dinner plates, have never been proven to harm humans. They are beautiful, and graceful, and when I saw that butterfly turn to ash, I felt a deep well of sadness rise in my throat.

Although the Federation will not admit it, we, at the CAEP, know that the force field is actually only effective against insects and smaller animals. For a large animal, it will merely singe its thick skin while it crosses the barrier, which may create enough pain to deter it … or not. The force field gives the population a false sense of security.

My own lock-down habitation is the standard one issued and built by the CAEP. It is a utilitarian design, made to house two agents adequately. I suspect the hospital-white, sterile décor is done on purpose to drive out any notion of comfort and sloth and keep the mind focused on getting the work done.

Where I used to live with my parents at the CAEP compound in Sector Seven, the house was full of colour. My mother would draw on the walls of our old home with petals of withering flowers she collected from the CAEP gardens. She depetaled the flowers, separated them by colour and then soaked them in what she called her 'magic' solution, which I later found out to be a mixture of salt, vinegar, water and alcohol. When the petals had bled out their colour, she then recruited both my father and I and the three of us would paint our home using our palms and fingers. I loved every moment of our days dabbing at the walls. It felt a little like we were marking our story similar to how the ancient cave people used to do on the walls of their dwelling.

The CAEP compound in Sector Seven where I grew up was a large area with tall spruce and pine trees and a carphite wall around its perimeter. My parents opted to live in a small, non-lock-down habitation at the edge of the compound. They had to get all kinds of permissions and exemptions before it was allowed. My father told me with a sense of pride that our house was as close as one could get to the ancient homes humans used to have — no force fields and no sensors. He said that it was how humans normally lived, among the natural environment and animals and not just among other humans.

I recall seeing giant butterflies and sometimes an acorn-sized ladybug flying around inside our habitation. I can still hear the sound their giant wings made. I would dance around with them. My parents wanted me to have a different kind of living environment than the other children — they wanted something closer to what was once considered normal.

An icy gust of wind plucks and throws my hair around, making me look up from my pad. The sky is turning a deeper shade of blue and some stars are beginning to come out, as is the crescent moon. The air is dry, and I catch a hint of tree bark and leaves. I recall jumping around in thick piles of leaves during this time of year when I was still living in the compound. I pull my shawl tighter around me.

I will be twenty-five in a month. Since before my parents died, now seven years ago, I would wait impatiently for this age to arrive, imagining all the 'adult' things I could do and all the countries I would visit. Now the birthday feels unremarkable.

The horizon of trees silhouetted against the sky, the colour of a dying fire, looks like soldiers standing at attention. Looking at a view like this, it is easy to forget that we are facing a possible annihilation of our species if we do not choose our future path well. The Animal Wars that still rage in some countries are brutal, bloody events that rarely end in victory for humans. Here we've managed to negotiate a truce and ceasefire with the Federation Peacekeepers to stop the animal massacres and it appears to be holding — but for how long?

While scientists scramble to find the cause of the animals and the hybrids' enhanced biology or even how to reverse it, the killing continues. I think we are spending too much time trying to understand why our world has evolved as it is now instead of just living with the consequences as amicably and best we can. As my father used to say, "Don't look for Whys, look for Hows."

I get up from the chair I was curled up on, and stretch. Taking a last intake of crisp autumn air, I enter my habitation, sure tomorrow will be another day just like this one.

CHAPTER 2

"Earth provides enough to satisfy every man's needs,
but not every man's greed."
– Mahatma Gandhi

The CAEP was formed five months after the start of the Animal Wars, in September 4793, when our founders were outraged by acts of cruelty to animals. People were killing indiscriminately, regardless of the creature's hostility, seeing danger now in any non-human life. People were torturing and making a spectacle of "reclaiming their power" over animals. Many species were completely eradicated. Fear, it seems, can make monsters of us all.

The CAEP is involved in a variety of projects, but our prime mission is to protect the animals, hybrids included, that we have left. We work with the Federation government who allows us limited and highly monitored access to all sectors that have been overrun. We conduct field studies, monitor behaviour and movements, and share our findings with them. Our presence also allows us to monitor any human activity. It is no secret that there are often groups of people who believe that they can reclaim territory by hunting down the giant animals and killing them with weapons and bombs. They inevitably end up destroying not the animals but the wilderness, leaving in their wake large, gaping blast areas devoid of life. Many are ignorant of the fact that all the animals today can more acutely sense the presence of humans.

The environmental arm of the CAEP works with botanists, entomologists and apiarists to preserve crops and non-animal food sources. Meat is no longer available because farm animals have died of the airborne virus that plagued their species. The virus stopped their hearts and thankfully, caused death to come quickly. The aftermath of the Great Livestock Death was ugly because decomposition developed far more rapidly than usual and within two hours of death, the stench of rotting meat overtook the entire FSA.

With the disappearance of animals for food, Federation bio-scientists started producing laboratory protein compounds that taste similar to chicken and beef to assuage the general population's desire for meat. Toxic effects from these compounds appeared in some people after about a year of consumption, which confounded the bio-scientists. Once the toxins appear in the body, mostly blue-black, grape-sized protrusions, it is a matter of days before death claims the person. There is no known cure for this sickness yet.

More and more cases surfaced to such an extent that the Federation halted the production and sale of bio-meat. In the mean-time, secretly, they continued to research new ways of producing protein and used the population as test subjects. These days, in their desperation to stave off hunger, people eat whatever they can access. Effects of the new compounds vary, but are often still deadly. Due to demand, a flourishing black market appeared with various producers of the sickening bio-meat.

To make matters worse, early this year the Federation discovered, an airborne, flu-like virus killing thousands in all the human-inhabited Sectors, which they nicknamed the Mammalian virus or M virus. By summer, the Federation government claimed they had it under control, that they had discovered a cure. They say the M virus was caused by mammals, one of which is the Bantou, a giant hybrid of the ancient bat, which raised the anti-animal sentiment level in the whole country to a new high.

I am not convinced that the theory holds because the viral outbreak is limited only to the cities. My intuition tells me that it is more likely caused by something that is in the human zones and spread through bodily contact. But the population believes the Federation reports and anti-animal sentiment continues to rise.

I was raised vegan, like all Caepians. Mission Control has spectacularly large gardens and fields where we grow fruits, vegetables and flowers from heirloom seeds. Their mission is to continue to extract as many seeds from each crop and keep them for future generations. We eat only what we grow, so we have assurance that what we are putting into our bodies is organic food without genetic alteration. Green leafy vegetables are still farmed but overall output is decreasing, so today, we eat mostly root vegetables and grains. Bees are slowly disappearing from global warming effects and years of being exposed to industrial agricultural pesticides. Most insects, bees included, remained at their normal sizes with the exception of a few species of bugs and butterflies. The CAEP bee keepers have been collecting and farming honeybees for pollination of fruits and vegetables. When they too are gone, there will be famine.

As Caepian children, part of our education revolves around agriculture and gardening. Experimentation with species is strictly forbidden and at the academy, we were told stories of some Caepian scientists who had been banished because of meddling with the natural world. Their intentions may have been honourable, but it violates our core belief, which is to live and co-exist with nature without alteration.

I often wonder what would happen if we could have predicted our current situation — could we have prevented the disasters that happened? The Nuclear World War was probably man's single most devastating act against our planet because it led not only to the melting of the ice caps, the Ocean Surge and extreme weather conditions, but also the start of the Tectonic Motion and the destruction of forests that changed the balance of the atmosphere and warmed the planet. In fact, our planet changed so much that it was renamed Neo-Earth in 4600.

Humans, it seems, are taught to live for the moment, but it's obvious to anyone who cares to consider the facts, that in our quest to live fullest in the present, we forget the importance of the future.

We have, if we are lucky, a century to live.

The CAEP was founded by Leo Sanderson, a multi-billionaire philanthropist. One of his grandchildren, Rupert, now runs the organisation, but Rupert is grooming his only daughter, Olivia, to take over the CAEP as he approaches retirement.

The family lives on a floating, state-of-the-art, island fortress up in the north, disconnected from the world for their own protection. Caepians are not popular. After all, they call us Sympathisers because we assist and protect animals. Many people do not believe in our cause and call us terrorists of the earth. Many want us dead.

Each agent habitation is protected for that reason. Only the Federation and the CAEP possess details of our locations. The CAEP Defence Unit is tasked with keeping us safe because the Federation is not concerned about guarding us — the less we are out in the wilderness, the more animals they can eliminate. It is no secret that the CAEP's mission vastly differs from that of the Federation. They would like nothing more than to see all animals wiped from the face of our planet. Our presence is a hindrance to their goal.

Thankfully, the Sandersons have the WPO's full support and sympathy and they ensure that we have the FSA's 'cooperation'. The Federation acquiesces to our presence and grants us access to the wilderness in exchange for our expertise on animal behaviour, genetics and data on their migration. But our relationship with them is controversial and fragile, based on mutual benefit and begrudging respect. We have long suspected that they use the information to eliminate the animals, but we lack concrete proof. The founders keep them close to monitor their activities.

In the FSA, our Mission Control is located in same compound where I grew up, in Sector Seven. There is no force field around the perimeter, in keeping with the CAEP's philosophy of not harming any living thing. As the CAEP is the only organisation allowed in Sector Seven, everyone there is under strict orders not to leave the compound. It is more than just a place to work. It's a city all on its own. We have an academy, a hospital, a Defence Unit, a communications office, a science and research facility, a physical training facility, and large vegetable, fruit and flower fields. Senior members of the CAEP are given private habitations, while others live in smaller ones in large buildings. Through the years, people started calling this little city Seven.

I'd like to think that Seven resembles ancient towns, while human habitation zones today are displays of carphite-concrete multi-level habitation structures, sky-towers and work buildings. They are all stripped of plant and insect life, each a forest of carphite-concrete and glass.

In Seven, there are spruce and pine trees that line the streets and wildflowers and weeds that peek out through the cracks on the concrete sidewalks. Birds find their way onto the spruce branches and greet passers-by with calls and songs.

Before the CAEP took over the compound, Seven was a town of nearly ten thousand. None of them survived the first wave of animal attacks and so the city laid in ruins until we arrived and rebuilt it. It is now a functional place with office and habitation buildings on both sides of a main road that leads from the airfield to a large, white gravel square in the centre of town. Some remnants of the old city remain. There is a partially broken, concrete sign at the entrance that reads: "Welc_m_ _o WAR__N". As children, we used to fill in the gaps and make up all kinds of words — welcome to Warren, Warden, Warton …

On some corners, there is a bench under a simple shelter, which I assume was where public transportation used to stop. On a side street from the main thoroughfare, are austere statues in bronze of a middle-aged woman in a dress that covers her feet, sitting and looking up at an older gentleman with a curly moustache who appears to be reading to her from a book he holds in his hands. At the bottom of the statues is a plaque in embossed bronze that reads: "Icelandic settlers". As a child, I used to sit under the statue after my classes and imagine stories of who these settlers could have been.

Seven is currently on loan to us by the Federation. My parents became permanently stationed there as scientists and researchers when I was six and I lived there until I obtained my first field agent posting out of the compound fifteen years later.

Before we moved to Seven, when my parents were still doing field work, we lived in a non-lock-down habitation in the centre of a jungle zone, in the south of Sector Three. It was a dark green place among trees and plants. We stayed until I was five, and I have a handful of fleeting memories of that house, almost swallowed by vines and foliage.

I don't recall much because I was very young then, but random memories pop up, such as showing my parents my blackened feet, from running shoe-less all day long in the dirt following a giant beetle. I also remember my father making me promise never to venture beyond the metallic poles he planted around the house. I found out later that they contained perimeter sensors. I recall the bird songs outside my window at dawn just before my mother came into my room to prepare me for breakfast. I even have a vague recollection of the smell of the area — a clean scent, like freshly cut grass.

That was when my father began carving small, wooden animals for me. He started this when I was a baby. By the time I was six, I had amassed a large collection, from Liogers to Bees.

Contrary to what many had thought would happen, the animals never invaded our space. My mother told my five-year-old self that we were learning to live with animals, which I now know as an experimental living arrangement to assess the possibility of co-existing with animals. I was too young then to know the importance of that statement and the impact of the experiment. But one day, out of nowhere, I remember my mother carrying me out of my room, waking me in my sleep. There were men in black uniforms all around us as we ran out of the house towards a waiting hovercraft. I cried ceaselessly the following week because I missed the forest. The memory of the animals there is gone now, layered over by grief and circumstance, but I still recall playing with them. And on some mornings, when I am still halfway between the dream world and this one, I have a flickering memory of soft, white fur caressing my cheeks.

My love of animals is instinctive, not nurtured. I was told that as a child, I was gifted with animals. They were drawn to me, and were playful and relaxed around me. My mother told me that it was as if they could understand me beyond words. I have no recollection of this.

I have not been within touching distance of an animal for years. My field work involves monitoring animals and evaluating their movements, tracks and what we can learn about their behaviour, but always from afar.

Lately, attack reports have been down. This is welcome news to everyone, but I was told that the same happened when the animals went into hiding for a few years before emerging as giants.

I have been posted in Sector Five now for just over a year — my very first solo posting, which I obtained after only three years of joint work in the Lake region. Normally, no one gets a solo assignment until they have completed at least five years of field work, but there is a decreasing number of field agents at the CAEP these days. Many young people leave after graduating from the academy, to join the WPO or the Federation government. Under normal circumstances, a solo posting requires proof of experience, not to mention skill in the job. Sometimes I question my own experience, and I worry that one day I will be exposed as ill-equipped for this work. I wonder if I was given the opportunity because of my parents who held senior positions within the CAEP and had many friends.

In my first joint assignment, I shared my habitation with an experienced Caepian and highly reputable Spatial Ecologist named Kate Winters, who was also my field trainer. Her toughness did not make me feel at ease around her, and even the Peacekeepers would not trifle with her. I learned swear words I never even knew existed from this formidable woman.

She has worked for the CAEP for almost forty years. At the time, she was not much older than I am now. Kate has seen animals smaller than they are today and been to Old India in the pre-Animal War era as a child. She told me the memory of the visit was "burned deep into her soul." Her own city, which was in the northern part of Sector Eleven, was destroyed and her family was killed. Despite this, Kate signed up and rose through the ranks to become Deputy Director and next in line to manage Mission Control.

Kate is now probably in her early sixties, but no one dares to ask. In today's world, that is a feat in itself. With disease, animal threats, and bio-food poisoning, most people do not live long. At almost two and a half decades, I have probably already lived half my existence. Despite her years, Kate has beautifully chiselled features and thick, silver-white hair that used to be golden in her youth. I have seen digitals of her when she was about my age and she cut a stunning figure in her CAEP military uniform and combat boots. I was told that they used her digitals in programmes promoting the CAEP. She has the most startling, magnetic, lilac eyes — almost unreal in their brightness. Even before we worked together, I used to wonder as a child whether they will glow in the dark. I asked my parents, only to be met with laughter.

Kate knew my parents well. She attended the same training as my mother when they both joined the CAEP. As social as my mother was, I think that Kate was her only real friend. They used to spend hours chatting over hot tea at our kitchen table, about everything from work to men, while my father would respectfully make himself scarce. My mother, I recall, enjoyed playing the matchmaker for 'Aunty Kate', as I used to call her when I was a child. I have a faint memory of having been afraid of her loud laughter and strong hugs. I believe that it was Kate who had been my father's accomplice when he was choosing an engagement ring as he was preparing to propose. I can see it in Kate's eyes that their passing distressed her as much as it did me. I sense that she has changed since then, as I have.

Today, Kate appears curt and impatient, but the underlying kindness is still there, reserved exclusively for people she cares about. She accepts no compromises and expects the same of me. She tells me that what we do is important for the survival of the planet and all species and that we are the original Peacekeepers. Without the CAEP, all the animals would be wiped out and without animals, the human race would not survive. It is already evident that the worldwide famine is caused by the rapid disappearance of bees on Neo-Earth. As apex predators, the planet can do without humans but we cannot do without the interconnectedness of all the species on Neo-Earth.

Kate is convinced that the animals have as much a right to live and thrive as we do. She is of the opinion that when the threat of animal extinction is no longer there, the animals will revert to their original sizes and aggression levels. I have trouble believing this part of her theory. We have seen, through thousands of years, that evolution does not happen backwards.

I am lucky that Kate taught me as she did; she was an exceptional mentor. In our walkabouts, she would point out sounds, animal cries and plants and told me what they were, what made them and why. Even the Peacekeepers who accompanied us often stood closely just to hear what she had to say. She was the one who pushed for my fast track to a solo posting. I had been hesitant, convinced that I could not do it alone. But she had taken me aside and told me that I was a Stollen and Stollens do not fail. I smile now when I think of that. She knew that my parents were my heroes.

I was not quite eighteen when both my parents died. I remember seeing Kate walk into my classroom in the middle of the afternoon with a look of terror on her face, or was it despair? My heart had started racing as soon as she came in. I knew something was wrong.

She told me later, in the privacy of the Samuelson that came to get me that their HMPT lost control and ran off a precipice. I was told it was a quick death, but how could anyone have known that? I remember feeling the bottom had fallen out of my world and I was falling, but I could not react. The pain that came later was something I hope I will never experience again. Their death nearly killed me too.

I still dream of them although their faces are starting to get less defined with each new dream. I know this to be a sign of healing, or at least this is what Kate tells me.

All field agents are posted in remote forest sectors away from human zones and we are strictly prohibited from leaving the habitation unless it is for a walkabout accompanied by a Peacekeeper. Even if I wanted to leave, without weapons or vehicles, it is dangerous.

My duties in the CAEP vary, but most often involve data and sample gathering and analysis during walkabouts in the wilderness. I have endless reports to write. I am required to know in which part of the wilderness each animal colony resides and where they move during each season. The sheer number of colonies and their migration patterns make this part of the job the most complex.

Mission Control does not trust animal behaviour and forbids us from making any physical contact. This is why it is a requirement to be accompanied by at least one Peacekeeper when we go into the wilderness for our walkabouts. They have their own based, located about five kilometres from my habitation.

Except for our Defence Unit, members of the CAEP are forbidden to carry weapons. This minimal armament is the organisation's way of cooperating and working with the Federation in a non-threatening way. As much as their goals differ from ours, we are still required to work together. Therefore, any reports I send to the CAEP are automatically sent as a facsimile to the Federation.

Over the last three months, I have begun omitting or falsifying some migratory and residential information in order to safeguard the locations of the animals from the Federation. If the Federation cannot find them, my hope is that the species will be safe from slaughter. I hear talk from some of the Peacekeepers who have accompanied me on my walkabouts in the past, that the Federation president has requested more Sectors to be reclaimed for human occupation and this only means that animals in those sectors are expendable.

I am particularly interested in the wellbeing of a pride of white Liogers that has arrived, in the last month, to Sector Five. The sound monitors caught their roars one day around a month ago. I was told they that their hunting grounds were further up north in Sectors Two and Three. They seem to have migrated to my Sector recently, the reason for which I am still trying to figure out. Even though I have not yet seen them, I know from digitals that they are magnificent creatures with soft coats of milk-coloured or jet-black, lightly-striated fur.

This will very likely get me into trouble both with the Federation and Mission Control, but somehow, I don't really care. I know that it is the right thing to do. After all, isn't keeping species safe what the CAEP was founded for? My mother told me once that I was meant for bigger things, that I will change the world. Well, I guess this is my way of fulfilling that notion.

In fact, her exact words, as I recall, were that "there were things in me that I cannot yet see, but that one day, I will change the world."

When I was older, I tried asking her what she meant by her words, but she only shook her head, and said, "You'll see." It was impossible to get a proper explanation from her. Her words still ring clearly in my head.

CHAPTER 3

"The frog does not drink up the pond in which he lives."
– Sioux Indian Proverb

The milky-white Lioger looks around at his pride from his perch on a large fallen trunk. He blinks slowly, liquid gold irises shining, and yawns. He is the oldest and has been the unchallenged leader of the group for years. With a five-metre body length and a shoulder height of two and a half metres, he is the largest of the pack. But he knows that his reign is coming to an end. He is not as agile. Some of the younger Liogers are starting to notice and sooner or later, his leadership will be contested. For now, however, he must keep his position. There is something he must do and he needs the pride united.

The hunt was easy and they have fed well on two large Black-tail Deer in the early hours of the morning. Some of the females are now lying down, sleeping, stomachs full. The cubs are the only ones still running around, testing their hunting skills on each other, a game that will serve them well in the years ahead.

The days are getting colder and the fur on their bodies is thickening, giving them protection in the winter months. The old Lioger can smell the coming of snow. The wind that is howling through the trees ruffles the thick mane on his head and he closes his eyes to sniff the air. He can smell prey from three kilometres away. Humans are often noisier and so easily avoided.

He is unfamiliar with the area, the pride having just arrived two days ago. They trekked hundreds of kilometres from the north, heading southwest. It is a journey that feels necessary. The old Lioger is pursuing his invisible compass and the others are following without contest. There is an urgent sensation in his bones. The leader feels he must get his pride to a location that only he can feel. There is a mission he must fulfil. He is the last of the old pride. The old Lioger is instinctively following a call to migrate; an urgent call to action. There is something he must find. He senses that the journey is nearing its goal. Once it is achieved, he can rest.

The next generation of Liogers does not feel his intuitive pursuit. Only he carries the connection.

Along the way, other prides are joining the group, expanding their numbers slowly. They hear the muted call to join the journey, although they too do not really know the reason why. The leaders of the other prides choose to follow the leader without question. They can feel that there is a larger mission at stake. Trust is a major factor. They rely on each other's strengths. The females are the experts of the hunt, while the male alpha leader is the protector of all of them. They may not understand his purpose, but they know he is doing this to keep them safe.

The only animals that challenge the Lioger pride is the troop of Primes that live in the mountains. Lately, they too appear to be on the move. It seems that something is happening in the FSA that is causing all the animals to grow nervous. However, as long as the Primes do not threaten his pride, he does not care.

CHAPTER 4

"Take only what you need and leave the land as you found it."
– Native American Arapaho Proverb

"I have good news, Marra." Kate's life-size, three-dimensional self is projected into the middle of my living area from the holographic communicator. She is smiling. It is evening and she is in her habitation, wearing a simple, white shirt and matching trousers. Her hair is down and it cascades in silver waves down one side of her shoulder, a look I rarely see and that renders her almost maternal. She sits on her sofa, holding a mug of something hot, which I am guessing to be tea. They grow it in the compound crop fields.

I narrow my eyes and think, but cannot recall having asked for anything specific, nor for a favour. "What kind of good news?" I am at my kitchen table, having just finished my dinner of potato bread and soup. I was not particularly hungry.

"I am bringing you to Mission Control for a two-week visit." Another big smile as she sips her tea.

"Special occasion?" I ask, wondering why I am given this exceptional leave.

"No, but you have been in Sector Five now for over a year and I think you need a short break," Kate says, taking another sip of tea.

I get up from the table and walk towards the sofa. The three-dimensional projection senses my movement and flips around to face me at my new location. Curling my legs under me, I sit down. This allows me time to think what to say next. I am not sure if I want to spend two weeks in Seven.

"You're stalling," Kate knows me too well. It's slightly irritating.

"So, two weeks ... October?" I wonder if she is planning something for my birthday, which is in the beginning of that month. I dislike being reminded that I am officially a year older. I don't see the point of it. My father was the same way and my mother and I always had to trick him into being present for his birthday celebration.

"Yes," Kate draws out the 's' at the end, sounding not too amused with my questions.

"Alright," I reply, knowing that it would be useless to protest. When Kate wants something to happen, it does. She reminds me of a military commander, focused, driven, seldom distracted..

"Right then. The hovercraft will pick you up at eight hundred hours on October first. See you then," she says, and then on a gentler tone, "Keep well, Marra." Kate is a person of few words, which suits me. Unlike my mother, I prefer to keep conversations short and to the point.

"You too. 'Till then," I reply and wait for the image to blink out. I wonder why I am summoned to Mission Control. Kate rarely does anything without a specific reason.

Maybe she has realised that my reports are falsified? My heart misses a beat at the thought. I have been very careful to mix facts at just the right amount so that the lies are undetectable. I wonder if Kate has seen through it. There is no better qualified wildlife spatial ecologist at the CAEP than her and she is the head trainer for all field officers. She has an eye for details, which makes it difficult to fool her. I look down at my hands and see that I have been unconsciously picking on my fingernails. I hope that Kate has not seen that. I clamp my hands under my armpits to prevent further damage. I am going on my walkabout tomorrow. I make a mental note not to misstate too many facts in my report.

Solitary life in an isolated wilderness Sector is not for every-one. I liken my life in Sector Five to living on a deserted, green island. To survive, it is about developing a routine that keeps your mind and body occupied. For some, this life is a punishment, but for me, I welcome the silence and the freedom of my own company. Solitude is a kind friend who allows me time to think.

I decide to watch an Old Earth video log, an activity that I end up doing most nights. The sounds from the video soothes me. I can recite some of the narration from memory, I have watched them so many times. I choose a familiar log, a documentary about the ancient gorillas, before the growth. They are cousins to the mutated Ape hybrids we have today — the Primes, as we call them. My father found the log in the Mission Control video vault. It is decades old and a little grainy. The audio is slightly tinny. Nevertheless, I find it enchanting.

I watched this one the first time with my father. I was twelve, wide-eyed and entranced. My parents and Kate often spoke about the possibility of the animals returning to their former state, before the growth, rage and aggression. I am highly doubtful, but my parents were always optimistic. They cited examples of how moths and butterflies had changed their wing colour according to environmental factors affecting the forests, in order to blend into nature and avoid being decimated by predators. I suspect that the secret project my parents were working on had something to do with their belief. Sometimes I wonder if they were researching ways to return the animals to their original sizes and demeanours. But I will never know.

I wonder what happened to all their work and who, if anyone, is continuing their research. Kate was evasive when I asked her years ago. Since then, I have not ventured to ask more about it. I know that Kate will only continue to stonewall my questions.

My eyes flit back to the video. I am lying upside down on my sofa, on an 'experimental' whim, and watching the scene from an inverted angle, my hair falling off the edge of the seat in straight, dark-brown strands.

The Gorillas are all sitting calmly plucking leaves from a branch and eating them, and a female is playing with her offspring. No matter how many times I watch this documentary, I am always astounded by how different these handsome creatures are from their future selves. My father told me that purebred Gorillas were believed to still exist in the continent of Neo-Afrika, hidden from humans. They are apparently giant beasts like all the other animals.

In the FSA we have Primes and Liogers. They are not native and rumour has it that over half a century ago, before the animals became giants, they were taken into the FSA for biological study and testing — but they escaped. We suspect these beasts evolved from laboratory subjects that the Federation kept for medical experimentation. This may explain their overt hostility towards humans.

The Primes are a genetic cross-species between the ancient Gorillas and Chimpanzees. Most of the other primate species have become extinct through years of poaching, killings, and habitat loss. Visually, they resemble Gorillas quite closely except for their size and the colour of their eyes. The Primes have very light eyes, almost silver and frankly quite beautiful. A full-grown male is a giant, standing at an impressive three metres tall, and is a formidable fighter when enraged. These hybrids have a far more developed brain than their ancient cousins, which helps them evade capture often. They are territorial, aggressive, and violent towards humans. The Primes are the lords of their new wilderness kingdom. The alpha-male is the only one with a spray of silver hairs on his back, which makes him easy to spot. He is the largest and meanest of the whole troop.

I monitor a band of Primes that is localised in the northern mountainous area of Sector Five via satellite video feed. To date, I have counted thirty members in Sector Five. As they are by far the most dangerous of all the hybrids, it is strictly forbidden to go into their territory, and if they come within ten kilometres of my survey area, I must pack up and get out. People often underestimate the speed at which they can travel and Primes are extremely unpredictable.

Long ago, before we knew much about Primal behaviour, one of our scientists was three kilometres from their territory. The unfortunate man was stalked, abducted and then pounded to death. His body could not be retrieved because after he was mutilated, the Primes proceeded to eat his flesh. This is how they project total dominance over their enemy. After this incident, the CAEP established strict rules on proximity based on species: ten kilometres for all dangerous species and two for the rest of the animals — dangerous species being all beasts that want to kill us.

At the academy, it is a requirement to study video logs of the mutated animals we have today. Ancient logs are not included in the curriculum, which is a pity because the insight we can garner from watching them is priceless. I feel that we can better understand the animals today from observing their behaviour before the change. My parents and Kate agree with me. This is why my father collected Old Earth video logs. My mother told me that he sometimes spent weeks or months hunting down a particular clip. Most of them were obtained through my father's historian contacts in the Coalition of Europe. The worldwide digital network no longer allows videos of any animals — another directive from the WPO to keep the world population calm.

Like my mother, my favourite animal in the FSA is the *Panthera Liogrispardus*, or what we simply call Liogers. They are a cross-species between Lions and Tigers, possibly mutated from escaped zoo animals. They have inherited all the strength and agility of the combined genes they possess. They also have a highly refined sense of smell. Liogers are formidable hunters and can climb trees easily. A full-grown adult male is as big as the Humpt in height and length, although not as wide. They look similar to their ancient cousins, except for size and eye colour, which is gold. Their coats are also different. This new hybrid is born either creamy white or jet black with light striations, regardless of how the parents look. A pride of Liogers is a beautiful collage of black and white, like a chess board.

This genetic trait baffles bio-scientists. To date, however, no adult Lioger has yet been caught for studies, at least to the knowledge of the CAEP. The Federation once made plans to capture a cub, but that was soon abandoned. An angry Liogress will kill every living thing in its path to retrieve her offspring.

Liogers are migratory, the pride moving anywhere where there is an abundance of prey, but mostly, they stay within the lowlands of Sectors One, Two, Three and Five. Each group can be twenty Liogers strong. Their favourite food is the Giant Blacktail and Whitetail Deer, which are indigenous to Sectors Five, Two and Three. With humans no longer able to hunt, deer are abundant in the whole of the FSA. Hence the Liogers are, on the whole, well-fed and healthy beasts and growing bigger and stronger with each new litter.

The animals here and maybe even everywhere else on Neo-Earth seem to sense the areas where humans live and avoid them. I think they just want to be allowed to exist in peace without interference from us.

They are the next step in the evolution of the animal kingdom. I believe that they have emerged to survive humanity's destruction of their species. This makes me think perhaps my parents are not so far off their mark on the theory of the moths and butterflies.

I have learnt most of what I know about the Liogers from my mother. She earned a reputation for being the foremost expert of this hybrid. According to her, they are not as aggressive as the Primes, are loyal creatures, possessing the ability to recognise kindness. When I asked how she knew that, she merely said that she had studied them long enough.

My mother was a woman of secrets. She was not as easy to speak to as my father. She spent long hours in her laboratory, a room in our habitation that was her place of work. She kept it under constant lock and key. Only my father held the duplicate. The only time I have entered the laboratory was after their death. We had to break open the door. The room had been emptied of its contents. Not even Kate can explain — or maybe she chooses not to. Over the years, I had tried to find out what went on inside that laboratory, but my mother never gave me the opportunity to sneak inside and she would get irritated when I question her about it. I still wonder to this day what they were working on inside the laboratory — a cure for the animals' aggression? A new species?

From the changes Mother Nature has started worldwide. It is getting more difficult for *homo sapiens* to survive. At the CAEP, we casually call this Mother Earth's Centuries of Reboot. Nature appears to keep coming up with ways to rid herself of human occupation. Our food sources are depleting and we are slowly exiled into smaller territories. We are becoming the unwanted guests of a planet that has been our home for millennia. It is as though she is shedding old skins in order to emerge renewed and clean.

The winds have started howling again like a wild animal, which is normal for this time of year. The sounds are beautiful to me.

I am not unhappy in my chosen solitary life. I look forward to my walkabout the following day. My heart expands with contentment when I am in the wilderness. Something about the of trees, soil and surrounding animal sounds and smells that calms me. It is as if part of me belongs in the green world.

I am awkward in the world of carphite-concrete habitations, sky-towers and even to the certain extent, among people. This is something I have noticed and not spoken about to anyone, not even to my parents. How can I explain that I prefer to live in the forest? How can I say that I want to live among the animals, even if I have to leave them behind? And now, the opportunity to speak is gone, evaporated like morning mist; no more future conversations to contemplate; no more secrets to divulge. I can be anyone I want to be without contest. Although I enjoy being on my own, I sometimes miss having someone to argue with, to find flaws in my plans.

My parents were wonderful, kind and yet mysterious people. As a family, we kept to ourselves with the exception of Kate. She was the only person in Seven that spent time with us. They were constantly working, and even the conversations they had at home would inevitably turn to work. They were passionate about the genetic project they were engaged in before they died, but they never discussed any of it in front of me. I used to think that they wanted time with me to not be affected by work, but I am not so sure now.

As a teenager, I had assumed that it was an 'adult' thing to do, to keep secrets from children. As I grow older and more aware, I realise that some of their behaviour towards me might have held something more.

CHAPTER 5

*"When one tugs at a single thing in nature, he finds it
attached to the rest of the world."*
– John Muir

I am wearing my walkabout puncture-proof outfit — a hideous
military, digital, jungle-camouflage print for both shirt and cargo
trousers. It was designed with large men in mind and not small
women. The material is resistant to animal bites and claws,
although I have not yet had the opportunity to test its worth. It is
supposedly breathable but I think that they are lying about that; I
feel like I'm wearing a portable sauna. I honestly don't believe that
the outfit will increase my chances of survival should an animal
attack. Hybrid canines are sharp and can tear through a lot thicker
material than cloth, even if reinforced.

I shove my gloves into my trouser pocket. I normally do not
wear them because they make my fingers feel clumsy.

It is almost nine hundred hours and the day promises to be
clear. The line of trees in the distance stand swaying in a dance
with the wind, like ladies in orange, red, yellow and green dresses
at a ball. The field of grass surrounding my habitation has grown
long and turned brown in preparation for winter. The grasses
resemble the savannah plains of Neo-Afrika and often I pretend
they are.

I place my helmet on the porch and stand, waiting for my
assigned Peacekeeper to arrive. I see the dark green vehicle in the
distance. The air is crisp and cold, and smells of autumn leaves.

The sound amplifiers on my porch are not emitting the usual animal noises, which I find strange. I wonder what is going on?

I am interrupted in my thoughts by the sound of the HMPT, or what we privately call 'the Humpt', approaching. They are completely fortified and armed, military vehicles made to withstand animal and laser attacks. I will not know if he is the same Peacekeeper who picked me up the last time until he exits the tank. The carphite derivative, glass-like windscreen and windows on Humpts allow the driver to see out but not anyone to see into the vehicle.

The front side window rolls down and a head pops out. He is a different Peacekeeper. I wonder if the last one resigned or was reassigned to another sector.

"Ready, ma'am?"

This one is polite for a change. "Yes, thank you." I pick up my fieldwork equipment, a rectangular padded bag where all the containers required for my samples are safely placed in different compartments. The CAEP ensures that our equipment is simple and lightweight, because a walkabout in a wilderness territory is dangerous and may require us to evacuate quickly in the event of an animal attack. I head to the opposite side of where his head is. The door is already slid open and I place my bag in the back of the vehicle, secure it so it does not slide around and then seat myself next to the peacekeeper. The strap automatically comes across the front of my body.

The Peacekeeper is even younger than the one before him. They must be recruiting them right off secondary education level. Protecting Caepians must be an initial task given to new recruits, like an initiation into the Peacekeeping role. I feel sorry for him all of a sudden. He looks very young, possibly around twenty. He is thin, his Adam's apple prominently displayed on a scrawny neck. He has not yet donned his helmet and I can see his recently shaved head is glistening and clean like a newborn's. From his long, blond eyelashes I am guessing that his hair will be the same colour.

"You know which area we are going to today?" I ask.

He simply nods while turning the vehicle and driving towards the wilderness zone.

I used to ask their names, but I no longer do that. What's the point of knowing who they are when they don't actually stay with me long enough to form a true friendship?

I had one Peacekeeper who was assigned to me continuously for four months. His name was Yon Hunter, but that was a long time ago, and I don't know what has become of him. I developed a bit of a crush on him and had mistaken him as a friend. When he stopped coming without so much as a goodbye, I felt hurt for a few weeks. Although nothing happened between us, there were moments when we were in the wilderness when I had imagined holding his hands — and maybe even getting my very first kiss.

It was then that I realised Peacekeepers are only there to do a job to which they are assigned. I am nothing more to them than a body they are required to protect. I am sure that they are not fighting among themselves to be appointed to a Caepian in a remote Sector. There are surely more interesting places they can be than here.

I am tempted to ask the Peacekeeper if this is his first visit of the wilderness but decide not to. I will find out soon enough when we arrive. Both his hands are on the steering wheel and he looks preoccupied with driving.

It is hot inside the vehicle, especially wearing my walkabout uniform. "Can I slide open the window a little for air?" I ask, knowing full well the answer will be 'no' but giving it a try anyway.

"No, ma'am, it is against regulations, but I will switch on more air for you." His voice matches his looks, a young man's voice that still has not deepened with age. He speaks with a strong Eastern Federation accent, pronouncing 'more air' as 'moar aih'. A subtle hissing sound comes out of the front panel. I dislike canned air.

"Thank you," I tell him, and silently sigh to myself.

It is a hundred and eighty kilometres to the zone where I will be surveying, an approximate two-hour ride on a dirt road that snakes through the wilderness. I wish I brought my music with me.

"I'm wondering, ma'am, have you ever seen a Lioger or Prime?"

I smile at him. "No." I detect a hint of relief as his shoulders drop. I decide to give him more reassurance. "Normally the animals stay away during the walkabouts. Believe it or not, as much as they dislike us, it's not in their nature to attack without provocation. So, if we are careful and keep out of their way, they let us do what we want in their area."

I see the straight line of his back curve as he relaxes.

My curiosity is piqued. I wonder what they tell the Peacekeepers before they go on a mission with a CAEP field agent. "What do they teach you abou the animals back at your base?"

"To shoot if I see one," he says without hesitation and emotion.

I am appalled by his instructions. "Absolutely do NOT just shoot if the animal is not attacking! In fact, only shoot if I tell you to, is that agreed?" I had no idea that this is what the Federation is telling the Peacekeepers to do. I wonder if Mission Control is aware of this. I know that it has been the FSA's wish for some time now to rid the country of all the animals in the wilderness. They are under pressure from its more affluent citizens to reclaim the country for the population.

"My mandate is not with you, ma'am." Then he adds, "Respect-fully."

"I don't care. If you shoot without provocation, you will bring the whole animal species upon us and we will both die because no amount of weapon fire will be enough to keep up with the number of animals that will attack us. They are extremely fast!" I hope to frighten him enough for him to listen to me.

He now looks a little uncomfortable. He bites a corner of his lips. "How will I know if the animal is not attacking?" I notice his eyes widen and un-widen with his words, something he may not be aware of doing.

"I do and I will tell you." Then more softly. "I promise. Trust me and we will be fine, ok?"

He nods and says nothing more. I am getting worried. An inexperienced Peacekeeper is not what I call an ideal protector in the wilderness. He will more likely get us killed than he would ensure our safety. The animals in the wilderness normally avoid contact with humans as much as possible. They sense our presence acutely and often disappear or at least move out of our range of detection. However, if one animal is hurt by a human, the whole species will come charging. The hybrids are highly protective of their kind. Their intellect has, after all, evolved one step closer to us, humans.

"So ..."

I hear the Peacekeeper begin and turn to look at him.

"Are the Liogers really as big as this Humpt, ma'am?" he asks

"I hear they are," I tell him and add, "and it's Marra, not ma'am." I see my hope of a quiet ride to the walkabout zone evaporating like dry ice exposed to air. His mouth twitches with the advent of more conversation. He seems happy with my reply.

I decide to change the subject before he asks more 'animal' questions, "Where were you based before Sector Five?"

"Sector Nineteen, FPB, ma' ... " he stops abruptly, still uncomfortable to use my name. I know that the Federation Peacekeeper Base is located in that sector. I remember Yon telling me that it is a large base. They all start out there. They say that most of the people living in Nineteen are either military or scientists.

"My whole family is from the East," the Peacekeeper continues. He will be easy to break under interrogation, I think, having forwarded information without being asked. The thought almost draws a chuckle from me.

"Are they also in Nineteen?" I ask.

He nods and smiles. My stance on Peacekeepers softens a little. He is but a boy who happens to be working for the Federation. "Are they military, your parents?"

"Yup!" he says, with a marked amount of pride. "We're a military family, all the way back to great, great, grand-dad." This question appears to lower his guard and he is almost slouching now on the wheel.

"So, you've always wanted to be a Peacekeeper?"

He shrugs. "Never thought of it that way," he says.

"How?"

"You know, everyone in my family, we just know that we'll enlist."

"Have you not thought about doing anything else?"

Another shrug. "Nah ... besides, what else is there to do?" I can see that my question has him reflecting, possibly for the first time, judging from the frown that now wrinkles his otherwise baby-smooth forehead. "Nah ..." he says again, as if to dismiss all other doubts.

I let a little silence pass between us. "How long was your training?" I ask.

"That's the fun part!" he grins, mirth returning. "Training is for like, three weeks. Man, it's tough! The captain like, screams at you ALL, THE, TIME!" he drags out the last three words, managing to roll his eyes and keep them on the track ahead at the same time. In another life and situation, this boy could be my friend, I think. He is endearing, like the pets I see on my video logs.

Three weeks is a short time to train these young boys to be combat ready in the presence of a giant animal. I feel sorry for him. Giving a weapon to a young boy, with minimal training and then putting them in a forest or jungle sector is criminal. How can they be expected to survive and protect a Caepian at the same time?

"They teach you about the animals?" I ask, curious.

"We were presented with a video on the Primes and Liogers," he says. "Shows you like, how big they are and what to do when you meet them, you know, which is pretty much, Pzzew, Pzzew, Pzzew!" he imitates the sound of laser fire, while I sit there a little stunned by what I hear. I am about to voice my shock when he continues, "But when you pass the basic, then it's super! You get to go on these assignments. The Digits are not great, but it's the experience, you know?" I am not surprised that the Federation does not pay these Peacekeepers much.

"Did you ask for Sector Five?" I enquire, deciding not to pursue my indignation of his training on how to handle the animal species. I doubt if he will understand.

"Nah, they give you the assignments. If I could choose, I'd

prefer to be in Twelve!" he laughs. "Closer to the human zone, you know?" which I do, "And warmer! Man, I hate the winters up north! Crazy cold!" he shudders for effect.

Our conversation is putting the young man at ease. There is a hint of a smile on his lips. I ask no more questions and stare out at the passing trees. I hear a sigh and we both settle back to enjoy the rest of the ride in silence.

Upon reaching our destination, we park in a clearing that has been identified in advance by the CAEP and that is about a five-minute walk to the edge of wilderness survey zone. I exit the vehicle like a teenager released from detention. Slinging the bag across my shoulder, I smile at the young man and motion to him with a nod that we can begin. He dons his full-face helmet and checks his High Energy Laser, or HEL, with the care of someone doing it for the first time. I wonder if it is not the Federation's intention to send the most inexperienced Peacekeepers to protect CAEP agents.

HELs are the standard weapons of all Peacekeepers and Warriors. They are the FSA's pride and one of the country's prime sources of income. The thing with HELs is, that while effective against soft-tissue objects like humans, they are less useful against the hybrids we have today. With their unusually thick skins, it takes several shots of lasers before they are hurt, much less killed.

I voice-adjust my visor to total transparency as we crunch through the fallen leaves and the undergrowth. I love the sound it makes; it triggers memories of walking home with my parents as a child in autumn. I see that the Peacekeeper also has his visor at transparency. He looks a little concerned, a whisper of a frown wrinkling his otherwise smooth forehead.

I have designated zones where I have to collect soil, plant and water samples. I am then required to retrieve the sound monitors where I left them the last time in order to move them to a new sector on my next walkabout. All specimen collecting areas and locations for the sound equipment have already been predeter-mined by the CAEP. I am only required to follow the coordinates given to me via data streamed directly on my visor. I have about six different species to track, from Primes to the Blacktail Deer, and so the walkabout normally takes two or three hours depending on the distances between the work areas. Often, I work slowly so that I can spend as much time in the wilderness as possible.

I love this part of my work. My heart sings when I am here.

The wilderness is getting denser as we walk further in. I am ahead and look back at the Peacekeeper. He has his HEL, pointed in front of him. I hope that he has the safety on because if he starts shooting, he will hit me.

I stop and listen. There is very little sound. This is unusual and my heart starts to beat faster. In all the time that I have been coming to this area, it has never been this quiet. All I hear is the hissing of leaves swaying on the branches.

The animal sounds are not increasing as we walk deeper into the wilderness. I voice-activate my infrared thermal imagers and the wilderness becomes a monochromatic picture. We use grey scale because it is easier to see thermal signatures in this colour range. Strangely, I don't see any animals around and yet, I feel watched. I am getting nervous. The Peacekeeper walking close behind me seems oblivious to the unusual silence. He even appears to have relaxed. I check my wristband, which is connected to satellite feed and it is not vibrating, signalling that it has not picked up images of any animals in the perimeter. I switch back to normal vision.

Despite the absence of animals, I am not feeling confident that we are alone so I quicken my pace. The sooner I can finish my work, the faster we can leave.

We arrive at the area and I start my sample collection. There are at least five sites where I have to take samples and I am now not wasting any time.

Looking at his young face, I decide not to let him know of my uneasiness about the situation. I do not want him trigger-happy, which will complicate matters more.

I work in the most efficient way possible and choose the shortest routes between zones. The hour ticks by and everything is going smoothly despite my unease. I now need to retrieve the sound monitors in two locations before we can head back to the Humpt.

We walk briskly to the next location, the echo of our boots crunching the undergrowth sounds louder in the stillness of the wilderness. As we turn a corner, I hear startled shrieks of Bantous. They are harmless to humans. But it is unusual to hear them so early in the day because they normally cannot withstand light. I look up and around me, just in time to see two large Bantous fly into the trees.

The Peacekeeper imitates me and looks up at the flying creatures, an expression of apprehension forming on his face. I decide that I must stay calm so he diligently follows suit.

"Just harmless Bantous," I tell him casually and continue walking, choosing not to reveal that under usual circumstances, these creatures would not normally be out in daylight. Sweat is now soaking my shirt. It is sticking uncomfortably to my back like a wet towel. Beads of moisture are also forming on my forehead and one is running down the side of my face. I raise my hand instinctively to wipe it away and it collides clumsily with the visor, stunning me for a second. I steal a quick look at the Peacekeeper who is at my side. He does not seem to have noticed. His jaw looks tense and a deep furrow is etched across his brow. My heart is pounding. Something is amiss but I cannot pinpoint the exact problem.

We reach the location and I am about to retrieve the first sound monitor when my wristband suddenly vibrates, startling me and I momentarily freeze. This means that the satellite thermal scanner has picked up large animals within the ten-kilometre perimeter from where we are. The buzzing is loud enough for the Peacekeeper to notice. He looks at me with fearful eyes, his face betraying the dread he is starting to feel. I take a look at the wristband and a computerised woman's voice tells me, "Animals at ten thousand metres ..." That is still too far for my visor infrared thermal imager to see. I check the satellite feed and see large blobs moving quickly in our direction.

A mighty roar reverberates through the thick wilderness; we can almost feel it shuddering the trees. A flock of birds leave their perch on the branches, shrieking and frightened, scattering foliage to the ground. The roar could only come from a full grown male Lioger. I freeze, my first fear response activated. The Peacekeeper stands there, not moving as well.

"Ma'am ... Marra, we should go. That sounds close," he says, clutching his HEL tightly in one hand, I see his knuckles are white.

I abandon all thoughts about the monitor and get up to follow the Peacekeeper. My heart is beating so hard I can hear it, making it difficult for me to concentrate. A second roar tears through the trees. I look around terrified, expecting it to appear through the bushes. Lioger roars can be heard as far as ten kilometres. Although my wristband is telling me that they are over five kilometres away, they sound much closer. The Peacekeeper is aiming his HEL in different directions, presuming the same. Meanwhile, the computerised voice on my wristband continues the countdown, "8500 metres ... 8000 metres ..."

I decide not to switch to infrared thermal imaging because at that distance, I will not be able to see them yet.

"Come on, let's go, let's GO," the Peacekeeper is leading the way. His voice is edged with tension and he is glancing around trying to catch sight of the Lioger. We start to jog in the direction of the Humpt.

We hear more roars now and short ones. There is more than one Lioger. These abbreviated vocalisations are how these hybrids communicate with one another. A male Lioger will utilise it to signal the others to follow. The sounds are even closer than before, as if it is stalking us from somewhere behind the bushes. This time, I switch to thermal imaging, but still see nothing.

"Run," the Peacekeeper says, panic lingering just below the surface of his voice. I disregard protocol and remove my helmet. It is impossible to run with it on. I am breathing hard. I am not as fit as the Peacekeeper, who still has his helmet on, and am finding it difficult to keep up. My wristband continues the countdown:

"5000 metres, 4500 metres …" Thankfully, the Humpt comes into view. The Peacekeeper is already barking orders for it to open its doors and start up. By the time I reach it, I am breathless and about to faint. I hold on to the vehicle for support as I try to catch my breath. The Peacekeeper quickly pushes me into it. The Humpt surges forward, kicking up gravel and speeds away, leaving behind a swirl of dust.

I check the satellite thermal scanner on my wristband. The computerised voice is now counting upwards, "5500 metres … 6000 metres …" I breathe a sigh of relief as we distance ourselves from the animals. The satellite feed indicates a group of animals closing in on the territory where we were. I assume they are the Liogers from what we heard in the wilderness. I am unable to see details of them. Although technological advances have been made for satellite thermal imagers, heat signatures still show up as undefined blobs, because of the satellite's distance from Neo-Earth. What is intriguing is how the Liogers can sound so close and yet not be there? There is an incongruence between the satellite images and the sound — which is not a good sign.

The Peacekeeper still looks terrified and is driving as fast as the Humpt can go. He is gripping the steering wheel tightly with both hands. I say nothing. We both need time to calm down. In all my years of walkabouts, this is the first time where I have heard Liogers in such close proximity. My adrenaline is still pumping. I am both frightened and exhilarated. This is my first contact, though I am not quite sure if this would be classified as such, but for me, it is still a connection of some kind.

"Where were they? The Liogers?" the Peacekeeper's voice betraying the panic he is still feeling.

I shake my head. "I don't know. I didn't see any heat signatures. They must have been several kilometres from us."

"They sounded closer than several kilometres away, ma'am, " he says, without looking at me. I realise that his training to call me 'ma'am is deeply ingrained and I do not correct him.

"Did you see any thermals on your satellite scanners?" I ask.

He shakes his head.

"Then, they must have been several kilometres away. They just sound close." I want to say more but decide to leave it at that. There is no point to frighten and worry the young man. This is his first time in the forest and, I want him to return. Too many people assume that the world's jungles and forests are worth destroying because they are home to dangerous animals, which in reality make up only a small percentage. But today, even if I want to give him an explanation of what happened, I am unable because I don't understand it myself.

"They sounded like they were right behind the trees, ma'am," the Peacekeeper insists. And he is right. It was as if they were not more than a few metres away from us. I cannot explain this anomaly in the systems and saying more would only increase his suspicion.

"It must be the way the sound travels in the wilderness," I say, blatantly lying and mentioning whatever that comes to my head. With his inexperience, he is likely to believe me.

The Peacekeeper shoots a glance at me, a look that says that he does not quite believe me but who is he to argue with a CAEP field agent? He falls silent, which is the goal I want to achieve.

I turn my attention to the scenery blurring past us. He obviously wants to return to the safety of his Federation compound as quickly as possible. My mind is a jumble of questions. Liogers that sound closer than what the satellite indicates is a situation I have never encountered. I am certain that the animals were stalking us closely, but why did they not attack? And why could I not see them on the thermal imager if they were behind the bushes? What were the animals on the satellite feed, assuming they were not the Liogers?

For fifty-five years since the first animal attacks, the world has managed to contain the problem through technology. I take a moment to think through the implication, and feel very uneasy: this incident might mark the beginning of a new challenge we had not encountered, as humans, before.

CHAPTER 6

"Study the past if you would define the future."
– Confucius

The Peacekeeper leaves as soon as we arrive at my habitation and unload my bag from the Humpt. He backs up and drives off so quickly that I am left standing there, in the swirling, dusty wake of the vehicle. The incident replays in my head on a continuous loop. It is confusing, to say the least. I am still wondering if my thermal imager has malfunctioned. My equipment checks the night before showed no signs of defect. And even if my equipment has malfunctioned, the Peacekeeper's thermal imager should not have. The probability of both failing is exceedingly small. This may imply an overhaul of my devices if it really is a systems failure, which would leave me virtually blind and is not ideal especially, based in a remote sector like mine. I am almost certain that Kate will have me evacuated in urgency to Seven. Safety for us depends upon our ability to detect.

I stand there in my driveway for a few seconds, watching the trail of dust speeding off into the distance. I doubt if I will see the young man again. His first walk in nature is surely not what he had expected. I look up at the sky. Grey clouds are gathering and covering the weak sun. The wind is picking up. If not for what happened earlier in the wilderness, this would be another normal day in autumn. The clouds are darkening to an ominous deep grey, turning the afternoon into evening. I glance at my wristband. A fluorescent number is blinking, indicating it is close to sixteen hundred hours.

I turn and drag my feet up to my habitation. I carefully put the sample bag and my helmet down on the table. My shirt has dried slightly from the sweat but it feels grimy and I start unbuttoning slowly to take it off. Two-thirds through, I decide instead to remove my field boots first. I lift the top flaps and free my socked feet. Shuffling to the sofa, I slump down onto it, letting my body melt into its softness. It dawns on me that I have to return to the same zone on my next walkabout to recover the sound monitors.

I sit up suddenly — a thought ripping through my mind. Having the two monitors there means that I can continue to hear the Liogers. I run to my computer and search for the recordings. Ignoring headphones, I locate the controls for the device placed at my last location before we left. I turn the volume up and hit the replay button from at least two and a half hours ago, about when the Liogers came into the scene.

I hear leaves rustling and birds for about five minutes and then there it is, the roar of the mighty, male Lioger. I turn the volume up. It is as I remember. This was when the Peacekeeper and I started running back to the Humpt. This next section of the recording interests me more. What happened after we left?

I hear more roars for a full five minutes and then a deep animal howl. I take a step back in shock. It is a scream that is easily recognisable because it is the distinct sound belonging to only one animal — a Prime. I did not expect any Primes in the area because in the last three months, they have not been located anywhere close to the zones where my walkabouts take place. Another scream pierces the air and this time louder, as though the beast is right above the monitor. Then abruptly, the device goes dead, the electrical buzz of static filling the air in my habitation. I check the other apparatus. It is located at least three kilometres away on the opposite end of the walkabout area. I rewind to a time that is at least twenty minutes before the other monitor disconnected and start playing it back. The scream of a Prime, like the Lioger roars, can be heard as far as ten kilometres and so this equipment, in theory, will pick up all the sounds.

I hear the Liogers as with the other monitor but not as loudly. Then I uncover something else that is not present in the other recording. I close my eyes to visualise the sounds better. I 'see' a group of Primes, grunting and growling as they shuffle noisily past the auditory device. The sounds are distinctive and clear and then trail off as they move away. How many of them, I cannot tell from just listening, but I guess that there might be about thirty. This is the size of the troop of Primes that we know live in Sector Five. I assume it is the same band because there are no others in this Sector.

Primes always travel together in a group, leaving none of their tribe behind and are led by the most powerful and vicious male, the alpha. They know that there is strength in numbers. The troop that I have located some months ago lives about forty kilometres away in the mountainous region of Sector Five, where the wilderness is very dense. As Primes are unpredictably aggressive, we do not go near their territory at all. It is unusual to hear them move into an area in the lowlands that is not theirs and distant from their mountains.

My mind refocuses on the recording when I hear the scream of the Prime that I heard on the other monitor. It must be the alpha male of the troop. This is when the other device is disengaged. I continue to keep my eyes closed to visualise the sounds.

The Primes and Liogers exchange roars of intimidation. It sounds like a terrifying confrontation is happening between them. I imagine that both species are standing their ground, with their compatriots on each side, growling and snapping at each other. The screams and roars reverberate through the wilderness for two more minutes and then it begins to dissipate as if they are departing. I conclude that the two families of predators decided to retreat and go their separate ways. I continue listening for another fifteen minutes to see if the Primes retraced their steps. They did not. The wilderness is back to its uneventful state of normal bird calls, frog croaks and the chirp of the cicadas.

I switch the recordings off and stare at my computer for a few seconds, gathering my thoughts. This is the most exciting thing that has happened since I moved into this sector and this discovery brings an involuntary smile to my lips. I then sober up and realise that this will also bring a great deal of focus into the area, attention I don't welcome. I like the anonymity of my work, especially since I have been falsifying reports about the locations of all the animals, which will also call into question the validity of my work.

I have another sudden thought. Could what I have seen on the satellite feed be Primes, not Liogers? If that is the case, then this would confirm that my thermal imager has not malfunctioned. But it creates a major problem: why were the Liogers invisible to the heat signature scans? Could they be a new hybrid? To evade thermal scans, it would mean that they would have to be able to lower their body temperature. Is that possible? Would they look the same as the current Liogers we have?

Liogers are known to defend their territory and get aggressive when their young, food or pride is threatened. Otherwise, they keep to themselves and leave humans alone. Therefore, were they hunting in the wilderness when we were there? But I still believe that we were stalked.

Primes in the FSA, on the other hand, have been known to attack without reason. They will even fight and kill members of their own troop over food. Despite their aggressive behaviour, it is unlikely they will leave their breeding ground and territory unless they feel there is a threat. Were they threatened? Or were they hunting too, although this appears unlikely?

I wonder if what happened could be the beginning of a battle for territory. Or perhaps the Primes are moving down the mountain to find another breeding ground? That seems plausible. The Liogers would certainly show up to defend their claim on the land. Maybe the Peacekeeper and I just happened to be in their war path. I wonder if similar problems have been reported in other Sectors. Kate would know this and I am required to report the incident. However, I am concerned about how she will handle this situation. When it comes to rules, Kate has a black or white view and she may therefore take a decision that will not allow me room to negotiate.

I return to the comfort of my sofa. I realise that my shirt is two-thirds unbuttoned and rebutton it without reflecting. My mind whirls with thoughts about the encounter — something is happening to the animals. What exactly? Is this the prelude to the second big wave of Animal Wars?

I realise also that Kate will be expecting my field report. What do I send? I worry that if the Federation knows about the Primes leaving their mountain, it will give them the reason they have been waiting for to send platoons to kill them. They have tolerated the existence of these beasts because the CAEP convinces them that the animals are happy to remain in the mountains and pose no threat to anyone. I am certain that the Peacekeeper will have reported about the Lioger incident. Reluctant though I am to get up from the comfort of my sofa, I grudgingly do. I am beginning to feel the commencement of an ache in my legs from muscles that have been overworked and they are begging for a warm shower, which I oblige by going into my bathroom.

Emerging steaming clean and refreshed, and in shorts and a clean shirt, I hobble to the living area and sit by the desk and ponder. The bag of samples is still there, unopened. I reach over and click the clip to release its hold on the strap. Flipping the bag open, I remove all samples carefully and begin the tedious task of cataloguing and reporting my findings.

It takes a numbing hour to document my sample findings. When it came to 'auditory observations', I stop. What do I report about the sound recordings? This is not easy to lie about because I have to send the samples and recordings to Mission Control. There is a monthly courier who collects the specimens and also delivers my food supplies. Digital reports and recordings are required to be data transferred after every walkabout. The academy teaches us basic computer skills but unfortunately not how to hack into and manipulate binary information.

Then I remember that Kate is expecting me at Mission Control in about twelve days. She will probably be bombarding me with questions. She may even fly me there earlier than the appointed date, given what happened. I will not be able to circumvent the facts this time. I sigh and proceed to report on what happened, making sure that the information is as close to the truth as possible without being detailed. I know that Kate will challenge me on this but I will cross that bridge when I come to it.

The communicator beeps suddenly, making me jump. I quickly look at the time, a little over nineteen hundred hours. This will be Kate. Only she would still be working at this hour. The young Peacekeeper must have reported to his Captain and news will have travelled to Mission Control. I brace myself.

"Answer," I say to it, mentally preparing for the worst. I remain at the work table.

"Marra," Kate says as she materialises into a three-dimensional projection. She is still in her office at her desk, a frown on her forehead indicating her concern.

I smile, trying to look relaxed and fail.

"Anything to report regarding the walkabout?" Kate's right eyebrow is raised in suspicion.

I clear my throat, then cough, trying to buy myself a few seconds of reflection. "I've just finished the report for you. I would have sent it within the hour." I pause and see that her right eyebrow is raised higher. Her stony stare is more terrifying to me than that of a Lioger.

"Um, everything is in it and when I go to Mission Control in twelve days, I will bring all of the samples," I continue, but I can see that she is not interested in that information.

"You heard a Lioger?" Kate goes straight to the point. Her face is a picture of grimness. My initial feeling of Kate's reaction is already beginning to surface.

"Yes," I say, then add, "towards the end of the walkabout."

"And?"

"It must have been more than a few kilometres away because my thermal imager didn't pick up their signs," I continue. "And we left quickly."

"The PK's thermals didn't detect anything either?" 'PK' is Kate's diminutive for Peacekeeper.

"None," I say, hoping I look calm. My elbows are on the table and I am absent-mindedly wringing my hands from nervousness. Realising it, I quickly cross my arms across my body, pinning my hands under them.

Kate gets up from her desk, comes to the front of it and sits on its edge. "What kind of a roar was it?" she asks, knowing that I am trained in identifying the differences.

"Well, there was a loud, territorial roar," I begin, "then I heard a series of coughing roars, which ... "

"... which indicates that he was summoning more Liogers to where he was," Kate finishes the sentence for me. I swallow as discretely as I can. "What did you tell the PK?"

"I told him that the Lioger was kilometres away," I reply.

Kate smiles. "We certainly don't want the Feds where it does not concern them." Then she looks at me seriously, "Do YOU think the Lioger was a few kilometres away?"

I clear my throat. "He sounded closer."

"How close?"

"A few hundred metres." I look into Kate's judging eyes and quickly add, "maybe less."

Kate stands up and starts to pace slowly. "No heat signatures ..." she says, more to herself than to me.

"None," I reply anyway. "Not even on satellite."

Kate pales and looks like she has just been told that these Liogers are right outside the perimeter of Seven. Her reaction is just what I expected.

"Let's postpone all walkabouts for about a month," she says. "And you're coming to Mission Control tomorrow."

I am taken by surprise at this last statement and start to protest, "But Kate ..."

She shakes her head. "Just a precaution. The Liogers may be checking out the territory. No walkabouts for a month. Let them move on."

"But ... " I begin again and stop as I realise that my report will make a mention of Primes and my argument for staying becomes invalid. Their presence in the wilderness lowlands pose an even greater threat for me because that would mean they are migrating and may travel down to my habitation. The sinking feeling of having to move from my current sector is making me feel queasy.

"It's only a month, Marra, not a life sentence. Think of it as a small break from duties. This could be fun! It will allow you to catch up on other ..." she searches for the correct word and, finding none, says, "things."

I wonder if she is expecting me to extend my two-week stay in Seven to a month.

Kate, perceptive as usual, replies, "Yes, no walkabouts for a month means you are staying a month in Seven. Don't look so alarmed, Marra. You might enjoy your time here. Much has changed since you left." She smiles.

I want to tell her that I don't consider Seven a place to enjoy myself, but decide against it. Kate still considers me her ward following my parents' accident and somehow feels protective of my well-being. I smile and nod.

"I'll see you tomorrow, Marra," she says this in an unusually soft tone that I am not used to. She looks genuinely concerned. "Send me your report," she continues.

"I will. See you tomorrow, Kate." I think I sound more disappointed that I want to. I wait until her image blinks out before letting out an onerous, audible sigh.

I lie back on the sofa and look at the plain, white ceiling. I idly think that if my mother was here, she would paint clouds on it, possibly rainbows. My mind has been wandering frequently to my parents lately, accompanied by a nagging feeling, like when you enter a room to do something specific and cannot remember what it is.

I have not returned to the compound for so long that I worry how I will feel about it when I am there. I wonder if our home is still intact. I wonder if any other families have lived there after we left. I decide to take a look when I am back.

I have avoided Seven since I left four years ago because my

parents' 'presence' is everywhere and in almost everything there. If I did not have to report to Kate, I would probably be eluding her too. Having spent sixteen years of my life at the compound, I have built up many memories. I remember when I was moved from the place where I grew up to Kate's sterile habitation after my parents' funeral and feel a lump rise in my throat. My heart shattered into little pieces that day — I had lost my best friends and my home. Going back to the compound is like re-opening a time capsule, but the problem is that I am not sure that I am ready to do it.

I sigh audibly again into the bland, white ceiling. I pry myself slowly off the sofa and head for my bedroom to pack for my journey the next day.

CHAPTER 7

"A journey of a thousand miles begins with a single step."
– Lao Tzu

The view from the hovercraft is magnificent. We have been flying for over two hours, and the morning mist has almost dissipated. We soar over tree tops and I can see the wilderness in patches, extending out as far as the eye can see like a thick, dark-green, red and yellow tapestry over the land. In the distance, a large, V-shaped flock of geese is flying south to warmer regions before winter blankets everything in white. They glide in perfect unison like military jets at an air show.

Neo-Earth is an unbroken canopy of autumn trees in their multitude of colours. The planet must have looked like this millions of years ago when dinosaurs roamed the lands, before men existed. I recognise a sense of calmness in seeing the world from up here. Would all of Neo-Earth resemble this one day?

We are flying eastwards towards Sector Seven. I am accompanied by two Defence Warriors from the CAEP, both seated across from me — large, bearded, muscular men with permanent scowls for expressions. They are preoccupied by the communication pads in their hands, possibly using the quiet time to check on personal affairs. The sound of the engine is muffled and all I hear is a faint and slightly hypnotic 'thwop-thwop-thwop' of the blades.

I look down at the zippered specimen and equipment bags at my feet. I have decided, after Kate's call the night before, not to send her my report since I will be seeing her face to face. It will be easier to gauge her reaction when she reads the full summary. A holo-screen, while useful for communication, can never replace the human aspect of connecting to another person. My mother absolutely hated holo-screen communication. When we were in Seven, she would trudge kilometres to anyone if she wanted to speak to them. She told me that she preferred looking at an actual face than a hologram. Being where I am, I don't have the luxury of human connection anytime I wish. The Peacekeepers, are the only people I 'connect' with in person.

What will Kate do when she reads that the Primes of Sector Five are now in the wilderness lowlands? I believe that this is the first incident of this kind. I don't think any protocol exists to deal with it. Will I be asked to leave Sector Five altogether? A pang of sorrow rises up at the thought. I have become accustomed to the area and am enjoying my work there.

The view outside the hovercraft window is unchanged except that we are now flying over a mountain range. We will be in Seven in another hour. I lean my head against the window, enjoying the sight and the soothing sound of the hovercraft blades.

I must have dozed off because a sudden thud shakes me awake. Outside, a weak sun is attempting to push through the clouds. I recognise the landing zone of the CAEP's compound. The Defence Warriors are already unbuckling their seat belts and preparing to disembark. I proceed to do the same and sling the bags across my shoulders.

We file out of the hovercraft and at the far end of the landing area is Kate, standing with her arms loosely crossed. She looks her usual elegant self in a pair of dark trousers and a white shirt. Her white hair is up in a tight bun. She waits for me as I walk towards her, but even from this distance, I can see she is very tired. I wonder what is keeping her awake at night? Was it the Liogers and what happened during my walkabout? My instincts tell me that she has much more to say about what happened. Although I am grateful and happy to see her, I feel my muscles tense up. Despite every-thing and how long we've known each other, Kate still sometimes makes me nervous.

She opens her arms and I enter her embrace. One thing that I can say about Kate is the strength of her hugs. She has arms made of carphite.

"It's good to see you, Marra," she says into my ear, not yet releasing me. Finally, after a few seconds that feel like a whole minute, she pulls me back to arm's length and stares into my face. I realise that I am turning slightly pink and sensing this, Kate turns, drapes an arm around my shoulder and ushers me forward.

"Good flight?" she asks. Small talk is not her forte. "Let's go to my office, or would you prefer to settle into your habitation first?" It sounds like she prefers we get straight to work and so I acquiesced. "Let's go to your office," I say. Kate smiles, pleased with my agreement.

The airfield is at the northern end of the compound and about six kilometres from the centre of Seven. We get into a matte-silver Samuelson. I see that my small backpack has been removed from the hovercraft and transferred into the vehicle. The two muscular Defence Warriors have somehow disappeared from view. They must have returned to their base without my knowledge. The Defence Unit is located close to the airfield.

The Samuelson crunched out of the landing area and onto a gravel road that leads to the heart of Seven. I am not paying attention to Kate next to me but am more interested in looking out of the window at the large spruce and pine trees all around, like a child returning home after a long absence. The trees are as I remember them, tall and majestic.

About one kilometre before we reach the centre of the compound, there will be a large, gravel track to the left that leads towards its eastern perimeter. At the end of that pathway was where we used to live. I keep my eyes peeled for the wooden signage marked with an arrow that my mother had playfully written: "Stollen, not bought". My father had nailed the signboard on a wooden spike and then hammered it into the earth to mark the turn. I vividly remember how she had howled with laughter at her own pun when she created it. It eventually became some kind of landmark for many people — the 'Stollen Path', they used to call it. I don't know if it has been taken down since I transferred out of Seven.

Kate seems to sense this and keeps silent all through the ride. That side of her is something that I truly appreciate. She has an innate ability to understand what I am feeling and has the kindness to permit me the space to experience the emotion.

"John, please slow down a little," I hear her tell our driver as we draw near to the location. The Samuelson's speed decreases perceptively. I give Kate a grateful look, then turn back to search for the rectangular board.

I see it in the distance getting larger. Kate must have signalled to John to slow down even more because when we are within a metre of it, the vehicle crawls pass. The signage is intact and exactly as I remember it, scrawled in my mother's uneven handwriting. My eyes well up with tears, which I try discretely to wipe away. I feel Kate's warm hand on my back.

"I made sure they left it as it is," is all she says. I nod at the window, not wanting her to see the tears. I am unable to speak because I know that my voice will falter.

By the time we reach Kate's office, I have managed to regain my composure. She works in a white building where a few Mission Control management cadres are located. Her office is a large, bright room enclosed by tall, carphite-glass windows. She has an enormous desk at one end and two armchairs and a comfortable, wide sofa at the other. I have a feeling that this is where she sleeps most nights, being the unrepentant workaholic she is. I sometimes get digital written messages from her in the early morning hours.

I hand her my specimen bag and a digital pad that contains my full report. Kate accepts it, waves me a seat on the sofa and chooses the armchair for herself. For the next few minutes, she is engrossed in reading the document. I stand up and walk towards the large windows. I can see the whole central zone of Seven from here. Right below us is a big, ugly square. The road from the airfield ends there. It is a bare space with white gravel created for major gatherings when an important announcement is required. The academy building is situated on a street directly left of the square, while the hospital is down the road on a street to the right. All habitations are clustered about a kilometre away, and built next to the main thoroughfare from the airfield. Everyone walks here and so for efficiency, distances between two points are minimised.

"Primes!" I hear Kate exclaim behind me. I turn to her shocked face. She has finished reading and the digital pad is on her lap. "You didn't tell me about this last night!" She sounds annoyed.

"Since I am here anyway today …" I trail off because I realise that my words are not having any effect in alleviating her displeasure.

She stands up and walks to where I am. "This changes many things," she says gravely. "We may have to move you permanently out of Sector Five." Her voice is tinged with concern but also something else that I cannot recognise.

"Kate, the survey zone is close to two hundred kilometres from my habitation, still very far from where the Primes are. And besides, this may be an isolated incident. Perhaps they are back on their mountain today. You, yourself, taught me that Primes dislike staying in the lowlands." I am about to continue speaking when Kate interjects.

"And what about the Liogers? Even if what you say is true, we still have them to worry about. Have you brought all your walkabout equipment?"

I point at one of the two bags on the floor near the door. Kate reaches the door in five wide strides, opens it and says something inaudible to a person outside. A few seconds later, a tall, young man with shocking, white-blond hair and tired eyes, enters and removes both packs. "Get the equipment checked and report back," she says to him. Then turns back to me, "We'll have to check the satellite feed on where the animals are now." Her voice holds a hint of nervousness, which may go unnoticed to those who do not know Kate as well as I do. I see a trace of worry on her brow.

She guides me back to the sofa and sits next to me. "Tell me again about the Liogers." Kate does not keep her eyes off me for a second while I tell her, as if searching for a sign of deception. I sense that she is more than just concerned. In fact, she looks almost terrified. Her pupils are slightly dilated and she is flushed.

"Kate, are you alright?" I ask her when I finish. I have never seen her in this state of agitation.

She shakes her head as if to dispel some unwanted thoughts. "Yes, yes, I'm fine." She stands and goes to get us both glasses of water. I recognise this move. I am the expert in stalling and buying myself time to respond. It is strange to see Kate using the same ploy. I wonder what is making her so uneasy.

She returns with the glasses and takes a sip in hers. I continue to watch her in silence. She is deep in thought, her brow knotted in stress lines.

"Do you know something I don't?" I ask her, less gently than I intend to.

Kate shakes her head. "I was just thinking ..." she begins and then appears to change her mind. "We'll know more when your equipment maintenance report comes back. This may be a malfunction," she continues.

"Not likely. I checked them myself the night before. They work perfectly."

"Let's just wait for the report before jumping to conclusions."

I am convinced that there is something she is not sharing with me, but I see no point in pushing the issue. Kate will tell me when she is ready, or at least I hope she will. It is unusual to see her this way, worried and almost nervous. Maybe she knows about these 'special' Liogers? Has she heard about them before? Has anyone else reported similar incidents?

"Let's speak about this again later. Now let me take you to your habitation. You can rest, shower, change and we will have lunch at thirteen hundred hours." She smiles as if on cue. I feel like I am being ushered out of her office because she no longer wants to discuss the issue.

For the visit, I am placed in a habitation building where guests normally stay. I prefer it to living with Kate because as much as we care about each other, we are awkward together. I suddenly wonder how I will last a whole month in the compound. The first day is already proving challenging.

Lunch is in a large hall where most of the management people dine. This is the only area where food is served once a day. I have forgotten what a small community Seven truly is. I am surprised when Kate walks me to a table occupied by a distinguished looking gentleman in a white shirt and a brown jacket. He stands up as soon as we arrive and smiles, his impeccable white teeth gleaming and perfectly contrasted on his dark skin. He looks Asian and resembles a tall, handsome, older alter ego to my favourite childhood hero, Clark Kent, with salt and pepper hair and a well-groomed, white beard. Ancient comic books are thankfully preserved in digital copies and as a child, I have been known to spend hours hiding in the Seven library reading them all. He even has Clark Kent's dark-rimmed, square glasses. I get the sense that Kate appreciates him a little more than just as a colleague.

"Marra, this is Doctor Liam Anders," she says, beaming.

I smile and shake his extended hand. A firm grip, which my mother told me once is a sign of confidence. "Nice to meet you, Doctor," I say. If he is startled by the unusual gold colour of my irises, he is good at hiding it because I see no flicker of hesitation in his gaze. It is a reaction that I normally get from strangers and while I don't admit it, it more than often stings my feelings.

"Please call me Liam. No need for formality," he says in a deep voice. He has a likeable demeanour. "Kate tells me you will be here with us for a month."

I look over to her. "I think so," I reply, still hanging on to hope that I can escape earlier.

"Yes, Marra will be spending a month here at Seven. A home leave, and she will also be able to get acquainted with all of CAEP's latest developments and progress." Kate affirms. She then turns to me and announces, "Liam is our Head of Research and Development. We are very lucky to have him working for us here."

I am not aware of the changes in personnel at the CAEP. Before her demise, my mother was the Head. "When did you join us, Liam?" I ask. "I don't keep up with the news much."

"Let's see … I joined two and half years ago now," he smiles. He speaks Americana with a northern European accent that I cannot place.

I want to ask more questions but feel it may come off as rude. I content myself with watching Kate converse with Liam. They appear relaxed in each other's company and I am detecting a mutual attraction, which makes me smile secretly. I want to see Kate settle down and happy. She deserves it and as men go, Liam is charming and there is no wedding band on his finger. He is an interesting person and speaks confidently. He is also quick to smile. Liam looks to be a typical product of Neo-Earth's migration — a dark-skinned Asian who is European. I wonder what he thinks of me and my heritage. He is after all a geneticist and must be intrigued with 'hybrids' like me.

"I hear you are taking care of Sector Five?" It was a question from Liam to me.

"Yes, I've been there over a year now. Have you been to the west?" I ask. My father had taught me that it is polite to ask something in return in a conversation. I smile at myself for having recalled this memory.

"I must admit that I have not." Liam shifts in his seat. "I was mostly working in the South-East, in Sector Nineteen, with the Federation before I joined the CAEP." He must have seen the surprise on my face because he adds, "I realised that I want my work to help and make a difference. I can achieve much more here."

It is not often that someone, especially a scientist of his calibre, moves from the Federation side to ours. Their philosophy on animal preservation differs fundamentally from that of the CAEP. In addition, it is no secret that they pay handsomely for someone with unique qualifications, which is probably the case with Liam, who appears highly educated and capable. He smiles kindly at me. He has not once asked about my parents. Kate must have warned him not to.

"Do you enjoy living here?" I ask with unpractised grace, not sure how else to keep the conversation going. My mother would be proud of the effort I am putting into socialising.

"It is …" he searches for an appropriate word. "Interesting," he decides. I hear Kate chuckle next to him, which has him turning to her and smiling. "It is a small place, but I have adapted and made good friends." He looks at Kate as he mentions 'friends' and her cheeks flush pink. The sight of it is quite endearing. I have not known Kate to be affected by words nor by any person. I have a gut feeling that she likes this man, because she seems somewhat giddy in front of him.

I later find out from her that he is currently the world's top authority on genetics and animal bio-neurology. He has published many papers and is sought after by every reputable research organisation. The fact that he has chosen the CAEP over the Federation is a great honour. I think that my parents would have liked him.

I let Kate and Liam continue the conversation for the rest of the meal, happy to chew quietly and observe their disguised court-ship dance. Liam asks me the occasional question to politely bring me into the discussion. He has no idea that I much prefer listening to speaking. I notice how Kate's expression is softened by the presence of Liam and I notice how he talks with gestures, moving his hands here and there to emphasise certain points. His eyes, however, are curiously still. The light within them remain constant, almost unmoving, even when he smiles. I have not seen that in anyone I know.

I am relieved when the meal ends. Liam walks us to the building, offers me his hand and then kisses Kate lightly on her cheek, like most Europeans do, before turning and heading in the direction of the Research laboratories in large, confident strides. The happy tune he is whistling fades as he moves further away. I have a feeling that I will see him again soon, judging from Kate's flushed com-plexion as we enter the building.

I spend the following two days in Kate's company being briefed on the organisation's latest news. Although useful, it feels like I am back in the academy. Kate is brilliant but lacks imagination. Her briefing sessions feel like classroom lectures.

There is still no verdict on whether I will be permitted to remain in Sector Five. Satellite thermal sweeps on Sector Five have revealed that the Primes have not returned to their home in northern mountains of the Sector. Instead, they appear to be slowly moving East towards the boundary line. Part of the Rocky Mountain range lies there. The big question is whether they will stop and make a new home in the mountains or continue on to Six. If they do, then we may have a big problem on our hands. Seven lies adjacent to Six, and our compound would need to be evacuated should the Primes continue their journey eastwards.

I watch Kate's frown grow deeper as she examines the thermals.

"Damnit!" I hear her curse under her breath. At times like this, I have learnt to keep very still and quiet. When Kate is angry enough to curse, it is advisable to let her vent until she runs out of steam. She is like a kettle on the boil.

She looks up at me suddenly, her eyes boring into mine. I can feel my heart rate rising slightly.

"Any reason why the Primes are moving towards Six? Haven't they always stayed on the northern mountains by the Sector Two and Three borders?"

"For as long as I have been monitoring them, they have not moved."

"Then WHY are they doing it now?" Kate says. I am not sure the question is directed to me or just rhetorical. I choose to say nothing. I am worried that if Kate feels the danger is still there, then I will never set foot in Five again and I will never have the chance to find the Liogers.

"But they appear to be moving away from the area I was, Kate. It is safe to assume that they are moving away," I say, hoping that Kate agrees.

Kate purses her lips, her eyebrows deeply knotted. "Let's keep monitoring that. Even if they are moving away from where the

Liogers were, we may have a different issue if they continue on to Sector Six."

I breathe a sigh of relief. My return to Five is still possible.

The Liogers, however, cannot be found. Only two conclusions are possible: they have moved on to another Sector, or they are cunning enough to avoid satellite detection. Despite all our advanced technology and equipment, it is not easy to locate all the animals in the wilderness. While infrared thermal imagers have progressed over the years, the resolution of heat signatures from space are still not high enough for us to see specific shapes. They look more like dots than animals. This is one of the reasons we have field agents. At the end of the day, 'eye and ear' witness accounts are still the most reliable. For more precise infrared thermal images, it is necessary to use a drone to fly over the wilderness area, but herein lies another challenge — where to look. The wilderness is vast.

On the fourth day, I am in Kate's office looking over the satellite feeds, seated across from her at the desk. The Primes appear to have stopped at the foot of the Rocky mountain range. Maybe they have made a new home there. We have to wait a few more days to see if this is true. As long as they stay there, they will be hundreds of kilometres from the area where the Liogers reside. This will make my return possible.

The maintenance report has confirmed that all my devices are functionally optimally, which is disconcerting to us both. I decided to plunge in and ask her thoughts.

"Kate, do you have a theory on why the thermal imagers did not detect the Liogers?" I ask her. she stiffens at the question and looks at me for a second before averting her gaze.

"I am not sure why it is happening, Marra," she finally says, not looking up from the logs she is examining.

"Do you think, it would be a new hybrid of Liogers?" That strikes a chord, because she looks up, her face slightly pale. Not to lose momentum, I add, "Is that possible? That a new genetic species of Liogers developed naturally in the wilderness?"

This time, Kate stands up and leaves her desk. She looks out of the large windows and sighs. I watch her without saying anything. She then turns to me and motions to the sofa.

"I think that it is time I tell you something." A shiver runs up my spine, I am both worried and excited at the same time, expecting a 'good news, bad news' kind of story.

"In the early years after your parents married," Kate begins, "they requested an experimental habitation built in the large forest, close to the border between Sector Two and Five. I'm sure you remember the place, even if you were just a child then. It was one with perimeter sensors, but no force fields." An image of our dark green house lights up my memory.

"Your parents were convinced that animals would only attack if they feel threatened and wanted to prove this theory. They believed that despite their enhanced sizes and strength, their fundamental behavioural patterns were the same as those of their ancestors. Your father had been consulting with zoologists in the COE. He believed that with ample prey in the forest and no danger from human hunters, the animals would leave them alone. These were the early days of the CAEP before field agents were deployed in all Sectors." Kate glances at me, a guilty look in her eyes. "I believed in their theory and helped convince the CAEP Director to allow them this experimental home."

"One of the conditions of living there was having a full-time Defence Warrior stationed with them. Your parents wanted privacy to conduct their research and somehow managed to persuade the CAEP director to allow them to have an Ukuu assigned instead."

"U-kuu?" I ask, never having heard of the word before.

Kate smiles. "They are a small tribe who used to live in Neo-Afrika, famous for animal tracking and hand-to-hand combat. There are not many of them left today. They were relocated to southern COE when their country fell and due to their fighting skills and extensive knowledge of wild animal behaviour, many were recruited by the WPO as specialised Peacekeepers.

Your father grew up with one of them, Kondo, and was close

to his family and tribe. It was Kondo who accompanied and lived with your parents in their experimental habitation. He resigned from his Peacekeeper role with the WPO in order to do that."

I search my memory and seem to recall fragments it: sitting on the shoulder of a tall, muscular, dark-skinned man with silver eyes; comparing my five-year-old white hand to a large black-brown one …

"The first two years went well and your parents and I were excited that their theory was proving true. There were no animal incursions and your parents' walkabouts indicated that while they were present all around, none of them ventured within the perimeter of the habitation, which was about two kilometres all around. We were ecstatic. It was the first concrete evidence of the possibility of co-existence."

CHAPTER 8

*"We are made from Mother Earth and we go
back to Mother Earth."*
– Shenandoah

August 4821

"Get your things quickly, Liebling! Hurry!" Rolf is telling his wife, Eva, as he urgently packs his digital pads and survey equipment into a large, black bag.

"No, not yet!" Eva stands by the window, looking out. She is trying to see if the Lioger is entering the perimeter. Its roar reverberates through the forest and now sounds like it is only about three kilometres away, far too close to the habitation and so Rolf decides to evacuate.

"Eva, please don't do this now. Pack up your things. We must go!" Rolf says, exasperation in his voice.

"No! It is not anywhere near the perimeter. In fact, I think that there is something wrong with it." Eva says. She is still at the window surveying the area.

Rolf walks over and turns her around by the shoulders. Looking at her directly, he says, "Liebling, the Lioger is too close to us. I will feel much better that you pack your things and we go, yes?"

"But Rolf, listen to it! It sounds like something IS wrong. I think we need to take a look," Eva's eyes grow large as she explains. She does that when an idea takes a hold of her and Rolf knows that expression too well.

"No, Eva," he lowers his voice, hoping she will listen. But she is already moving away from him.

She types something on her wrist communicator and stands there smiling at Rolf. "I've cancelled the evacuation request," she tells him. Rolf's stares at his wife as if she has lost her mind.

"Why would you do that, Liebling? That is crazy!"

"I'm not crazy and you have to trust me, okay?" She puts on her puncture-proof jacket and heads for the door. Rolf walks after her, "Eva, please listen to me. You cannot go out there. It is too dangerous!"

Eva continues to ignore his pleas. She turns to him, "Sweetheart, that Lioger may need our help. Let's go and do that, yes? Trust me."

Rolf looks to Kondo for inspiration, 'help me' written across his expression. When his wife puts her mind to something, it is hard to change it. Kondo only shakes his head and picks up his HEL. He is aware that Eva will not listen to any of them.

Rolf lets out an infuriated cry, picks up his weapon and follows his wife out the door. Outside, he stops her and put his wife between himself and Kondo and the three of them proceed in the direction of the roars.

They move cautiously. Rolf can pinpoint the Lioger's location with the satellite thermal locater on his wristband. The notation '1200m' is flashing angrily in red. They are getting close. The sound is increasing steadily. What Rolf fears most is meeting more than one Lioger because he knows that he will not be able to protect his wife. So far, however, the roar appears to come from only one animal.

They finally come upon the source of the disturbance. About fifteen metres in front of them is a Liogress, a giant, milky-white female. She is scratching at a fissure in a rock face as if trying to get inside or to retrieve something. The hole is fairly large, enough for a human but too small for a giant beast to fit. Rolf, Eva and Kondo stay very still in their place, not wishing to draw the Liogress' attention to themselves. Fortunately for them, she appears more concerned about the gap in the rock than her surroundings.

"Listen!" Eva whispers to her husband, pointing up in the air.

Rolf hears nothing but the roar. Before the next one starts, Eva taps her right ear with her finger, asking him to listen carefully. Kondo suddenly nods. He hears it. This time Rolf pays more attention. He closes his eyes to concentrate. Almost imperceptibly, he detects the muffled mewling of a cub. His eyes fly open and he nods at Eva. She points to where the Liogress is and with both hands, mimes a circle. Her husband knows that she is indicating the crack in the rock face and understands she thinks the mewling sound is emanating from within.

"I must get into that cave," she whispers into Rolf's ear. He shakes his head and lip-syncs the word 'NO'. Never will he allow his wife to do something so dangerous. Besides, how will she even be able to get anywhere close to the hole with the Liogress guarding it?

"I will get closer and you and Kondo will distract her for a few seconds. Then I can dive into the entrance," Eva hisses into Rolf's ear.

"No!" he hisses back. "She will kill you! Eva, there is nothing we can do here. We must leave!" His wife has a bad habit of over-simplifying situations. While it may sound easy to her, he knows from experience that it is suicide.

She looks at her husband, her eyes a mixture of anger and determination. Then without any warning, starts to move forward, towards to the Liogress. Rolf tries to hold her back, but she shrugs his grip off her furiously. He feels Kondo's large hand on his shoulder. Kondo's expression tells him to let her go and for them to do as she asks.

Heart racing, Eva moves slowly towards the rock face from the side, hidden by the bushes. The Liogress has detected her presence, but she is more worried about her cub inside the fissure. She casts a few angry growls in Eva's direction and springs forward as if to attack, but she is only trying to scare Eva into retreating. Eva is now about three metres from the cave, hidden behind bushes. She looks at Rolf and Kondo and nods. Rolf's heart is beating out of his chest, he is not confident that this plan will work. He and Kondo choose a spot about ten metres behind the Liogress. They want to leave enough space for the beast to charge at them and to move away from the rock face.

Then, they start shouting. Kondo trains his HEL on the Liogress while Rolf coaxes her to follow him. It is working. The Liogress slowly turns and starts to prowl menacingly towards them. She fixes her gaze on Rolf and contorts her mouth into a terrifying snarl. She is a giant beast, easily three times the size of Rolf. She can kill him with just one well-placed bite.

Eva watches intently as the beast slowly moves closer to where her husband is standing. When she finally leaves a space of about four metres from the rock face, Eva sprints, summoning all the energy she has in her legs and heads for the hole. The Liogress suddenly stops and whips her head around. She hears the echo of boots on the soil. Swivelling back, she runs towards the gap. Eva doubles her effort and speeds up. She must reach the cave entrance before the animal or she will kill her. She is only a few feet from it, but she knows that the Liogress is faster than she is.

They reach the gap almost at the same time. Eva dives head first into it but not before the enraged female takes a swipe at her with a giant paw with extended claws as sharp as knives. Eva cries out as a searing pain shoots up her right leg. She lands heavily inside the cave and then scrambles away from the entrance. The claw leaves an ugly gash above her ankle. It is seeping blood. She picks herself up, groaning as she puts weight on her injured leg. Although the wound looks threatening, she knows that it is not fatal. Outside, she hears the enraged roar of the Liogress as she begins scratching again.

Eva turns her attention to the surroundings. As her eyes begin to adjust to the dimness of the cave, she realises that it is about the size of a large room with a high ceiling. The ground is compacted dirt and slopes slightly downwards. At the bottom about three metres away, she sees a white Lioger cub head. It is an unusual sight because the head appears to be on the ground without a body.

Eva hobbles down towards it. The cub begins mewing again. It is frightened. As Eva approaches, she understands what she is seeing. The creature is stuck in quicksand and the more it struggles, the more it is sinking.

Fortunately, the quicksand area is only about three metres in diameter and Eva knows she can reach the cub's head easily. The difficulty will be to pull it out because it looks like most of its body is already sunk in. Eva takes her jacket off and places it flat on the quicksand close to the cub's head. Then she lies on her stomach and very carefully and slowly, crawls towards the terrified animal. Half her body is now above her jacket on the soft sand, while the other half is on solid ground. Although still very young, the cub is about the same size as Eva and probably twice as heavy. It growls at her as she wraps her arms around its neck, but it is unable to do more than that. Eva can feel its fear through its thick coat, its heart thumping frantically.

Eva pulls as hard as she can to try to dislodge the cub, but try as she may, she is not strong enough. Tears of frustration starts to fall from her eyes as she realises the poor animal may die. It is struggling, trying to paddle its way out, unaware that the more it squirms, the more it is sinking, dragging Eva down with it.

"Stop moving, little baby Lioger," Eva says soothingly to it in her maternal voice, but it only mews in terror and continues. Tears of fear are running down her cheeks as she tries again to pull it out, but instead, feels herself being slowly dragged into the pit. Suddenly, she feels hands grab her waist.

"Hold on, Liebling!" her husband's deep voice tells her. Eva cannot turn her head as her arms are around the neck of the cub, but a wave of relief washes over her. Rolf has come to her rescue.

"Hold tight!"

Slowly, she feels her body move back towards solid ground and she clings tighter to the young creature. Thankfully, it has stopped moving from exhaustion, and starts to pant. She hears Rolf grunt from the tremendous effort.

It is a gradual and energy-intensive process and after several agonising minutes, they free the young cub from the quicksand. Rolf takes his wife in his arms, glad that she is alive. The cub first lies on the ground, panting, exhausted from all its attempts to free itself, then slowly, it stands up on unsteady legs and heads up the slope to its mother, waiting outside. The roars stop abruptly as the family reunites. Eva and Rolf lay back, tired smiles on their faces. Her head is on his shoulder while they wait for a safe moment to leave.

"I thought the Liogress had killed you," Rolf says and kisses his wife on her sweaty forehead. "I heard you scream. I was so afraid …" his voice cracks with emotion.

"How did you get past her?" Eva asks, looking up at his worried face. Her heart swells with love for this man, who has braved an enraged Liogress to save her.

"Kondo was bait," he answers and then starts to chuckle. He does not tell her how he ran towards the beast without thinking when he heard her scream and how Kondo had to hold him back. They lie there quietly, listening to each other breathing. Eva has completely forgotten about the wound on her leg, but now that the adrenaline is wearing off, the pain returns. The blood is soaking into her torn pant leg and spreading.

"We must get you home," Rolf tells her calmly, aware of the gaping wound. Eva nods.

"We go now!" Kondo suddenly appears inside the cave and signals for them to move. He has a gift for appearing abruptly and using as few words as possible.

Rolf helps Eva up and as she hobbles forward, she leaves a trail of tiny blood drops. Kondo points to it, "she bleeds," he says.

Rolf has known this man all his life and understands how and what he means to say. Leaving a trail of blood is dangerous because it may lead animals to the habitation. Therefore, Rolf tears the sleeve off his shirt, uses it as a tourniquet to stop the bleeding and then lifts Eva up and puts her across one shoulder, carrying her like a sack of grains. He can move faster this way. She is so tired that she does not protest. She must be losing more blood than she initially estimated, he thinks.

At the habitation, he washes, sews and dresses her wound, and she is soon fast asleep. Rolf watches her for a little while and then joins Kondo at the habitation window to keep vigil. One Liogress means that there is a whole pride of them nearby.

A week goes by, however, and no Liogers appear at the habitation. Rolf and Kondo relax and life starts to return to normal routines. Then a week after that, in the early hours of the morning and while Rolf and Eva are still asleep, the proximity alarm screams. Rolf bolts out of bed and proceeds to dress as quickly as he can. Eva follows. The door swings open minutes later and Kondo strides in. "Come," he says, motioning to them with a flick of his head. Eva notices that he is already in his full combat outfit and is carrying his HEL. How he manages to be ready so quickly is a constant mystery to her.

From the window that looks out to the front yard, Eva is shocked to see a cub standing about twenty metres away from the front door, its body swaying a little from side to side. It appears to be the same one she rescued, judging from its milky coat, but she does not remember it looking so sickly. It is bald in patches and its eyes appear to be watering. Without saying a word, Eva opens the door and goes out before Rolf has time to stop her. She walks towards the young animal. It makes no move to leave and instead, sits heavily down, its body continuing to sway. It is as if it is on some kind of drug and is about to collapse. It is then that Eva remembers the mother. She looks around and sees the female about five metres back, lying on her side. Eva cannot see if she is alive. Her abdomen looks distended and her legs and paws are swollen. She is also balding in patches.

"Eva!" Rolf calls out to her. She ignores him and slowly approaches the young animal. It makes no effort to leave and does not display any hostile behaviour. Then, as if it can no longer continue sitting, its strength gives up and it slumps on its side. Its breath comes out in ragged streams. Eva kneels to take a closer look. Like the mother, its abdomen is distended and its legs and paws, swollen. There are black sores on its body that are oozing.

"Rolf, help me!" she calls out to her husband. He is already standing over her. "Help me carry it inside," she says. Then without waiting for Rolf to respond, she walks over to the giant Liogress lying motionless. She does not hear Rolf telling her not to go. As she gets closer, she realises that the female is still alive, although barely. Her breathing is ragged and shallow. It has the same sores that are on her cub. Given her size and weight, Eva knows that she will have to be treated where she is. Eva turns and runs back to the house to get her medical kit. She is not a veterinarian but has read extensively about the Old Lions and worked long enough alongside her veterinary colleagues to be able to understand Lioger anatomy. Her medical background helps and she is determined to cure the animals as best she can.

Rolf and Kondo place the cub on the large kitchen table, lying on its side, eyes closed. Rolf begins to take samples of the pus oozing from its wound as well as the liquid from its eyes. Kondo stands back, still holding the HEL.

"Go look after Eva," he tells him in his native, Neo-Afrikan language, which Rolf speaks fluently. "I am fine here." Kondo quietly leaves him and heads out to where Eva is outside.

She is bending over the giant mother, doing the same as her husband. She uses her stethoscope to listen to the animal's lungs and heart and then drawing out a large syringe, she very carefully finds an artery in order to draw some blood. The Liogress momentarily raises her head and growls, sending Eva scampering back. Kondo raises his HEL, ready to defend her. Then the beast lowers her head again, too weak to fight back. Eva resumes her action, with more caution this time.

She draws several vials of blood to carry out her investigation. Then she takes all her specimens back into the habitation, but not before bringing the Liogress some water and pouring it into her mouth. The huge beast licks the clear liquid down, but is too weak to raise her head. This is the first time Eva comes close to a Liogress, and she cautiously strokes her body, in awe of its size and beauty.

Eva and Rolf race against time to find the cause of this strange disease. The hybrid's blood, Eva and Rolf discover to their great surprise, is similar to human blood through its genetic evolution and mutation. This means that it is easier for them to find a cure because there are less compatibility issues if they need to use human blood for transfusions. Nature has somehow altered the animals' biology and brought them closer to humans. By mid-morning, Kondo joins in the effort. His task is to keep the animals hydrated and warm.

While waiting for a cure, both of them are injected with an antibiotic, normally reserved for humans, which appears to stop their deterioration temporarily. Eva also keeps the animals slightly sedated, upon Kondo's insistence. It is dangerous if the Liogress suddenly decides to attack.

Eva and Rolf work ceaselessly for the following few days to understand the nature of the bacterial infection and to try to develop an antidote. In their research, they find out that the animals have ingested a poison that is giving them the sores and making them sick. While they stay to work in the habitation, they send Kondo to find the source of the toxin. Rolf knows that if anyone can track and locate anything in the forest, it will be him.

Kondo returns two days later, with a bottle of clear liquid. It is water from a drinking hole, fifteen kilometres away. He has tracked the source of the poison there by following a trail of dead animals. Sadly, he has also found the pride that both the Liogress and her cub belonged to. The contaminated liquid has killed all members and they have lain decomposing for several days, exhibiting the same sores found on the two animals. They now understand why there are no other Liogers in the area. The female and her offspring probably drank from the poison pool a few days after the cub was rescued from the quicksand pit. This gives Eva an approximate timeline on how long it takes the poison to take effect.

With the source established, it is not long before Eva and Rolf finds a cure for the toxin that causes the bacterial infection. It is found in human blood. The poison is engineered to kill only hybrid animals by attacking a specific protein in their blood. Due to the hybrid's near compatibility to human blood, it is possible to counter the effects of the poison by replacing the damaged protein with that from human blood. To create the cure, Eva isolates and extracts it from her own blood and then injects into the animals. Once the protein is repaired, it is a waiting game to see if the animals' bodies will rally and repair themselves. Six days have passed since the Liogress and her cub collapsed at their habitation and Eva realises that time is of the essence. She draws a small pack of her own blood and also one of Rolf's and commences the process.

The next day, they inject the protein into the animals. The antidote appears to be working as the sores start to heal, but the animals are still weak. Rolf and Kondo carries the Lioger cub from the habitation and places it next to its mother. After that, it is a question of waiting for the cure to take effect.

It takes another twenty-four hours before further signs of improvement start to manifest, which is faster than Eva anticipates. She deduces that Lioger blood, given the correct assistance, actually repairs itself quickly. Eva, Rolf and Kondo watch their patients from within the habitation like expectant doctors.

At the end of the eighth day, the Liogress sits up uneasily and starts licking her offspring. They are weak from not having eaten for over a week. Rolf has instructed Kondo to hunt a giant rodent and puts it close to the mother. It is not ideal, but these are extraordinary circumstances. The Liogress and her cub feed tentatively on the carcass, eyeing the humans the entire time. When they finish, they slowly walk away, casting a final glance at the habitation.

Kate looks at me, trying to read my expression. I am stunned. I wonder why my parents have not told me of this.

"You see," she continues. "Because of the transfusion, I believe that the Liogress and her cub became the first of their kind to receive our blood. And I believe that they evolved further." Kate sighs. "Your parents told me what they did and I kept their secret because if the CAEP had known of this, they would have been banished. I don't condone what they did, but I understand."

Condone? I am surprised that Kate disagrees with what my parents did. I feel even prouder of them knowing what they did.

"So ..." I say, "you think that the thermals did not detect the Liogers during the walkabout because they are newly evolved hybrids?"

Kate nods, "I think so. That appears to be a logical explanation. They must have developed other abilities in order to become undetectable to thermal sensors. I believe they may have migrated down to Sector Five."

It is a plausible explanation. "So only you know this?" I ask.

"And now you do too," Kate affirms. "In all honesty, this happened over twenty-five years ago and in all this time, we have never had a problem with Lioger incursions and therefore I thought the new breed didn't survive."

"And what will you do now?" I ask her. I worry that Kate will tell the CAEP and drastic action will then be taken to hunt down the animals. Beasts that are 'invisible' to sensors will be considered a major threat to humanity.

Kate stands up and walks to the window. After a moment she says, "I don't know," and shakes her head gently. She looks conflicted.

"Did the Liogress and her cub return to the habitation?" I ask with interest.

"I asked your parents the same question and they said they never saw the animals again."

"What about the poison? The Federation?"

"Yes," Kate replies. "Your parents returned to the water hole to cover it up so no other animal could drink from it and ran into the Federation warriors and scientists at the site."

"What happened then?" I ask. Knowing my mother, she would not have let her feelings about it remain unspoken.

"There would have been an altercation if not for your father. He convinced your mother to hide and watch from a distance. She recorded the Federation personnel on a video."

"Where's the recording? Did they report the incident to Mission Control?" I feel outraged, even though this had happened twenty-seven years ago. I am beginning to understand why my parents had never trusted the Federation and had often told me not to, when I was old enough to understand.

"Yes, they did, but the Federation received nothing more than a hefty fine by the WPO for poisoning the animals. Your mother was disappointed ... furious." Kate continues, "In fact, that was how the Field Agent Programme started. It was your father's idea — a way to increase the CAEP's presence in the forests and wilderness of the FSA.

My heart swells with pride — my parents not only saved a Liogress and her cub but also created the Field Agent Program. Kate smiles at me. "Your parents were very well-respected and your mother," she laughs, "a force to be reckoned with!" Her mood returns to seriousness once more. "But, I still don't know how to solve our current problem," she says gravely, referring to the new, Lioger hybrids. Not being visible on thermals implies that they can approach any human habitation without detection.

"Will you report this to the Director?" I ask again.

Kate looks thoughtful. She knows that reporting it will endanger the survival of the new hybrids, but not reporting it would mean her dismissal.

"You know what they will do if you report this, Kate," I tell her, appealing to her empathy. The Federation will send Peacekeepers to hunt down the new hybrids and the CAEP will not have any authority to stop it because the WPO will agree with the Federation that they pose major human threats.

"How can we protect anyone if we cannot track these creatures, Marra?" Kate looks perplexed.

"Let me return to Sector Five," I say. "Let me find them. Once I have located them, we can continue monitoring them. Let me use the portable drones to locate them. The satellite may not see them, but maybe with drones, they might be visible."

Kate studies me, and I can see doubts clouding her thoughts.

"I'll think this through," she finally decides. "I'll let you know my decision soon."

I open my mouth to say something more and change my mind when I see her frowning at me. I nod. "I'll return to my habitation and continue looking over the satellite feeds there."

I take a last glance at Kate as I leave. She is at the window, looking uncertain. I don't see how she can disagree with my plan. There aren't any other alternatives.

CHAPTER 9

"Look deep into nature, and then you will
understand everything better."
– Albert Einstein

It is early and the sun has not quite risen, as swirls of purple and orange sky begin to part ways. A round of Robins are singing their dawn songs. It is cold and my breath is visible in puffs. I smile remembering how, when I was child, I used to pretend I was an ancient steam train and 'chugged' to school, billowing 'smoke' from my mouth.

I am on my way to see Kate, having been summoned the night before. A boy with blond hair unevenly flattened by sleep, walks past me on the wide pavement, his shoes tapping the concrete in quick succession. He must have just woken up not too long ago, as his eyes still carry a remnant of sleep. As he passes, he turns his head and winks, which takes me completely by surprise and I suppress a chuckle. I wonder which adult he learned that from — an older brother or his father?

More children are passing me from behind and one or two are running, holding hands and giggling about a shared joke. Young, carefree faces, still unwrinkled and hopeful. They are moving towards the street where the academy building is located. I remember when I was one of these children, making my way to class, in braided pigtails and holding my digital pad. Did my face have the same look? I stand at the crossroads where I know our paths diverge and watch the students walk, run towards the white building of the academy. The winking boy is far ahead of the others. He walks with a lot of determination for someone so young.

I take a breath of cold air, look forward and continue my walk towards Kate's office. It has been two days since I last saw her. Maybe she has come to a decision about my returning earlier to Sector Five, at least I hope so. I feel compelled to return to the wilderness, knowing that there is a pride of new hybrid Liogers there. The fact of this new species is a great thing — a break-through. But the question is, will Kate let me go back?

The day is grey and the wind is playing with the fallen leaves, creating swirls on the pavement. A collective honking comes from far above me. Thick flocks of snow geese dot the sky, as they fly south. The air smells like dry ice and soon, it will be too cold to breathe it in.

I skip up the flight of steps to the main door of the building where Kate's office is located. The magnetic door slides open and instead of taking the lift, I decide to take the stairs. I am feeling a little anxious and the activity will ease my nerves. Her office is located six flights up and I take the steps two at a time. By the time I arrive at her door, I am breathing hard. Her young assistant with the shocking white-blond hair is looking at me strangely, probably wondering why anyone would choose to run up on foot. I flash him a quick smile.

"She's expecting you, you can go right in," he says in a thick, mid-European accent that I did not expect. I gaze at him, a little surprised, but he has already returned to staring at his computer, a bored expression etched on his face. I wonder if he enjoys his work. He appears no older than I am.

The door slides open. Kate is seated on her sofa, laughing and chatting to a young man with cropped, dark blond hair, on the armchair. His back is towards me, but at the sound of my entrance, he turns and our eyes meet. My heart stops and my body freezes. I have met him before. He is handsome with deep-set, piercing eyes, the colour of leaves in spring. His short hair stands like soldiers on his head. He gets up from his seat and stands there smiling.

"Hi Marra," he says in his velvet baritone voice and displays a dazzling set of perfect teeth. I continue to stand there looking stunned. He was the Peacekeeper who accompanied me on my walkabouts about a year ago, Yon Hunter. I have never seen him with hair and he looks even better than in my memory.

"You remember Yon?" Kate breaks the spell and I turn towards her. My face feels warm. I walk to the sofa and sit next to Kate, nodding, then, remembering my manners, return Yon's smile, muttering a "hello."

He is still standing, smiling and eventually takes his seat. The memory of him and how I used to feel about him comes flooding back. My heart is beating like an infatuated schoolgirl. I wish that Kate had told me that he would be here so that I can be more mentally prepared. It is then that I shift my attention abruptly back to her, thinking to myself: "Why is he here at all?"

Kate clears her throat, anticipating my question. "Marra, I agree to you returning earlier to Sector Five to track down the Lioger pride," she begins, "on the condition that you have a protector with you. So ..." She pauses for dramatic effect, then turning to Yon, she says, "Yon is assigned as your partner."

My eyes grow large with alarm. That means that we will be living together in my habitation! I am not prepared for that. I have only ever lived with my parents and Kate. Letting a stranger into my private space feels like a violation. I sense that I have just walked into a baited trap — I get what I want but only under specific conditions. "Kate," I start, "I don't need a protector. I ..."

"No, no, no," Kate says, shaking her head. "To keep this ... incident between us, we cannot use Federation Peacekeepers." She looks at Yon, who is listening.

"But he IS a Peacekeeper," I say, realising too late that I sound like a protesting child.

"Not anymore," Yon suddenly speaks up. I have forgotten how I have enjoyed the tone of his voice and try to distract myself by focussing on my outrage. "I joined the CAEP Defence Unit after I left the Peacekeeping Force."

"When was that?" I ask, sounding defensive.

"Right after I left Sector Five," he says. This must be why he stopped coming for the walkabouts with me. I remember sleepless nights thinking about where he was, trying to figure out what I had done for him to leave so suddenly and without warning. Then when the pining stopped, the anger began. I thought that we were friends and friends certainly would not abandon one another.

I concentrate on Kate. She is looking intently at me and so I walk over to the window to distance myself from her gaze. I often feel like Kate can look into my soul, in a way, and it is unnerving. With Yon there, I feel doubly strange; I feel like I have been left out of a conspiracy between them.

"I cannot have you look for the hybrids on your own," Kate says. "It's too dangerous. I took a look at Defence Warriors we have here and came across Yon's profile. He was stationed in Sector Five last year and was with you for four months. He is perfect for this mission."

I say nothing. Kate is right. Yon has been with me longer than any other Peacekeeper and he had always been inquisitive about my work. I have no doubt that he is the right choice, but I am uncomfortable with having to live with someone I have known only from the field for a few months. And then there's the fact that I'm likely still infatuated with him. Worse than that, he might catch on — and I don't want that to become a hindrance to our fieldwork.

"You both will leave for Sector Five in two days. I want to get Yon up to speed on what is happening and also get him all the proper equipment for his work there with you ... a crash course on field agent work. She then stands and Yon follows, as a sign of respect. "I will file all the relevant documents for you to be assigned to Sector Five and to report to me," she says to him and extends her hands out to shake his.

He towers over her, as my father once had. I look at him in his black, Defence Warrior uniform that silhouettes the sculpted body underneath it, and my stomach flutters as if a million butterflies are frantically trying to escape. I wonder if he will be in civilian clothing when assigned with me. After shaking Kate's hand, he strides over and extends his hand to me. I find the formality awkward, but accept it. My hand disappears completely, enveloped in his large grasp and my heart rate quickens.

"See you soon, Marra," he smiles, and I blush despite myself. Is there no 'Off' button for my facial colouring? I mutter something along the same lines, but cannot quite recall the exact words. I feel like a teenager meeting a boy for the first time. Pathetic. After he leaves, the room falls into an uncomfortable silence. Kate looks at me from the sofa, trying to read my thoughts.

"You like this boy!" she says, happy with her deduction and looking smug. It is no extraordinary feat because my face is as transparent as carphite-glass. I ignore her comment. "Should we talk about locating the Liogers?" I say.

Kate is still chuckling when I seat myself at her large desk. She walks over and places herself across from me, still smiling. She puts her reading glasses on and keys in the coordinates of Sector Five on a console. Half of the large desk lights up with a colour satellite view of the area. I don't have this technology installed in my workspace in Sector Five, which is a pity because I find it a wondrous thing to be able to view maps intimately this way. We can enlarge and minimise it from hand gestures on the screen, which enables us to zoom into a particular location. The satellite map shows details of the land, including trails, trees and animals. We assume that the shapes on the mountains would be Primes because those are their locations of choice. Looking for Liogers in the vast expanse of wilderness of Sector Five where there are other lowland animals is similar to looking for a single leaf in a forest of trees. To add to the difficulty, normal satellite view is useless if the Liogers are under the canopy of trees. This is when thermal imaging is required, but thermal image resolution is similar to the normal satellite view, nothing more than blurry shapes. The best way to locate the Liogers is to use portable drones to scout the Sector, flying below the tree line.

"On my last walkabout, I was in this zone," I point at a coordinate on the satellite map.

"So, this boy, Yon," Kate suddenly says without looking at me. I raise my head in surprise. "Anything happened?"

I stare at her, words refusing to form on my lips, warmth creeping up slowly from my chest to my face.

"Well?" Kate now looks up at me, smiling nearly from ear to ear, a playful glint in her eyes.

"No, he was just a Peacekeeper," I reply with no conviction in my voice. I look down at the map, trying to look preoccupied.

"It's good to have a friend," Kate continues in a casual tone and smiles at me when I look up at her. Then, sensing my discomfort, she says, "So. Let's plot a search area for you and Yon …" She draws out his name and I am sure it is done on purpose.

But I am grateful that she has chosen not to pursue the inquiry. I am not used to expressing how I feel. That kind of conversation doesn't come easily to me.

We scour the map, our heads bowed over the digital projection. Based on our understanding of the species, we estimate a route the pride would take and so begin plotting out search areas. There is no question that it will be a dangerous assignment even with drones because the Liogers may circle back and stalk us like what they did to me and the Peacekeeper during the last walkabout.

Liogers, in general, are stealth hunters and move quietly through the foliage to ambush their prey. They normally circle their quarry from all directions to prevent escape, before attacking as a group. Without being able to read their heat signatures, they will become even more dangerous to track. I cannot say that I am not nervous about the mission. There is a high probability that Yon or I or even both of us may be hurt, if not killed. But my determination to keep the Liogers safe far outweighs the fear for my own safety,

As my eyes go over the wide area in Sector Five where we will be searching, I notice that Kate is very silently saying something to herself. It is barely perceptible but I can hear it. I didn't realise that she reflects by speaking out details to herself. When I am working,

I find sounds distracting, even music. I smile quietly to myself; this is something new I have learned about Kate. Then, a thought hits me and an idea starts to take shape in my mind.

"Kate," I say, "If we cannot see them, maybe we can hear them." Kate looks confused and so I continue, "Can we get one of the engineers to make a highly sensitised ear piece for both Yon and I, that can extend out say … ten kilometres or more? That way, we can hear them before they get close to us."

"That's an excellent idea. Let me ask engineering." She pushes a communications button on her desk and a few seconds later, a holographic woman with dark, limp hair and wearing a green laboratory coat appears in front of the desk. A pair of glasses is hanging on a chain from her neck. She grabs and perches them on her nose, brushing a stray hair out of her eyes. Then, seeing that it is Kate, she flashes a tired smile.

"Deputy?" she says. Kate explains to her in very few, precise words what is required and Abigail frowns.

"Is it possible? We need two pairs," Kate tells her.

The engineer is scratching her chin and looking thoughtful. "It can be done. I have to consult with one or two other engineers. When do you need it?" she asks.

"Forty-eight hours," Kate says.

Abigail's eyes widen momentarily and then she sighs. "Let me discuss this with my assistants and I'll let you know."

"I can't give you more time, Abigail," Kate says, "I'm sorry."

The engineer stares blankly at us for a second or two. Then, her face moves and she purses her lips. "OK. We'll get on it and do the best we can. Two pairs, you say?"

To this, Kate nods. Then, she adds with a smile, "Thank you, Abigail … and your team." She switches off the communicator, not waiting for the other woman to respond.

It is not surprising that Kate does not have many friends. Then I remember Doctor Liam Anders. I bet she doesn't behave the same with him. By hierarchy, he reports to both her and the Director. I remember her softened expression when she was with him. He's the first man to whom I have seen her express kindness for the sake of itself. Maybe with time, Kate is changing.

Will I become Kate when I grow older? Am I becoming her even now? I feel something stir in my chest and I take a deep breath to still it.

We continue plotting out possible areas to locate the hybrids. Once or twice, I steal glances at Kate. She is looking older than I remember. Deep lines cut into her forehead like creases on cloth and dark circles frame her lilac eyes. I wish that she would speak to me like she did to my mother. I know full well how it feels not having anyone to confide in, and I feel my parents' absence like a deep chasm in my heart that I cannot cross. Often, I want to just tell Kate to trust and talk to me. I may not replace my mother, but perhaps in each other, we could fill that empty space.

"You know that I am still not one hundred percent convinced that I am doing the right thing, allowing you to return to Sector Five," Kate suddenly says, straightening up and removing her reading glasses. She sighs, looking at me with eyes full of concern.

"I know," I tell her. "But it is the right thing to do."

Kate does not reply and so, I repeat, "It is the right thing to do, and I'll be fine, Kate. Besides, you now have Yon with me."

"You're right," she says, but I hear no conviction in her tone. "You promise me that there will be no heroics when you are in the wilderness? Let Yon take care of you?"

I look at her like I don't know what she is referring to, which draws a smile to her face. "You don't realise that you are as stubborn as your mother," she laughs. "Even if you are your father's daughter."

In the afternoon, Yon joins us in Kate's office. He returns wearing a white shirt and a pair of khaki cargo trousers, smelling of soap. His presence is distracting and I find it hard to concentrate on even the simplest details. I find myself noticing little things about him I had forgotten, like putting checks on a list of items in a memory vault: how the skin on the outer edges of his eyes crinkle when he laughs or smiles, how there is a tiny red mark on his neck, from a nick with a razor blade when he shaved, how his shadow beard becomes more pronounced by late afternoon, how I know the faint trace of black ink under his left shirt sleeve is an ancient design tribal tattoo that covers the top of his arm to just below his neck, like a shoulder guard (he had removed his shirt once to show me).

I remember the first time he stepped out of the Humpt as Peacekeeper over a year ago. Time slowed down as I watched him move in slow motion out of the vehicle. I had found him so handsome, my heart was beating a rhythm I didn't recognise. He used to tell me terrible jokes to pass the time when we were on the road — "*Did you hear about the restaurant on the moon? Great food, no atmosphere!*"

By early evening, a rumble in my stomach announces my need for food. I peer at Kate and see with relief that she has not heard it. Yon runs his hands through his short hair and stretches out his torso and his arms over his head. It is an unsubtle cue that I am grateful for because Kate promptly removes her reading glasses.

"Let's call it a day. We'll resume tomorrow at ten," she says. "Marra, will you join me for breakfast at my habitation?" she asks, to which I agree.

Yon and I leave her office together in awkward silence, trying too hard to be polite with each other: "*After you.*" "*No, after you!*" chuckle, chuckle, chuckle. At the bottom of the building, he narrows his eyes and asks, "Can I walk with you?" I must have looked alarmed because he adds, "It is on my way."

"Sure," I say, not feeling sure at all.

"So, have you continued practising the knife throw?" he says. I had forgotten all about that. During one of our walkabouts, Yon had given me a small knife and shown me how to throw it. I discovered that day how absolutely untalented I was in handling weaponry.

"No," I laugh, remembering that the knife is now in my kitchen. "For everyone's safety, I have decided not to pursue that … art."

Yon smiles. I search my brain for something to say. "The knife is great for chopping vegetables though." And I hear him laugh. "Are you staying at the Defence Unit barracks?" I ask. That is almost six kilometres away.

"Yep," he says.

"How will you get back?"

"It's not that far on foot," he laughs. "Besides, a bit of jogging is good for me."

I laugh, more from nervousness than actual mirth. I see the habitation building where I am staying, not far ahead and feel relieved. Small talk stresses me.

"I actually miss the walkabouts with you," Yon says out of the blue and looks at me. I am not sure what to reply. I had missed him but am not about to tell him that. He does not appear to mind my silence. We reach my building and I turn to him. "Thank you," I say, like an idiot. Do I extend my hand to shake his? I am confused and feel skittish, my heart performing somersaults without my permission. As if he understands my dilemma, Yon suddenly steps forward and envelops me in his huge arms in a bear hug. My initial surprise subsides and I hug him back. His body feels like a furnace and he still smells of good soap. I sense his eyes burning into my back as I enter the building and run up the stairs to my habitation on the tenth floor, telling myself over and over not to turn and look at him.

Early morning the day of our scheduled departure from Seven, it is still dark outside. The trees are swaying to a music I cannot hear. I am already packed and eager to leave, looking forward to being back in Sector Five, and sleeping in my own bed. I realise, with a start, that I have somehow now considered Sector Five as home. What an odd discovery! When I was first assigned there, I had felt nervous because it was a Sector far removed from the human zone and I was afraid that I would fall short of Kate's expectations as a good field agent. Now I feel I am master, or trying to be, of that space.

I carry my equipment and specimen bags, as well as my small backpack, down the building. Abigail and her team are true to their word. The newly engineered long-range sound amplifiers are safely packed in a box. The devices are small and fit snugly into each ear. Abigail has explained that she has made them not just as amplifiers that work with the helmet visor, but also a normal hearing piece for the communicator. They will pick up sounds as far as fifteen kilometres, with the help of satellite enhancements.

At the bottom of the building, I am surprised to see that Yon is already there, waiting by a Humpt. He is in his black Defence Warrior uniform. I assume that he has driven all the way from his base by the airfield.

"Good morning!" he says in his happy, morning voice, or maybe this is how he sounds like everyday? "Let me take all of that from you." I smile and hand them to him. I wonder if Yon is capable of having a bad day. I find it hard to read him. I had lain in bed staring at the ceiling the night before, heart beating like drums, his warm hug lingering on my body like a shadow. He probably slept like a Lioger after a good kill.

Footsteps approach us and I turn to see Kate walking in large strides towards where we are. She gives me a hug upon arrival and shakes Yon's hand.

"You are both early, I see," she says. Kate's nose is pink from the chill and she places her hands back into her coat pocket for warmth. The weather is a little colder now, especially in the morning and her breath appears in visible wisps. "I will not accompany you to the airfield, Marra," she tells me. "There is something important waiting for me in my office. But I will call you tonight once you get settled back in your habitation." I am surprised to hear this, because it is unusual that Kate does not see me off.

"Shall we go?" Yon's voice brings me out of my thoughts.

"Yes," I say and turn to give Kate another hug.

"Take care, Marra," Kate tells me, smiling with affection and searching deep in my eyes for an acknowledgement of mine. Then, she turns to Yon. "And you, take care of her!" It sounds like a command.

"Will do, ma'am," he replies, nodding.

As the vehicle speeds towards the airfield, we pass my mother's signage and a stab of nostalgia surfaces. I have not taken the time to visit my old home. I can easily blame it on lack of time from working with Kate, but deep down, I know that yet again, I have avoided the situation. I am not as brave as I pretend to be.

As the hovercraft carries Yon and I above the treeline and mountains towards Sector Five, I take a long look at the childhood home I leave behind. It is perfectly camouflaged within the wilderness that surrounds it. I think of my parents and how they may have created a new hybrid with their blood. What a pity they did not live long enough to know about this. My mother would be pleased. She might even have named the new species after herself and my father. They would not want this new hybrid destroyed. It is ironic, but these new Liogers carry a little of my parents in them and just for that I am determined to make sure they survive.

I look over to Yon. His eyes are closed and his head is back. He is fast asleep. Some people are gifted with being able to fall asleep easily and anywhere. I close my eyes. Tomorrow is an important day.

CHAPTER 10

"Nature does not hurry, yet everything is accomplished."
– Lao Tzu

Yon and I are walking through the third zone we have mapped out as a possible area to find the Liogers. Close to winter, Sector Five's wilderness canopy is thinner because many of the leaves have fallen in preparation for the cold months. This is letting in more light into the area. The dead foliage is also providing a thick layer of cushion on the hard ground, which renders our footfalls more discrete. The wilderness smells of rotting dried vegetation, mainly old leaves that have fallen in dense bunches on the ground, and the winter chill makes the leaves look like they have come from a refrigerator. The weather has turned colder and I am in my winter wear, bundled up thickly, making it awkward to walk. Yon, with his natural body heat, is still in his normal Warrior combat uniform. He would probably light up like a beacon on thermal imaging.

I am in front and he is about three steps behind me. Today is our fourth day, and our first three have not been fruitful. There are giant deer and rodents about, but no Liogers. Our portable drones are flying in different directions in the wilderness and are also not picking up any signs of the animals. Yon is in charge of monitoring them as I am still a little unfamiliar with their controls. Although it is possible that they may have left the Sector, my intuition tells me otherwise. I sense strongly that they are still somewhere in the vast wilderness.

Although I cannot see Yon, I can hear him. The earpieces that Abigail has made for us are more powerful than I anticipated. They pick up every minute sound from all directions. In fact, it is too loud for me. I prefer not hearing every rustle of leaves or the snap of branches that the jungle produces naturally. I discover to my amusement that Yon hums while he walks. He does it almost imperceptibly, but with the sound amplifier, I can hear him quite distinctly. In the beginning, I tried to guess the song, but have given up. They are probably songs from southern COE where he was born. They sound, however, suspiciously like children's nursery rhymes. Does he have children?

We have not discussed our personal lives ever. There is a possibility, of course, that those are the only songs he likes humming. I can ask him, but somehow, it feels like prying. Besides, this is not the place and time to get into that kind of conversation. It would spoil the quietness of the forest. I have always preferred silence to speech, especially when I am on a walkabout.

I am getting slightly more relaxed around Yon. Living with a man is different. Some things I used to do are no longer possible, like walking around in my underwear, drinking water straight from the container or showering with the bathroom and bedroom doors open. I mourn the disappearance of those little habits. What I have lost, however, is compensated in other ways.

Yon, I discover, is a decent cook and enjoys it far more than I do. My repertoire of recipes stops at two dishes, rice with sautéed or steamed vegetables, and soup. I can eat the same food every day and not tire of the same feelings on my taste buds, a trait I share with my father. For us, food is merely fuel, not pleasure, much to the distress of my mother who loved to eat. I recall that dinners were culinary feasts at our house and there would often be guests. Kate was there at almost every meal, but sometimes we would get my father's COE colleagues visiting from afar or mother's work colleagues. I used to dread these encounters because there would always be comments about how tall I had become, how grown, how pretty, how tall ... and the unavoidably question of the unusual colour of my eyes. My parents used to tell them that it was genetic evolution and somehow, they always managed to placate the crowd.

My mother blossomed during these elaborate mealtimes. She would cook pumpkin, broil potatoes, sauté vegetables ... She often called her cuisine a fusion between East and West, making up names for her dishes. My father and I were spectators of her show. It was often during those moments that I loved watching them — my mother, the cooking adventurer and socialite, and my father, her adoring fan. Even while entertaining, my mother would throw glances at my father, so full of affection that was thick as honey.

Yon is not the culinary artist my mother was, but he is a better cook than I ever will be. So, he prepares the meals now. He tells me that it calms him, but maybe it's his solution to not eating my two dishes continually.

Yon whistles strange songs when he cooks, just as he hums while he walks. They are unlike the strange child-like tunes he hums on the walkabouts and resemble either a love ballad or a rock song. He sometimes sings, although he mostly forgets the words and then just makes noises to compensate. He walks around the habitation in a pair of shorts and his Defence Unit exercise shirt, no matter what the temperature is. He tells me he does not feel the cold easily, which results in us bickering over the habitation temperature and finally settling on a compromise.

I must admit that he is likeable even if he continues to tell the most terrible jokes, a trait he has not lost. More often than not, he is a boy who is trapped in the body of an adult. There is an ease to him, which I envy. He does not find anything awkward, unlike me who feels self-conscious in his presence. My words are measured in company, while Yon seems to say the first things that pop into his head. He is 'censor-less', which I admire. My mother was the same way. Maybe this is why I prefer my own solitary company. With no one around, I am at ease to express and be myself.

Yon is not afraid of conversations. I enjoy listening to his stories, watching his every facial expression as he recounts. I have not been anywhere outside of the FSA and am curious to how life is beyond our shores. I find out that his parents are well and alive and living in South COE in a small commune. They are farmers and tend to a small patch of land shared with three other families. Natural earth-grown food is scarce and rare and therefore crop patches are highly valued. Families take turns guarding the land against raiders. Yon tells me that crimes are frequent and although his parents and the other families have chosen to live outside the city, it does not reduce the danger. He is the middle son of three. His two brothers are also farmers and help his parents. Yon is the only one who aspired to change his lifestyle and when the Global Peacekeeping Force went to his village to recruit, he left the farm to join them, much to his parents' regret. After extensive training in Northern COE, he was permanently posted to the FSA five years later.

He tells me that farming is not for him, that he prefers learning how to fight and to protect people. "It's a skill that is far more useful in today's world," he says at one point during our conversation, but with a look of dejection. I wonder if he regrets leaving his family behind. I wonder if he misses them. I could ask him these questions but somehow, I decide that when the time is right, he will tell me himself. I believe that there are moments when questions are needed and there are times when it is sufficient to just be present to listen.

Yon appears oblivious to the effect he has on me. I don't know if I feel happy or not about his indifference, but my ego is definitely bruised. There was a time over a year ago when I believed he had feelings for me, but maybe he has found himself a girlfriend, a wife? He is after all thirty years of age; he has forwarded that information over breakfast one morning while asking for my age. I am almost certain he doesn't lack female attention. His ring finger is bare but that does not mean anything. My parents rarely wore their wedding rings, especially when out in the field.

When Yon was still a Peacekeeper, I would look forward to every walkabout because it was when I would see him. I would even try to look as presentable as possible, a fire of hope burning in my heart that he would suddenly take me in his strong arms and kiss me like heroes do in all the ancient romantic movies. My heart would flutter so much that I had trouble controlling my breathing and my voice. I thought I caught him looking at me sometimes, a hint of admiration in his eyes, but I may have been mistaken. I read that our mind lets us see things we want to see and I certainly wanted him to see me in an amorous way. He would have been my first romantic relationship, had something happened between us. Now, he is just a colleague. Based on how he is around me, he sees me as nothing more ... I think.

An icy wind circles the trees, blowing up loose leaves from the ground and stinging my uncovered hands. My mind refocuses back on the present.

"How are you doing?" I suddenly hear Yon's voice in my ears, a velvety baritone that has an irrational tendency to quicken my pulse. I continue walking without looking back.

"Good, you?" I say, happy that he cannot see my face, because it has broken out into a silly grin, just listening to him speak.

"We've been walking for almost two hours now. Let's take a break." I feel a hand on my shoulder, stop and turn back to look at him. He has set his visor to full transparency and I can see him smile, the skin on the outer edges of his eyes crinkling. "There," he says and motions with his head to an enormous trunk covered with dark green moss. A ray of sunlight has found its way through the canopy and settles on a spot at one end of the trunk. The image is almost spiritual, like nature's chapel in the wilderness.

We head for the tree and I sit on the ground, leaning back against the majestic log. It is only when I sit that I realise how exhausted I am, the muscles on my legs stretched out are thanking me for the respite. Yon lowers himself heavily to my left, leaving a space of about two feet between us. We remove our helmets and drink water from our canisters at almost the same moment. I discretely watch him while he gulps. I can see his powerful neck muscles in motion, which momentarily transfixes me. He exercises vigorously every evening in the habitation, which gives him his extremely fit physique.

"Do you think the Liogers have moved out of Sector Five?" he asks as he places his canister down and I quickly look away, feeling guilty like a stalker.

I shake my head and look around at the green world that surrounds us. Few people understand the majesty of the wilderness. Humanity almost decimated all of it in years past. The emergence of the giant animals has given forests, jungles and the wilderness, on a worldwide scale, a renewed chance to grow and survive. "I don't know, but I feel they are still in the area, somewhere," I say.

A buzzing sound heads towards where we are sitting and I spy the two small drones coming towards Yon, like trained birds.

"Come to me, my lovelies," Yon says, grinning like a circus ringmaster. The small drones, about the size of his palm, land lightly on the ground next to him. "Better than trained birds, eh?" he winks at me. "Wish we could have more than just two. We could have them fly all through Sector Five, while we sit here and rest."

"That would be ideal," I say. "You can ask Kate for more drones when you speak to her next."

"I actually already tried that and she only gave me two," he says. I am surprised. I can only surmise that drones are not easy to come by at the CAEP. They are sophisticated machinery and not cheap.

I hear him sigh quietly. "Well, the Liogers are doing a good job of hiding, even from these," he says as he carefully packs the drones into his pack. I assume he will release them again later. Then, he leans his head all the way back, gazing at the tops of trees. Shifting his head slightly in my direction and he looks at me from the corner of his eyes, which are startlingly dark green in the light. "I actually don't mind too much that it is taking time locating the Liogers. I am enjoying being back in the wilderness," he smiles. "This is much better than being at the Defence Unit barracks."

"It is beautiful here," I nod. "I forget often that it is full of wild animals."

"… that we have not seen," he says and chuckles to himself. "We haven't even seen a deer!"

It dawns on me that he is right and a sense of dread washes over me. Before I can say anything, Yon sits up, his expression serious, his eyes searching for something in the air. He hears something. I can see from his face that he feels that we could actually be in some danger at that moment. My heart starts to race. He puts a finger on his lips. I close my eyes and listen. I hear a distant grunt and growl. We both slip our helmets back on and get to our feet.

"Move," Yon says, his eyes tell me that this is a serious request. All humour leaves his face and he looks ready to fight.

The range of the sound amplifiers is fifteen kilometres. That must be where the animals are situated from our position. The heat signatures will only be visible when they move closer. I am about to check the satellite thermal scanner feed when Yon urgently says in a low tone, "Primes! We have to return to the Humpt! Run, Marra!" He is almost shoving me forward, as I try to coordinate my feet and body with the force of his strength. Our vehicle is almost five kilometres away. Yon puts himself in front of me and motions for me to follow him as he runs, holding his HEL in both hands, ready to fire if necessary. Primes can travel faster than us, so we move as quickly as we can.

All of a sudden, I feel a strong vibrating sensation and look down. My wristband satellite proximity sensor is activated, indicating that the animals are ten kilometres from our location. As I run, a computerised voice is counting down the distance between us: "9000 metres, 8500 metres …" My heart is hammering in my chest. I try to keep my breathing steady in order to keep up with Yon, who clearly has more endurance than I do. This is a déjà vu from a few weeks ago.

Then, out of the corner of my eye, I catch a movement in the bushes. My heart nearly stops. "Yon, there is something in the bushes," I say into my visor between breaths, without slowing down.

"I see it," his voice comes back, tense. He is breathing hard too.

"Just keep going, Marra," he says, "not much further now!"

I know he is only saying that as an encouragement. I estimate the vehicle is still about three kilometres away. The computerised proximity report is telling me that the Primes are now three kilometres from us and getting closer.

I hear a terrifying scream and Yon slides to a stop as a monstrous Prime appears from the bushes and stands there beating his enormous chest. The Prime towers over us at almost four metres tall with a wide chest. This may be a new hybrid given that it is almost a metre taller than it should be. It flashes its teeth, displaying large canines that can tear flesh from our bones in one bite. Yon moves backwards, shielding me with his body. He is holding his HEL forward but has not fired it. A cold sweat is breaking out and soaking the shirt underneath my jacket. My legs feel weak and my knees wobbly and I am breathing in short bursts. I recognise the signs of panic. Where there is one Prime, there will surely be others not far behind. I look around waiting for another to come charging at us from the bushes on our right.

The beast abruptly lunges forward, catching Yon off guard. I see a flash of laser fire but it only grazes the creature on its right shoulder. It lets out a blood-curdling, furious howl and sends Yon flying into the bushes with a swipe of its mighty hand. I scream involuntarily. There is now nothing and no one between me and the giant animal.

I slowly and steadily retreat, trying to put distance between me and the beast. My legs are so weak that I am mostly crawling in reverse. The Prime's silver eyes are completely dilated, making them look black and menacing.

"Yon!" I whisper in desperation, as I continue to crawl backwards, my voice quaking with fear. No response. I try again, a little louder. I take a quick glance and see that he lies crumpled in a heap. I hope he is still alive. He has fallen against a large bush, that will have cushioned his body from the impact of landing. If it had been a tree, he may have been broken into two.

A growl sends my attention back to the beast in front of me. It is advancing slowly on all fours, baring its teeth and canines. I see silver hairs on its lower back and know that I am in the presence of the alpha male. It is then that I remember my training and quickly look down, while continuing to retreat. I hope this will show the Prime that I am acknowledging his status and encourage it to move away. *Please let it back away,* I silently say to myself over and over again between panicked breaths, praying that the mantra will become reality. It is my only salvation.

The Prime releases a bone-chilling, furious scream and despite everything I have learnt not to do, I look up. I have just enough time to see it lunging at me, jaws wide open, exposing sharp and long canines, ready to kill. Instinctively, I crouch down and cover my head with my arms, bracing for the end of my existence.

I feel myself being pushed to the side and out of the way of the charging Prime. It is a powerful shove that leaves me breathless and dazed. I lay a few metres away from my previous location, on my side and unable to move. My chest feels like it is on fire. I try taking in a breath and am rewarded with extreme agony. I groan, stopping all movements; I think my ribs are broken. Although I still have my helmet on, my face has slammed against the thick, hard, visor and I feel it throbbing with pain. I idly think that my head would have been crushed had I not been wearing my helmet and make a mental note not to complain about it ever again. My body feels like it has been hit by a Humpt. My vision is blurred, but I lift my head carefully and painfully to try to see what is happening. I hear animals fighting furiously, but my line of vision is blocked by something large and black. I lay my head back on the ground. There is a coppery taste in my mouth. I must have bitten my lips and my tongue during the fall. My mouth is dry from fear and my own blood tastes putrid.

Something hard with uneven edges clamps on my right shoulder and pulls me backwards. I surrender to my pain and lose consciousness. The last thing I hear is a horrendous scream of an animal in agony accompanied by roars that rip through the silence of the forest.

I don't know for how long I am lying here, but when I open my eyes, it is pitch black. I blink a few times, but the darkness remains. My visor is no longer working, nor will the night vision automatically activate. I pry it off my head. I remove my ear pieces too. They are useless without a functioning helmet. It is an uncomfortable sensation to have my eyes open and yet be blind. I feel like I am in a cave somewhere shielded from all light. It smells of moss and decaying leaves. But I am still alive.

I marvel at this small miracle. My head and ribs are in horrible pain, even when I breathe but especially when I move. The air feels cold on my face. The ground is hard and feels like rock, confirming my guess at being in a cave. I want to call out for Yon, but I don't think that he is anywhere close. Is he still alive? Has the Prime pounded him to death? In fact, where is it?

My head is throbbing and waves of nausea are threatening to take over. I think about getting up, but to go in what direction? I can hardly move from the pain. I wonder if the CAEP knows where I am. I had not hit the distress signal on my wristband while running — I was too busy trying to stay alive. I feel for my wristband. It is still there, but from the inactivity, I know that it too is dead.

I close my eyes again. Maybe if I continue to sleep, the morning will come quicker. As I silence my mind and drift off to oblivion, a snort sounds to my right. Then, it becomes a gentle panting. My eyes fly open. I am finding it hard to breathe and my heart is once again on the run, galloping like a horse out of control. Who is panting? What is panting? Is it Yon? I want to call out and ask, but realise that if it is him, he would call out my name. It could only be an animal. I can almost feel the adrenaline coursing through my veins, it is dulling my pain and lifting the fog in my brain. I stay appropriately still and listen, my breaths coming in short bursts. I put my hand on my mouth to try to muffle the sound, tears involuntarily streaming down the sides of my face. It is said that only when death is close do we realise the truth about our yen for life. I can truly say that I am not ready to die. I think about all the places I have not been to and the experiences I have not yet had.

There are more sounds of breathing; I estimate at least two or three animals around me. I survived a Prime only to be food for other beasts. Will it hurt when they start to devour me alive or will I become unconscious first?

Seconds go by, then minutes and nothing happens. Why am I not being eaten? Have they already feasted on Yon and are reserving me for breakfast? Are they feeding me to their offspring later? My adrenaline is wearing off and pain is returning to various parts of my body. Are these creatures purposely not attacking to put me in a false sense of security? The breathing sounds are as harmonious and rhythmic as a meditation mantra and my eyelids feel like lead. I finally surrender and close them, saying a final goodbye to my life.

"Ma'am, are you alright?" It is a male voice. He is gently shaking me. It is still pitch dark out but now I see people everywhere and torches and lights. I blink.

"Get ready to move her out!" he shouts to someone behind him.

Hands appear from everywhere and my body rises and lands on a stretcher. Blankets wrap me warmly and a mask is placed over my mouth. I smell sweet oxygen. Pain is everywhere and despite the mask, breathing is difficult. I am passing in and out of consciousness. I wonder where the animals around me have gone. Or maybe I have imagined it all in the delirium brought on by the pain?

"Yon," I say through the mask, weakly to the man who appears to be in charge.

"We've found him," he replies. I don't know what that means — found him alive or found his dead, mutilated body? I am about to ask him more, but they are carrying me away and he is no longer listening. Through the fog in my brain, I discern that we exit a large cave and continue on through an area of few trees and bushes. I don't see any other stretcher. Where is Yon?

I close my eyes, and the throbbing in my head is so severe it feels like my eyeballs are about to pop out of my skull. I see shadows of large men jogging next to my stretcher. I think that they must be our protectors. We arrive at a location brightly lit by floodlights. I close my eyes and squint to shield them from the light that is burning into my skull through my eyeballs. From my horizontal position, I can see a hovercraft high above the treetops with two cables hanging from it, extending to the ground attached to a kind of platform. They strap my stretcher onto this platform. Then, the two men who carried me jump onto each side of it and I feel us moving upwards towards the waiting aircraft.

In the cabin, I see another stretcher with Yon. He is unconscious and an oxygen mask is over his nose and mouth. He is alive. Feeling relief, I close my eyes and surrender to the pain and heaviness and allow darkness to engulf my senses.

Fingers are caressing my arm. For a moment of confusion, I thought it was my mother waking me. Then, reality materialises and I feel disappointment. My eyelids feel like they are glued shut and I open them with difficulty. The light feels too bright. I wince.

"Welcome back." Kate's voice is gentle.

I turn to look at her. Her dishevelled hair tells me that she has slept on the chair next to my bed. Her eyes are red. Has she been crying?

"You are in our hospital." She says. "You gave me a fright." She smiles and holds my gaze in hers.

I try to move and a sharp pain shoots up my side. I grimace.

"Try not to move too much. You have two fractured ribs and a bad bruise to your forehead, probably from the helmet visor knocking into it, and a concussion."

My lips feel strange.

She notices my movement. "And swollen lips," she says. I try to smile but even that hurts. My tongue feels raw and sensitive.

Kate shakes her head, as if trying to dispel a thought from her mind. "You are badly hurt … " she appears to want to say more but does not.

"Yon," I begin, which sounds more like, "Yuh." I can hardly open my mouth and my tongue is uncooperative.

"He's fine," Kate replies. "He's in worse shape than you, but he will live. You're both very lucky that he hit the distress signal or we may not have found you so quickly!"

I am surprised to hear that. Yon must have activated the signal while we were on the run. Without it, the CAEP would not have even known that we were in danger. While they can locate us easily from our Nano Locators, they will not look for us if they are not alerted to our distress. He has saved our lives.

"We won't talk about it now. We will wait until you are better, but there will be questions and reports to be made, alright?" Her normal Kate voice is returning. Unable to speak properly, I nod. "I'll be back later," she tells me and with that, she leaves. As she walks out the sliding door, she nods to a Defence Warrior standing right outside my room. "*Why does Kate think I require protection?*" I want to ask, but I hear her heels clicking away from my room until silence reigns.

I notice a small red spot on the plain, white ceiling. I wonder if it is blood and how did it get there? A scarlet drop that hides a tale. I touch my forehead and grimace. There is lump like half an egg buried in my forehead. I close my eyes and hear the breathing sounds ricochet in my mind.

Then I remember: Liogers. It must have been. But why did they keep me alive?

CHAPTER 11

"We will be known forever by the tracks we leave."
– Native American Dakota Sioux Proverb

4841 – Kate, the day of

I am trying to read these field reports, but I have been staring at the same sentence now for a while without quite understanding the words. Again, I hoped that work will help to take my mind off Anthony.

I push myself away from the desk in disgust and walk to the window, taking deep breaths to calm down. I look out at the white gravel square of Seven; it is just past noon and some people are already on their way, walking in groups, to the dining building, laughing, some holding hands. I used to be one of them. My throat tightens and turn my back on the scene. I stand facing my empty office instead.

Eva told me that anger was part of the process of grief. Am I grieving? My feelings are closer to murderous than sorrowful. If I had a HEL and if Anthony was standing here in front of me, I think that I would probably shoot him to pieces. I loved him, trusted him. And he betrayed me.

My fury keeps me awake at night listening to the loud, rapid thudding of my heartbeats while my mind replays the events that lead to my predicament. But in a way, I prefer the anger, because when it subsides, even for a second, a deep sense of loss and helplessness sweeps over and covers me like a thick, suffocating blanket.

How could this have happened to me? I pride myself on my intuition and my ability to grasp the unspoken or unknown. Did falling in love dull my senses?

My fingers wrap around the closest thing to me on my desk and I hurl it across the room. Its impact with the wall breaks it noisily into various pieces. For a split second, the sound resonates with how I feel and a small elation passes through me. Then, the realisation of what I have done brings regret. I have destroyed a small clay figurine of 'Otto', the extinct polar bear of Rolf's bedtime tales that Marra had moulded and baked for me with Eva's help when she was eight. I walk quickly over to the wall to pick up as many pieces of it that I can find.

Eva and Rolf told me to let it go. They were kind and gracious about finding their habitation ransacked by Anthony searching for the nano-drive, and their sympathy frustrates me. I think that they chose not to make it an issue seeing that I am already hurting and this kindness makes me angrier. I don't want their pity. I want them to be furious with me, to shout at me for having told Anthony about the drive, to scream at my stupidity!

The evidence was nearly stolen because of my indiscretion and without it, we have no proof of the Federation's involvement in the manufacture of the deadly virus and the massacre of the animals four years ago. Thank God the nano-drive is still with Rolf because he has the foresight to keep it on his person and not hidden in the habitation. My guilt will be worse otherwise, especially since Kondo had obtained the nano-drive in exchange for his life.

Rolf said that Kondo must have known his cover was compromised at the Federation, and therefore had concealed it in the hilt of his dagger, which he knew would be passed down to Rolf upon his death. Unfortunately, Rolf only discovered the evidence recently, while cleaning the weapon, a year after Kondo intended for it to be found.

Kondo had volunteered to be placed in the FSA Peacekeeping Force years ago so that he could keep an eye on what they were doing and I had helped with his posting. The Federation said that he died from heart failure while sleeping. Kondo was a senior trainer and although he was fifty-nine at the time, he was in excellent physical condition. His death had shocked Eva and I. For Rolf, it was more than that. He was devastated; they had grown up together and he had lost a brother. Had the nano-drive not been found, Kondo's death would have been for naught.

Anthony Kilmer arrived two years ago. A biologist by training, he was square-shouldered and as tall as Rolf, blond with smouldering, blue eyes, which he jokingly said he inherited from his Viking ancestry. He had been funny, good-natured and handsome, like no one I have ever met. He had shown interest, which surprised me. I have never thought of myself as a woman that a man like him would like. I fell, first slowly and then headlong with blinding speed. He was intelligent, charming and everything I had hoped for in a partner.

I thought that I had finally found the person to confide in, to share my life. I must admit that I have always been a little envious of the bond and love between Eva and Rolf.

Anthony and I were together for a little over a year. He had said all the right things and made me feel like a desirable woman. I now see it for what it was, because it had blinded me to his pretence and deceit. Had I really been so in love that I did not suspect his frequent disappearances, his excuses to go for a run to remote corners of Seven? I can see clearly now, but it comes too late. Anthony has disappeared since, his Nano Locator, disabled.

My eyes are moist and I dry them. I take a deep breath in and exhale, trying to dispel all negativity from my mind. I must stop feeling sorry for myself.

Since the discovery of the drive two months ago, we have managed to pinpoint a location where the Federation had tested their laboratory-engineered airborne virus on the animals. We think it is situated in a small area in the South-Eastern part of Sector Three, close to the borders of Five and Two, where from past records we know that Primes resided. It is not easy to know precisely because the stamp on the video merely indicates 'South Sector Three', and it is a large area.

The recording was filmed via a drone. This was likely how they dropped the gas in the area too. From the facial haemorrhages on the Primes and all the other animals struck down by the biological agent, Eva guessed that the federation had somehow revived and bio-engineered an ancient, extinct virus and made it airborne to produce a deadly disease that could infect through inhalation. This new strain worked quickly. The sight of the twitching bodies of animals haunts me as they slowly bled and laid dying in agony. The gas appeared to be purposefully disseminated in the area where the Primes were living, possibly to test its potency on the species, but the winds must have carried it further out and hence killed deer and rodents as well. It was a small mercy that we saw no Liogers.

I glance at the digital timer on her wall above my desk; Rolf and Eva are still on their way to Sector Three, to the location of the massacre, to collect soil and water samples. They estimate that it will take them a whole day of driving. They hope that although a year has passed, there could be some traces left of the biological agent. We have agreed that it would be safer to use the Humpt instead of the hovercraft, so as not to attract any attention. We are not sure if Anthony acted alone or had an accomplice who might still be in Seven. For any eyes watching, it will appear that Rolf and Eva are going for a routine walkabout.

I look forward to their return tomorrow. We have planned to bring all the evidence to the Mission Control Director and maybe even to Mr Sanderson himself. Finally, after so many years of waiting, we may have our first incriminating proof of the Federation's intent to kill all the animals of the FSA.

This thought gives me some comfort and relieves me a little of my fury. I return to my desk and place all the pieces of my broken 'Otto' into the little plate that is normally under my potted plant. I will somehow put 'Otto' back together again. I resume reading the reports, remembering how my mother used to tell me that the best way to forget was through hard work.

Just as I am hitting my stride, I hear the door buzzer sound. It echoes through my office, owing to the sparse furnishings and bare walls. My assistant must be asking if he can be excused for lunch.

"Come," I say, while still reading my report. I want to finish the last sentence. While I am doing this, I sense that he is already standing in front of my desk, which is odd. Francois normally waits by the door. I look up smiling, but instead of him, the Mission Director is standing there, hands in his trouser pockets, looking uncomfortable like a person about to confess to a crime.

I stand up, perhaps a little too abruptly. "Director! I'm sorry, I ..." I begin. He holds his hand up, telling me to stop and shakes his head, a pained expression on his face. Something is wrong.

I go around my desk and motion him to the sofa. His steps are slow and deliberate, his frown deepening. My apprehension grows, like expanding fog. The Director looks like he is about to announce that my services to the CAEP are no longer required. Can the Federation have such influence? Does this have anything to do with the nano-drive?

The Director crosses his leg and clears his throat. "Kate, I have received some bad news." My heart stops for a split second and then starts to race.

"Rolf and Eva ... they had an accident," he continues, looking down at his hands. I feel blood drain from my face and my body feels limp and paralysed.

What accident? I want to ask, but the words will not form.

"We received a distress signal from Rolf and then the signal died. So, the Defence Unit traced their Nano Locators and it appears that they are not moving. Their location, however, is one where the Humpt could not have gone ... " He continues to say more, but I only see his lips move, as if in slow motion; there is a pinging sound in my ears, as if I am tuning in to another frequency.

I try to say something, but no words will materialise. My thoughts are a confusing jumble and only specific words jump out at me: distress signal, Nano Locators, not moving ...

"... I have them looking at the satellite thermal feed, but the view is unclear. The Defence and Medical Units are flying there as I speak to assess the situation." The Director's voice comes back into focus.

"I should have gone with them," I say absently, finally finding my voice but it sounds foreign, thick and tense, as if another person is talking.

"Kate, we are taking care of the situation and I don't want you there." The Director gets up from the sofa, walks over the desk and pours me a glass of water. "Here, drink this. You don't look well," he says, seeing the pallor of my face. I take the glass, it feels cool in my hands, but I am unable to act. The air in the room appears to be slowly sucked out, leaving me breathless.

The door opens all of a sudden and a woman enters. I recognise her as a nurse I met once in the CAEP dining hall, but I draw a blank at her name.

"Kate," her voice is calm and kind, as if talking to one of her patients. I cannot bear all of the fuss and stand up. I realise that the Director thinks I am about to break down and I am not fragile!

"Andrei," I say, looking at the him. "I'm fine!" My voice, however, is an octave higher than intended. "Let's go to the Defence Unit. I want to hear what they have found," I say.

He looks at the nurse and she at him, silently exchanging thoughts. I decide to take matters into my own hands, leaving them to their telepathic communication and storm out of my office. I hear Andrei's shoes tapping on the floor, running after me. A hand grabs my elbow and I am forced to stop.

"Kate," he says. "Calm down." He is unaware that the worst thing anyone can say to someone agitated is to ask the person to calm down. But he is the Director, and taking a deep breath, I stop and turn to face him.

"Let's go to my office," he offers. "The Defence Unit will report directly to me there." This sounds reasonable enough and I nod.

The Director's office is in another building about two minutes away on foot. It is a strategic decision to locate each high-ranking cadre in different structures to ensure safety in the event of an attack. This way, everyone cannot all be killed in one place. I notice that the nurse is following us with quiet steps, looking inconspicuous. Does the Director feel that I will require her assistance?

I think of Eva and Rolf as I walk. Are they alive? Not moving means that they may be unconscious, not dead. I really should have insisted a Defence Warrior accompany them. *Please*, I recite a silent prayer, *don't let them die.*

I remember that Rolf has the nano-drive. They had decided that it was too dangerous to leave it with me because Anthony might get other spies to ransack my home and office or even to attack me. If Rolf and Eva die, the drive is lost along with all our hopes of bringing the Federation to justice!

We wait in the Director's office, uncomfortable in each other's company, but thrown together by circumstance. It reminds me of a funeral gathering. I stand by the window, looking out. Everything appears normal and everyone is going about their day, oblivious to the fact that the next hour may change my life forever. The nurse, Janet (I remember her name now), is sitting on the Director's tawdry green sofa, hands folded on her lap, a picture of patience and virtue. I wonder if there are more nurses outside the door waiting to take me away to the hospital should I become hysterical.

The Director is back at his desk. I can feel his stare burning a hole in my back, and I don't care. We've known each other for almost as long as I have been working at the CAEP. We have risen through the ranks together, and although he is always a step ahead of me, I know that his office will one day be mine. Therefore, this is not a time for me to lose composure.

I was shocked before, but I am ready now to accept anything that may happen next. My heart is heavy, but no one needs to know that. My intuition tells me that my best friends are gone, victims of the Federation's treachery, like Kondo, and that proof will be difficult, as usual, to obtain. If only I had not shared knowledge of the drive with Anthony, the Federation would not have known that we had it in our possession. Love has made me foolish..

The communicator beeps and three heads turn to it simultaneously. I return to the Director's desk from the window where I am standing. A hologram of a uniformed Defence Warrior is in front of us, surrounded by wilderness.

"Sir," he begins. "We found the Humpt. I will send you the image taken by the drone now. You can see for yourself." He is a burly man, approaching his forties. I notice his eyes are a clear blue, like Eva's, and my heart clenches.

The drone shows us an image of a wrecked Humpt at the bottom of a ravine. The visible door is slid open and a close-up shows the bloodied bodies of Rolf and Eva. I avert my eyes discretely, looking at the wall of the office behind the image. I am not bothered by blood, but the sight of the mangled bodies of two people on the planet that I truly love makes my stomach turn. I fight back an urge to scream and force down tears that are slowly forming. I will have time for all of that later. My private grief is no one's business but mine.

"Retrieve the bodies," I hear the Director say. The hologram of the blue-eyed Defence Warrior is back, to my relief. "And find out what caused the accident," he adds. The communication blinks out.

"Kate?" he asks me.

I look at him, my eyes dry. "Director, I would like full access to all the information on the accident," I tell him, and then add, "please."

He nods. Everyone in Seven knows how close I am to Rolf and Eva. We spend … spent almost every waking moment together when we were not in our offices working.

Then I remember Marra. She is still in the academy at this hour. I must tell her. News, especially bad news, has a way of spreading like wild fire.

"Director," I say, "I must go and tell Rolf and Eva's daughter, Marra. I don't want news to get to her first."

"Yes, good idea. Go, go," he says. Andrei is in his early-sixties, a year or two younger than I am. He is ambitious to a fault but on the whole, a good man. We have our disagreements about how to handle the Federation, but otherwise, he is a loyal member of the CAEP.

"Kate, are YOU alright?" he asks before I reach the door, the question that is playing in his and Janet's minds since the beginning.

"Yes, I am fine, Andrei," I reply in a level tone, not betraying the agony I am feeling. "Thank you," I add and walk out of the office in deliberate, even strides. I want to project a picture of control and calm even when on the inside, my heart is dissolving into a puddle of sorrow and guilt.

How do I tell Marra that it is my mistake that sent the Federation after her parents? How do I tell her that I am responsible for their deaths?

I doubt that the Federation will leave anything behind to incriminate themselves, but I intend to comb through the evidence in detail and find something, anything.

The biggest challenge we have always faced is that here in the FSA, the Federation exercise the freedom and means to do whatever they want, which is normal given that this is their country. The population is so busy trying to stay alive that they do not care what their government does as long as they are safe and fed. The only authority the Federation are mildly mindful of is the WPO. It is all about showing a good political front. This makes my blood boil.

It seems that the more we go after the government, the more deaths occur. Perhaps it is time I stop. This is getting dangerous and while I don't care about my own safety, I don't want Marra hurt. She is all I have left now of Rolf and Eva. They would want me to protect Marra at all costs.

As I walk towards the academy building, I practise in my mind all the ways to tell Marra of her parents' death. Maybe the best way is simply to say that it was an accident. I don't want her to go on the same mission and path as we had — Kondo, her parents and I — trying to expose the Federation for who they are.

She is young and her life is ahead of her.

CHAPTER 12

"In every walk with nature one receives far more than he seeks."
– John Muir

4841 – Eva, the day before

The bonfire Rolf has built in the back of our house is eating up all the work that we have done over the years. My heart cannot help but grieve. I am a scientist and destroying research is a betrayal to my profession. I look up at Rolf, standing next me. His hand feels warm and his grip is firm. I can see it in his eyes that he grieves too.

The fire curls around all the samples and bottles and digital pads, making horrific crackling and snapping sounds, like an orange monster eating noisily, I see Marra's face. This is all for her. After Anthony broke in, Rolf decided that it was no longer safe for us to keep any research about Marra. She must remain our secret.

We have argued. I suggested we hide all the work in a drive, but Rolf disagrees. He has a point, nano-drives can be stolen and then, Marra will be exposed. We do not want our daughter to become the subject of laboratory tests like an animal.

I suggested we leave Kondo's drive to Kate while we are away, but Rolf insists we hide it in our habitation along with a video for Marra, to let her know how she came to be, who she really is and how much we both love her. He tells me that this is only a pre-caution, in the event that we don't get the opportunity to tell her face-to-face.

I don't like to entertain the possibility of death, but he is right. What we are going to do is dangerous and I don't want to leave my daughter unaware. If we return from our mission safely, then we can retrieve Kondo's drive from the hiding place and bring it to the WPO with Kate and we can erase the video we made for Marra.

He tells me that he has hidden the nano-drive in something of hers, which no one can find. I trust him and do not let him tell me where it is, just in case I am caught and tortured for information. He just shakes his head and laughs at his dramatic, silly wife.

Rolf's hand squeezes mine and I look up at him. He has tears in his eyes, my handsome, kind husband. I turn and wrap my arms around his body, while still watching the fire monster gobble up all the work that we have done to try to reverse Marra's condition. It has been a futile endeavour that has taken up all of our time since her birth. It appears that the more tests we conducted, the more they have strengthened her. After eighteen years, Rolf and I know that her condition is permanent. The guilt I feel is still there and as Marra matures, she is starting to notice my unease and therefore, I am more careful around her. Rolf tells me we must let the guilt go, that Marra turned out to be perfect, but I can't help it. She is our world and our raison d'être — our reason for being. But my intelligent husband is right; it is time we accept her as she is. Perhaps there is a purpose, a destiny she is yet to discover and fulfil. She is an incredible girl, kind and gentle, like her father and I'd like to think, brave, like me. I chuckle. Rolf calls me reckless. Brave, reckless — merely semantics! They are the same word viewed from different points in the continuum.

I feel a kiss on the top of my head. The bonfire has consumed everything. A stab of sorrow hits me while I am looking at the laboratory, once we emptied its contents. It is almost like losing a child that we have fed and watched grow for years.

I have absent-mindedly locked the door behind us from years of habit. Rolf laughed, but mostly out of nervousness. He has not said much, which is typical of him, but I sense his inner agony. It is especially hard for him. He had grieved for Kondo a year ago and recently, with the discovery of the nano-drive, he has been grieving all over again.

Rolf and I decided not to tell Kate about Marra. While we trust her with our lives, Marra is our responsibility and the less people know about her, the better. I know that Kate is tearing herself apart with guilt about Anthony. Mistakes happen, I have told her, but I don't think that she is listening.

Rolf and I understand how she was deceived. We were too. Anthony was a picture of kindness, cheerfulness and good nature. I thought he was good for Kate. No one could have known his involvement with the Federation.

The airborne virus that we saw destroy the animals on Kondo's video is terrifying in its ferocity and efficacy. We are convinced that the Federation believe that by reviving and engineering a cocktail of viruses long extinct, they will find the solution to exterminate the animals. The Federation would have stored samples of those viruses in their deep freeze lockers to use at their disposal. Such short-sightedness! Viruses are akin to wildfires and there is a strong possibility of mutation. Like all living matter, they will seek out the best way to survive and propagate. The Federation scientists have no idea the danger they have put upon our world. Rolf and I want to get samples so that we can have a better idea of exactly what cocktail the Federation scientists have produced to confirm our suspicion.

In our long history of existence, mankind has tried to play God several times, each with disastrous consequences. I think of the mass exodus from all the old cities surrounding Lake Victoria on Neo-Afrika hundreds of years ago; the result of humans introducing the Nile Perch, a carnivorous fish, which over the hundreds of years progressively led to the extinction of other fish species in the lake. Then, coupled with human pollution of the waters, Lake Victoria eventually met its end. Huge swarms of lake flies are now the only permanent inhabitants of the area.

Nature has her own way and her own plans. She doesn't need anything or anyone to regulate her. If left alone, she will find her own footing.

As the last flicker of flame extinguishes, Rolf and I walk towards our habitation. Marra is still at the academy. Later tonight, we celebrate as a family. Early tomorrow morning, Rolf and I are leaving for Sector Three.

CHAPTER 13

"Over every mountain there is a path,
although it may not be seen from the valley."
– Theodore Roethke

Today is apparently my birthday. It is a strange feeling to reach another annual marker. When did humans start counting the number of years lived and why? Is it useful? I am twenty-five today and yet I feel no different. I never thought that I would be spending this day propped up on pillows on a hospital bed, drinking water from a thick straw.

I smell the threat of snow in the air, sharp like dry ice. It is a little too early to say for sure, but there is more and more evidence that the seasons on Neo-Earth are changing their schedule. I can see frost on the window across from my bed in the early morning when I awake — tiny crystal, spiky leaves and vines pasted on the outer panes — melting slowly as the temperature rises outside. Soon, they will remain there all day, like an extra layer of carphite-glass.

It's been eight days since my arrival in the hospital. The worst of the pain is over and I have refused to take any more painkillers in the last four days. The discomfort is bearable. I don't know how Yon is. He is placed in another ward. I am not able to see him because I don't have the means of getting to him. Kate tells me that he requires more time to heal because his injuries are more extensive. I cannot help feeling a sense of guilt. He was hurt trying to protect me.

I recall vividly the first day when I awoke in the hospital. Kate had returned as promised in the afternoon. "He's for your protection, Marra," she had said, when I asked about the Defence Warrior posted outside my door. My questions clearly made her uncomfortable and the next day, the Warrior disappeared.

Kate's daily visits are timed with the precision of a military exercise. She arrives every morning at exactly ten when the doctor happens to also show up and leaves half an hour later. We talk about inconsequential things — hospital food, body pain, medication, but she has not asked about what happened. She tells me that she wants me to heal completely before making the reports. She has, however, brought me a digital pad to note anything that comes to my mind about that day. This is Kate's way of asking me to record any memory before I forget. Even if I do not want them to be, the events of that day are permanently seared into my mind. When I close my eyes, I can still hear the breathing of the animals in the cave.

My doctor, Doctor Odam, is a grandfather-looking gentleman with eyebrows like white caterpillars. He tells me that he knew my parents and their loss was a great tragedy for the CAEP. I don't remember seeing him at the funeral, but I didn't notice anyone that day, my grief was so absolute. After he checks on me, with Kate standing there like a supervisor, he leaves with her and they talk in the corridor outside my room, away from everyone and far enough that I cannot catch their words. Oh, how I wish I still had Abigail's ear pieces. Something is happening and Kate is being stubborn as usual, not telling me.

Doctor Odam is astounded at how quickly my broken ribs are setting themselves. I am still wearing the custom-made digital cast on my torso in the daytime, taking it off only when absolutely necessary. I am told that at the rate I am healing, I will no longer need the cast in a day or two.

Three days ago, when I realised that I could stagger to the bathroom on my own, I removed my hospital robe and cast to look at myself in the large wall mirror. My body is bruised — dark blue patches marking places where the impact of my fall was hardest. I look like a strange spotted animal. Interestingly, I have four distinct round bruises, about one centimetre in diameter and closely spaced like large dots in a row, below my right clavicle. The same pattern is present on my back equidistant from where my clavicle would have been. It looks like an animal's incisors have clamped down on my shoulder, hard enough to leave marks but not to break the skin. I do remember feeling something with jagged edges on my shoulders and being dragged. That was before I lost consciousness. Judging from the incisors, I believe that it was a Lioger. A rodent's jawline is different, and the Prime at the time was busy trying to kill Yon and I. Even if it was a Prime, it would have used its hands. I frown, trying to understand — a Lioger clamped its jaw on my right shoulder and dragged me to a cave. Why?

The sound of the door sliding open directs my attention away from the window and my thoughts. Kate is standing there smiling, holding a muffin on a small plate, adorned with a single, lighted candle.

"Happy birthday, Marra," she says. I am not surprised that she remembers. Kate reminds me of my new age every year since the deaths of my parents. "Make a wish." She stands by my bedside, holding the muffin out in front of me.

I humour her and extinguish the flame with a single breath. Kate very carefully hugs me, not wanting to give me more bruises. The lump on my forehead is now a small bump and my lips have returned to their normal size, but my tongue still aches a little, although it is generally healed.

"Thank you, Kate," I smile. I see blueberries peeking out of the large muffin. My mother used to bake me these.

"I bet your wish has something to do with getting out of here quickly?" she laughs, placing the plate of muffin carefully down on the small table next to my bed.

"Maybe," I say. An awkward silence falls on the room like thick fog. Then, almost as if she has made up her mind about something, Kate pulls the chair in the corner up to my bedside. She sits on it with determination, looking like she is about to announce some important news.

"Are you feeling better today?" she starts. "Doctor Odam tells me that your ribs are healing very well and fast. That's good."

I nod and say nothing. Kate is direct when she is confident but goes around the subject when something bothers her. All her casual questions are 'padding', to help her launch into the crux of the matter. She looks at me with enquiring eyes and sighs before saying, "Have you ever been to any doctors besides your mother, Marra?"

The question is surprising and disappointing, an anticlimactic end to my wait. "No, she always took care of me," I say, deflated.

"Do you know your blood type?" Kate asks. This is another strange question and my curiosity is piqued. Where she is going with this?

"AB positive," I say. That is what is written in all my health reports.

"Marra," she says, "it appears that that's not your blood type."

Is that what she is worried about — that my mother made a mistake about my blood type? I feel the suspense deflate like a punctured balloon and smile with relief. "So Mom made a mistake," I say and smile.

Kate purses her lips for a microsecond. "No," she says, "it's more complicated than that."

A deep frown etches itself across my forehead immediately. "What do you mean?"

Kate takes in a breath and appears to hold it for a second of two before expelling it and telling me, "Doctor Odam is unable to determine your blood type. It appears to be new — never before seen in any human."

I take a sharp intake of breath. The information is so unexpected that it literally throws me against my pillows. I stare at Kate, unable to form any thoughts nor words, my mouth agape. What does that mean? What's wrong with my blood? It's not human? Why did my parents keep this from me? Questions rise to the surface like molten lava bubbles of a volcano about to erupt.

"Only Doctor Odam and I know about this," Kate says to fill the silence.

"That's why you had the Defence Warrior outside my door?" I ask, dread feeding my senses.

She sighs and nods. "I cannot have anyone else knowing this. Henri, Doctor Odam, is a personal friend of your parents and he has sworn not to discuss this with anyone else. In fact, he is now examining your blood, trying to figure out its genetic makeup."

I am still shocked. A thought crosses my mind. Am I my parents' child? Was I adopted? How could my blood be 'never before seen in any human'? I am confused, alarmed and sad all at once.

As if reading my mind, Kate says in a gentle tone, "You ARE their child, Marra. You were born in this very hospital and I was with your mother after you arrived into this world." Then, as if to further emphasise the point, she says, "You have your mother's dimples and your father's nose and you are a product of both their personalities. I see them in you."

Tears well up and I hasten to wipe them before Kate notices. She does and she leans forward and holds me in a gentle embrace. The kindness of the act takes me by surprise and I let the tears roll down. I feel Kate gently stroking my hair as my mother used to do and my heart aches. After a few seconds, I pull away and look down into my hands.

"What does this mean? I'm confused," I confess.

"It means that Doctor Odam and I will find out more about your blood and you have nothing to worry about. There is nothing wrong with you, Marra," she says.

"Except strange, non-human blood," I say. I try to recall if I was ever ill as a child and I am not sure if I was. I have not paid attention to details like that; I did not have to. I do remember that I received all my health check-ups from my mother.

"You are human. My choice of words is regrettable. You have human DNA with an extra something and your blood is a new type. Perhaps there are others like you we are not aware of. Our world is changing all the time."

I feel that she is saying this to make me feel better, but some-how, it makes sense. Our world IS changing. Have I become the first evolved human, like the animals?

"You cannot tell anyone about this," Kate says again. "Not even to Yon. At least not yet." I look up into her eyes. She is serious.

I nod. Why would I want to tell anyone about this? I am a strange hybrid, like the animals we have on Neo-Earth. I remember all too well the taunting I received at the academy, "*Lioger Eyes, Lioger Eyes!*" What would they call me now?

I am starting to understand my parents' secrecy all through my life with them. The silences when I walked into their conversations. The locked laboratory in our habitation. They must have studied me for years without my knowledge. What were they trying to do?

Kate hugs me and my thoughts stumble back into the present. "You'll be alright?" she asks with concern.

"I'm fine, thank you, Kate," I reply. She touches my cheek lightly and then gets up, and strides out, looking back at me once, her smile telling me that all is well. I feel, however, just the opposite. That nothing will be well for a while. I've just been inside a tornado and it has spit me out, transformed. Fear clots at the bottom of my heart like dirty blood and I can feel the clot increasing. My intuition says that my parents would have told me about this had they been alive. There had never been a moment in my life with them where I felt unloved or uncared for. They were genuine in their affection. Their plan was probably cut to shreds when they unexpectedly died. Would they have left me a note? Something?

I lie back on the pillows that are propping my back. Like a prelude to doom, the day outside has gone dark again and I hear rumblings of a potential storm. In the dim light of the day, I can see my reflection on the carphite-glass — a dishevelled girl, with a small cut just above her upper left lip, looking dismal and tired. Even from where I am sitting on the hospital bed, I can make out the dark circles under my eyes.

My eyes! Can it be? All these years, are my unusually coloured irises an indication of my 'condition.'

"*Lioger eyes, Lioger eyes,*" I hear the children chant in the echoes of my memories. Do I have Lioger genes?

I pull back the sheets and stumble uneasily out of bed. I stagger, as quickly and painlessly as I can manage to the bathroom and drop my robe and remove my cast. Standing there naked in front of the large, full size mirror, I see the fading marks where the Lioger had clamped its jaw on my right shoulder to drag me to safety. In the darkness, I could hear them around me, but they did not attack. Something pushed me out of the way of the attacking Prime; it can only be Lioger, I'm sure of it now.

Then I think back on the Lioger that stalked the Peacekeeper and I on the walkabout. It did not attack. Were the roars warnings for us to leave before the Primes arrived?

Why are the Liogers protecting me? Why am I important? My gold irises look back at me in the mirror, the same colour as those of Liogers'. There can only be one explanation …

I am one of them. *Freaking Hell*, I say out loud.

CHAPTER 14

"Nature always wears the colours of the spirit."
– Ralph Waldo Emerson

It is later in the day and Kate has not returned, nor has Doctor Odam. I imagine them looking over a projection of my hybrid blood, scratching their heads and chins for inspiration. Knowing Kate, she would by now have sequestered Doctor Odam to a secure room so that he can continue his work in secrecy. I feel sorry for him. Kate can be very forceful. I wonder how far he has gone with the research. He would have been working on it from the first day of my arrival at the hospital. I bet he has not thought of comparing my blood to that of a Lioger. Why would he, nor anyone?

I demand to be allowed out of my room, much to the amusement of the attending pink-cheeked, large middle-aged nurse. She listens to my 'demand' with the patience of a kindergarten teacher, which frustrates me. I change tactics and smile. If tough does not work, then maybe charm will.

"Pleeeease," I say, trying to make my eyes look like those of adorable small children.

"Doctor Odam said that I have healed really well. All I am asking is half an hour out in the wheelchair. I promise I will be extra careful." I continue looking at her with pleading eyes.

"I'll have to check with the doctor, dear," she replies, unmoved.

I slump back onto my pillows, dejected. Maybe I can steal a wheelchair? How hard can that be? I am getting stronger every day and there may be a wheelchair in the corridor, who knows? I take uneasy steps, to the door. The cast is comfortably snug and keeps my ribs secure. The door slides open and my head pops out. No wheelchair in sight.

"We don't keep those lying around, dear," I hear her say, and I jump. Where was she hiding? "Back to bed," she orders.

I stagger back to bed. If anything, the moving around does some good and I feel a little less 'constrained.'

The more I reflect, the more I am convinced that the Liogers that I heard in the wilderness were there to protect me. In the first incident, it was because the Primes were getting close to where I was. The roars were warnings. With Yon, they arrived as the Primes attacked. I remember seeing movement in the bushes as Yon and I ran. They must have stalked us knowing that the Primes were closing in. They must have also kept Yon alive because he was with me. They dragged me to the cave to keep me safe and then stayed around until the rescuers came. I must find out what Yon remembers.

My heart beats with excitement. My dreams are often about playing with a white Lioger cub. Maybe they were not really dreams but memories? I feel convinced that my parents would have left something behind that can explain all of this. The only place I can think of would be our old house in Seven. I must get out of this hospital.

The universe must have heard my thoughts because the door slides open and Doctor Odam and Kate walk in.

"How are you feeling? And I hear it is your birthday. So, happy birthday!" the doctor asks in his gravelly voice. I like him. His white caterpillar eyebrows and unkempt hair give him the look of a mad scientist.

"Thank you," I smile. "Can I leave the hospital?" the question comes out too soon, I realise, but I am feeling impatient.

I hear a husky chuckle. "Soon enough, soon enough," he replies. "But not yet. You are healing remarkably quickly. Far more than your friend, Yon. But I still want you here for observations." He walks around to one side of the bed. "I suspect it is not just your blood that is special. Your body is somehow healing much faster than I expected."

"Henri, I mean Doctor Odam, is right," Kate says. "We want you here for observations and to heal completely and …"

"Compare my blood to that of the Lioger," I interrupt her, unable to hold on to the information any longer.

"What?" the doctor's gravelly voice asks.

"My eyes!" I say. "Maybe my genetic and biological make-up created my eyes. Mom used to tell people that they were caused by 'genetic evolution'. She wasn't lying. I am evolved from something, and look at me, kids used to call me 'Lioger Eyes'. Maybe I have a bit of Lioger in me?" I say all this a little too quickly, which I regret immediately. The eagerness makes me sound young and impulsive, not the attitude I wish to project.

Kate stands there, looking stunned. She looks at the doctor and he at her. "Is that possible?" she finally asks him.

"I am a medical doctor. Animal biology is not my specialty. Kate, maybe we need to bring in someone with more experience in this field. A geneticist? A biologist?" Doctor Odam's eyes widen.

"We can't," Kate says. "I don't want more people knowing about this." But she looks conflicted.

"What about Liam Anders? Isn't he a geneticist? He does what mom did, right?" I ask, careful now to speak slower and with more deliberation.

Kate turns her attention to me. She is silently processing my words. I see not only concern in her eyes, but a hint of fear and confusion. I wonder what is bothering her. Doesn't she like and trust Liam?

"Let me think about this," she tells me. She turns to Doctor Odam, "Let's walk and talk."

"Wait!" I say quickly before they leave. "Doctor, please can I get a wheelchair and go to the recreation room?" I plead.

"I don't see why not!" the doctor says after a second of reflection. "I'll have them bring you one. In the meantime, rest."

Kate unexpectedly plants a kiss on my cheek. "I'll come back with an answer, Marra," she says.

Yon lies sleeping like a handsome, enchanted prince on his hospital bed. Even in slumber and unshaven, he is attractive. His left lower arm is in a digital cast as well as his torso and his left fibula. I remember the landing he had when the Prime hit him. It is a miracle he is alive.

The electrical wheelchair arrived as promised after Kate and Doctor Odam left and I was out of my room in thirty seconds, zipping down the corridor towards the other ward, looking for Yon. He is alone in his room and I have let myself in as quietly as I can.

His breathing is soft and even and has a calming effect on me. I park the electric wheelchair next to his bed. His eyelashes are the colour of his hair, a dark blond shade. They are long and slightly upturned, sweeping down his eyelids like the edges of feathers.

"Oh, we have a visitor!" a happy voice greets me and the enchantment is broken. I turn and meet a smiling, young nurse with short, blond, curly hair and a trim body. She looks to be about my age and pretty in an uncomplicated way. She walks to the other side of Yon's bed and starts examining all his vital signs. "He's been sleeping for a while now. He should be up soon. His painkillers, you know," she says.

He stirs hearing the young nurse's voice and I see his eyelids flutter and slowly open. I see green irises peeking at me, as if his sight is adjusting to my presence. Then, his mouth starts to break into a smile, and as suddenly as it starts, he winces. "Ow!" he says, his right hand flying to his lip and I realise that his lower left lip is split from the fall and still red and swollen.

"Hi Marra," he says, grimacing a little. He has the look of someone slightly inebriated.

I smile. "How are you, Yon?" My heart quickens.

"I want one too!" he says, pointing at the wheelchair and pretending unsuccessfully to pout.

"You'll get one when you are much better," the young nurse says as if speaking to a spoilt child. I have already forgotten about her. She has been standing there watching Yon wake up as I have.

Is she interested in him? She is smiling at him like he is a beautiful, naughty boy, and in that instant, I dislike her.

"Ah! My favourite!" Yon grins, long, deep dimples appearing on his cheeks, framing his smile like inverted commas, the pain from the split lip forgotten.

The nurse giggles like a schoolgirl. "Well, I'll leave you two. You must have things to talk about." She walks out but not before flashing Yon a toothy smile and a wink that grates on my nerves.

"Are you in a lot of pain?" I ask, turning my attention back to Yon and trying not to think of the pretty, blond nurse with the thick, red lips.

"Nah! That's what painkillers are for," Yon chuckles. "But I can't move much with all this," and he waves at all his casts with his good right hand. "How are you, Marra? I would go and see you, but I'm held prisoner here." He whispers the last sentence as if we were in a conspiracy. Even in pain, Yon has not lost his strange sense of humour. "A hug?" he asks, his arms outstretched. I feel that the painkillers are doing most of the talking but the prospect of a hug is tantalising.

I carefully get out of the wheelchair and approach him. It is an awkward hug as both our chest casts collide lightly. We must look comical, two bruised people trying to give each other comfort.

"Excuse the 'bed' breath," he says. "If I knew you were coming, I would have brushed my teeth and combed my hair!"

I smile. "You do have bad 'bed' breath," I tell him. Yon has a gift of putting me at ease. I hobble back to my wheelchair. "I'm sorry."

"Huh? About what?" he asks, an eyebrow cocked in surprise.

"They tell me that your injuries are extensive," I reply.

"So? That's not your fault. It goes with the job, Marra. Don't put that on yourself," he says, his tone gentle and serious. Then, in a more jovial voice, "I'd do it all again to protect you!"

I feel butterflies flutter their wings and take flight within my heart and smile. I let a few seconds pass in silence before asking, "Yon, were you unconscious the whole time after your fall or did you wake up in the night before the rescue team came?"

Frown lines appear on his forehead as he tries to remember. "I woke up with the worst pain all over my body at one point, I think," he says.

"Did you see anything? Were you 'moved'?" I ask.

"Moved?" he looks at me unsure of what I am asking.

"Were you in the same spot you fell when you woke up?" I rephrase my question.

"It was dark and I was not fully conscious all the time … but no, I don't think I was moved. And I don't remember seeing anything." Yon says. "In all honesty, everything was swimming around in my head and even if there was something, I probably wouldn't have seen it." He looks at me, his suspicion growing about my line of questioning. "Why?"

"Just a thought," I say and then I choose to correct myself, "a theory."

"You're not on painkillers, are you?" Yon teases.

"No," I roll my eyes at him. "They found me in a cave."

"Yes, that I know. I was told when I asked about how you were. How did you get there?"

"I'm not sure, but I think a Lioger dragged me there." Listening to the words from my mouth, I realise that I sound insane.

Yon's furrowed forehead and knitted eyebrows tell me that he thinks I have lost the plot, because what I have said does sound unbelievable. Why would Liogers want to save me?

"I'm serious," I say.

Yon smiles, "I know, but I'm just thinking why would Liogers do that? Have they saved humans before?" And before I can reply, he launches on another question, "How do you know you were dragged there by a Lioger?"

I stand up and walk slowly to his bedside and then remove my hospital robe as carefully as I can while not exposing more than he needs to see. It is a tricky process because the robe closes from the back and I must make sure that the whole thing does not fall to my feet. I carefully reveal my right shoulder where the incisor marks are and then turn slightly so that he can see the back of my shoulder where the corresponding marks are located. I feel Yon's finger touch one of the marks on my back and instinctively shudder. His touch courses through my body like an electrical current. I move back and quickly tie up the top part of my robe and return to my wheelchair, my face warming up.

"Oh! I'm sorry," I hear him say. "I didn't mean to do that, but the marks are amazing!"

I look down at my hands and take a deep breath to cool off my face and then look at him. He is staring at me and I am unable to read him. My heart is beating its familiar fast-paced rhythm.

"So?" I say, a little too strongly. "Do you believe me?"

Yon tries shifting his position on the bed and winces in pain. "I think my meds are wearing off," he says. "And man oh man, I need to pee."

I am exasperated. He has the attention span of a fruit fly. Yon appears to sense this and holds up his good hand to stop my descent into frustration.

"Hold up," he says. "I believe you. Don't get upset just because I needed to express my … you know," and he waves at the general area of his bladder.

"I'll go," I say, flicking on the electrical gears to move away. "We can talk again later. This is too soon and you need to rest." My voice sounds tense, which is not what I actually feel and I add in a gentler tone, "Do you want me to call the nurse in?"

"I already did," he grins, although it looks more like a grimace. I have forgotten that he is healing slower than I am and all of a sudden, I feel ashamed of my behaviour.

"I'm sorry," I say. "You need more time to heal and we can definitely talk about this when you are feeling better. I'm just too impatient." I smile.

"Marra, please come back and see me, okay? And we can talk more. If I can get a wheelchair, I'll go and see you but it looks like it won't be for another few days."

"I'll come back," I promise him and give him a smile to tell him that I understand.

The pretty nurse arrives as I leave. Is there only one nurse who takes care of him? I glance at them as I exit and notice that she has re-applied her lipstick. They are chatting like old friends and as my wheelchair rolls down the corridor, I hear her squeal of laughter.

I decide to take a detour to the hospital recreation room to clear my head. It is a big area with large floor-to-ceiling carphite-glass windows that look out into a compound of trees. The ground outside is a thick carpet of red and brown foliage, peppered here and there by yellow leaves. The trees look like giant stick people with nearly-bare branches for arms. Soon, they will change into their icy, white robes. For now, they are content to sway to the wind's songs. I often imagine the wind running around the trees, like a joyful animal, howling at the sky.

I wheel to the large window and touch the carphite-glass with my outstretched fingers. I think about what Yon said. He did not see anything and was not moved and yet he was not killed. A Prime would not have left him lying there, alive. I am convinced that the Liogers that protected me also protected him. He would most certainly be dead otherwise.

I have completed my report about the attack on the digital pad but have not given it to Kate. I will hand her the report when I see her next and I plan to leave the hospital in the next days. Time is wasting while I am here. I take a last look at the trees and flick on the electric gears of my wheelchair to return to my room.

The whirring sound of the motor is all I hear in the corridor as I make my way back. It is not loud, but in the quietness, it echoes distinctly throughout the corridor. I see Kate standing by my room as I approach.

"Marra," she smiles as I draw near. "I have decided to let Liam Anders examine your blood, but anonymously. I'll just let him know that it is from a new hybrid."

We enter my room together and she helps me into bed. "But won't he know that it is human blood?"

"Yes, but there is enough other material there that could give him doubt."

"How will you explain where you get it from?" I ask, not confident in her plan.

"He'll just have to accept it. I won't tell him it is you. This is too sensitive. I don't want you exposed. I will tell him that I came upon the sample from an unknown source," she says.

We look at each other in silence for a few seconds. "Do you not trust him, Kate?"

She sighs. "Let's just say that I prefer to make a non-emotional decision. Just because I like him does not mean that I should think irrationally. When the time is right, I will tell him, but not yet. I just need him to analyse and give me the facts."

I nod. I cannot argue with her logic. It is probably best that I am kept secret at this point. I open the drawer of the small table and remove the digital pad. I hand it to Kate. "My report is there. And Kate, when can I leave the hospital? I'm truly better now. I don't really need to stay here."

She smiles. "Just one or two more days, Marra. Patience." Her fingers lightly tap the digital pad. "I'll be back tomorrow. Thank you for the report. You rest now. Enjoy the rest of your birthday." She plants a quick kiss on my cheek, squeezing my hand lightly before turning and striding out.

There is so much I need to do the moment I am released from here. But I know what I must do first — return to my parents home. That's where this started, and that's where I'll find some answers.

CHAPTER 15

*"What the caterpillar calls the end,
the rest of the world calls a butterfly."*
– Lao Tzu

March 4848

"Are you sure about this, sir?" Simeon says. His forehead is beaded with sweat and a drop starts to snake its way down the left side of his temple. His mother used to tell him he was of a 'nervous disposition' and at this moment, her words come back to haunt him.

The Tall Man, the nickname he gives him, pivots his head slowly in his direction as if he has mis-heard Simeon's question. The glare is terrifying, like that of a feral animal about to attack.

"I, I mean, is, is this the right thing to, to do? I, uh, I, I don't mean any disrespect, s, sir," Simeon tends to stammer when he is frightened and at this moment, he is terrified. He swallows as discretely as possible.

The Tall Man turns back to face the large, thick carphite-glass window that looks into the sealed experiment room, uninterested in replying, as if Simeon's question is beneath his intellect to entertain. "Proceed," he says into a microphone at the side of the window that feeds into the room.

Two scientists in white BioHazMat suits nod. They remove two small intranasal spray injectors filled each with a limited amount of light amber liquid. Sitting on the examination table, bony, bare legs dangling, is a young man with sunken cheeks and dark-rimmed eyes. He is in a light blue hospital robe that is one size too large for him. He looks malnourished, typical of the population in the South Zone of Sector Nine who often live in poverty. His hair is still wet from the shower he took earlier and now hangs in thin, light-coloured, strands over his eyes. He scratches his right arm, an unconscious gesture from nervousness and also from a black sore the size of a grape — a sign of bio-food poisoning. He flinches slightly and inches his body away as the scientists hold up the spray injectors, pupils dilated in fear.

But this is why he is there, to participate in the experiment, the Tall Man at the window reminds him. His voice is calm and reassuring, like an old friend. David thinks about the five thousand Digits they promise him. That can buy his family many things, maybe even real meat. He looks once more at the man at the window on the other side of the room. He tells him that the spray injections are quick and painless. David looks at the men in the white BioHazMat suits. He wonders why are they dressed like that? He does not have a good feeling about the situation, but five thousand Digits can go a long way to helping him and his family. He stops moving and braces himself for the injection, heart pumping.

Simeon watches all this in silence. There were three before David. *Were they released after the failed experiments?* Simeon searches his memory. He has not seen them leave the facility.

To those who do not know the Tall Man, the smile is a warm assurance of trust and compassion. Simeon, having worked with him for almost three years knows the smile is as deadly as a giant cobra's as it prepares to strike at its victim. There is a vicious coldness to him that makes Simeon's skin crawl.

He rues the day he became part of this experiment a long time ago, but there is no way out of it now. He tried using parental illness as an excuse to quit and leave but instead of allowing him to do so, they suggested bringing his parents to live with him at the facility. Simeon had no choice but to rescind his request. He did not want his parents anywhere near there or involved in any way in his work. He regretted immediately even having brought it up because now they are watching him even more closely.

He was flattered in the beginning when Mr Edgar, the head of the Federation Research Laboratories or FeReL as most people call it, summoned him into his office to tell him that he was chosen to assist in an important project. Simeon is a respected virologist, but he also secretly thinks that he is better than all of his colleagues. He graduated top of his class and published countless research papers. FeRel houses some of the world's most deadly viruses, long ago eradicated from Neo-Earth, in their Viral Deep Freeze Lockers, and every virologist wants to work there.

Perhaps this was why he was chosen. He thought that after six years, they finally noticed and rewarded his talents. And he was ecstatic at first. He signed a Non-Disclosure Agreement and they warned him against talking to anyone about his work, including and especially to his family. Being a bachelor, that meant only his parents and his brother.

Simeon is nervous around women. They scare him, make him feel inadequate. Besides, he knows women normally prefers tall men with thick hair and muscles in all the right places. Simeon does not fit into all those criteria. He started balding even before he reached the age of thirty. In a way, Simeon is grateful he has no wife. That will make his situation even more unbearable.

For the project, they moved him from his office to a secured building and gave him special access clearance via retinal scan. His gut told him that the extra security was suspicious, but he gave it no further thought because he was happy with his 'promotion'. He should have asked to leave then, before the job started. Now it is too late. He is in this too deep.

He remembers the first few months he worked on the project: he and his colleagues, other virologists like him, were relaxed and happy in their new office. They all felt honoured to be the chosen few for this important work, which was to create a new virus from ancient strains that they had kept in the Deep Freeze Lockers. They were told that it was to eliminate all the animals in the FSA and maybe even in the rest of the world.

Everyone knows the animal problem is colossal and Simeon

was more than happy to help. He himself had lost friends and some family to the animal attacks. They will be heroes if they create this super virus! The difficulty, of course, is to create one that does not affect humans in any way.

They report to the Tall Man, but his name is undisclosed. Simeon was suspicious. Why all the secrecy? But the the money and the prestige of working for such an important project blinded his conscience.

In the beginning, the Tall Man was never present. They call him 'Sir', as if he is the commander of a secret army. He communicates with them via voice transmissions, a method that has fallen into disuse decades ago. It is unusual given that the most common way to communicate is through holo-screen. However, no one complained. The work was challenging and kept them busy, motivated and well-compensated.

Then, as the months and then the years progressed, the task became more difficult. During field tests, the viral strains killed certain animals but not all, and Sir became impatient and angry. It seemed some species of hybrid animals, specifically Liogers, had developed far greater immunity to the viruses. The problem was that there was no known sample of Lioger blood anywhere. Simeon needed to examine the blood so he could figure out how to engineer the biological agent. Short of going into the forest and hunting down a half-ton Lioger, there was not much they could do and Simeon told this to the Tall Man. Simeon thought he would be fired, but instead, the Tall Man had said nothing on the other line and after a second, hung up.

Simeon started to notice that colleagues, one after another, began to disappear — to leave, to supposedly get new jobs — replaced by new ones. But it was happening at an alarming rate; one every week or so. Pressure mounted to survive the cut; to survive possible death — because none of his former colleagues were ever seen again, and it became more and more clear that failure was not an option. Simeon waited for his turn. It made him ill to go to work each day not knowing what would happen. He began getting paranoid; every stranger became a spy or assassin sent to eliminate him; each knock on the door of his habitation, a killer waiting to slit his throat.

Not too long after his conversation with the Tall Man, he arrived at work as usual and was told he had been moved to head another work group. They told him his expertise was better suited to the next mission.

His heart pounded out of his skinny chest as he followed the two large Peacekeepers, holding on to his box of items, his hands shaking. He sweated profusely when they put him in a lift and scanned a card that took them to another floor he had never been on before. He thought it was normal they would kill him as discretely as possible.

On exiting the lift, however, Simeon was greeted by another scientist. The man introduced himself, took Simeon to a work-station and even brought him coffee, all while smiling widely. Simeon finally relaxed when the Peacekeepers left. He was not going to die that day. His new colleague told him that this new project involved bioengineering a different virus that was to be administered to humans.

Simeon looked at him as if he had just spoken in a foreign language. Why did they need a virus for humans? But his colleague only raised his shoulders and smiled. He said he was not paid to argue with directives. Simeon watched his enthusiastic, young colleague walk away and felt pity. He had that same optimistic look when the first joined. Now he wakes up every morning expecting it to be his last.

The new mission baffles Simeon. Creating a virus for the human population does not sound logical, but he is too frightened to argue. The virus needs to be airborne, highly infectious and carries the appearance of harmful symptoms without being lethal. This is a whole new challenge.

Once, Simeon tried to be brave and asked Mr Edgar why they were producing such a virus. The response he received was short: Do what he was told and don't ask questions as per his signed contract. Had he forgotten? Did he need to be reminded of it again? The last question sounded like a direct threat and Simeon made no more enquiries.

This is the virus they are testing on the volunteer now. The previous strains did nothing more than gave the past subjects bad colds and the Tall Man was furious. This is Simeon's last chance, he is told. Simeon is too soft and needs to prove his worth or his place in the laboratory will no longer be necessary. *That means elimination and certain death*, Simeon thinks and trembles. Therefore, he throws his morality aside and does as he is told. To make his human virus more potent, he adds more harmful strains, and produces a vaccine to counter it, should the subject fall violently ill. This is the only way he can engineer the virus with the required specificity. He sends the encrypted file to the Tall Man over a secured line and then spends two sleepless nights wondering if he will 'disappear' like his past colleagues. On the third day, he receives an encrypted message from the Tall Man on his digital pad — "Not bad" it reads and Simeon knows he has survived to live yet another day.

For the clinical test of this virus, the Tall Man makes an appearance in the laboratory for the first time since the start of the projects three years ago. He is impeccably groomed and dangerously polite. Everything about him engenders ruthlessness. Simeon thinks he fits the description of a textbook sociopath. When he walks into the laboratory that morning, smelling of expensive cologne, Simeon is shocked. He recognises him immediately, but he also knows that there is a reason why his name has been withheld all these years and kept secret. It will be unwise for Simeon to acknowledge him by name even then. Therefore, he mentally nicknamed him 'the Tall Man'. He is intimidating and even his deep and calm voice intimates violence. That is when Simeon's long forgotten stutter returns.

His attention stumbles back to the young man in the experiment room. He watches with self-loathing shame and dread as the scientists in the BioHazMat suits inject the sprays into the young man's nostrils.

Guilt nibbles at Simeon from the inside like a flesh-eating bacterium. He feels his humanity leave him at the first injected spray. He silently asks for forgiveness. He knows what he engineered is going to give rise to painful symptoms in the next two weeks. He realises there is a possibility that the vaccine may not work. Therefore, there is a fifty percent chance that David will die.

Simeon tries guessing the use for the virus, but cannot find any viable reason. Why does FeRel want to make humans sick? He doubts if they will ever tell him and he worries that sleep will never return to him, should the subject die.

Simeon watches the young man as he is led away to an adjoining room, where he will stay for the next two weeks for them to monitor the effectiveness of the virus he has just inhaled.

"Let me know if the symptoms begin early. Otherwise, I will call you in two weeks," the Tall Man says, walking away, whistling a tune. Simeon does not reply. He knows he does not need to. He stands there and watches the Man disappear behind the sliding door and listens for his footfalls to fade away before breathing normally again.

The virus Simeon designed is spliced from two ancient viruses. The first is a deadly flu strain that killed hundreds of thousands in the year 3246. A vaccine was eventually made that eradicated the problem. Millions of animals, mostly birds and bats, connected to the emergence of the virus, were culled. In 3248, the World Health Organisation announced that Earth was finally free of this virus.

The other strain was a variation of the Ebola virus that appeared in 2992, which was eradicated five years later in 2998, but not before it ravaged and killed about four million people worldwide. Samples of both strains had lain dormant in the Federal Deep Freeze lockers until recently awakened.

The new strain that Simeon has bioengineered exceeded his expectations. Instead of two weeks, the symptoms appear on the tenth day. The Tall Man return as soon as Simeon send him the results.

David, the young volunteer, first experiences severe chills from a high fever that wracks his body with pain. He starts coughing around the same time. He coughs so much that his throat begins to bleed. By the following day, a head-splitting migraine sets in. He becomes delirious and weak as the virus continues its warfare through his body. Finally, he begins to bleed from his eyes.

Standing there at the sealed window with the Tall Man, Simeon watches as the virus attacks David's body in full force. What he finds most horrifying and heart wrenching is hearing David's pleas and cries for help. Simeon wants to give David the vaccine that he has already prepared for the occasion, but the Tall Man tells him to wait. He wants to see the full extent of the virus' destructive power. Simeon looks away a few times as David's body begins to bleed profusely, from everywhere. He has never imagined that his creation will be so lethal and he feels profound shame. He has become a virologist to find cures, not to destroy a human being.

"S, sir?" he begins, "I, I think that … that David needs the, the vaccine … " his voice trails off as the Tall Man raises his hand to silence him. Simeon's heart is hammering loudly in his ears. Time is of the essence. The window for injection of the vaccine grows smaller.

Finally, the Tall Man nods to the lone scientist in a BioHazMat suit standing in the sealed room with David. The young man is so weak that he lies on his bloodied bed unmoving except for a faint rising of his chest. The scientist inject him with the vaccine and leaves.

"Now we wait," the Tall Man said, sounding pleased. He turns and leaves the laboratory, whistling. Simeon stands there, staring at the result of his work. He feels nauseous, guilt like a stone in his stomach. He knows this has changed him permanently. He is no longer the confident virologist who thinks his work could make Neo-Earth a better place. He has become a dark thing. If David's body had gone past the point of no return, the vaccine will not work. Simeon prays for a miracle.

"Congratulations, Doctor Olsen," the Tall Man tells Simeon as they stand watching David's recovery from the virus. It is three days after the experiment has come to a head. For a while, Simeon is sure that the young man will die. Who knew he had such a determination to live?

"Thank, thank you, sir," Simeon stammers. "We will keep him here another week or two to run more tests and then we will send him home."

The Tall Man laughs, which surprises Simeon. Did he miss a joke?

"As you say, Doctor Olsen," he says, flashing a perfect set of teeth that looks white against his dark skin. "Now that the virus works, I'd like you to produce six more vials. I tweaked your formula slightly for David, I had forgotten to tell you that before. So, use the new version. I've assigned you three new assistants for this project. You have three days." The Tall Man shoves a pad into Simeon's hands, does not wait for a reply and walks off.

New assistants, Simeon thinks, *what happened to the current ones? Why would he need six more vials? Who would he inject them to? Tweaked his formula? How?*

But Simeon has been reflecting, when he is lying in the dark on his bed nightly, too stressed for sleep to find him, haunted by David's agony: in the beginning, they had him work on a virus to eradicate the animals and now to infect humans. Are the two connected? Why infect humans with long-extinct laboratory-engineered illnesses? *Unless … unless …* Simeon thinks, *unless they need a valid reason to release the animal virus!* There are still people who feel that killing the animals is wrong. If this is really what he is involved in, then isn't he a witness, a loose end?

He can run, but where? And even if he could escape, what about his parents? He is sure that the Federation will take them into questioning or maybe even use them to find him. The only way to stay alive is to do as he is told. He has contemplated suicide many months ago, but he cannot go through with it. A laser weapon would be ideal as it will be quick, but he does not know where to get one and slicing the radial arteries of both his forearms is far too painful.

Simeon decides to simply hunker down and work. His new assistants seem oblivious to what is happening around them and ask no questions. The next two days, Simeon works to reproduce the virus. He sees that the Tall Man has indeed 'tweaked' his formulation to make the virus more resistant to varying temperatures. The vaccine Simeon has previously created will not fully eradicate this new virus and he wonders if he needs to create a new vaccine that will.

To appease his guilty conscience, Simeon visits the experiment laboratory and look in on David. It is as if David's well-being gives him hope that there is something that he did right, as if David is his moral compass.

David has improved. He is still weak from the effects of the virus, but with the vaccine, he has been on the mend, slowly but surely. Simeon does not speak to him. He just looks at him from the safety of the thick, carphite window.

On the third day, Simeon arrives as usual to the window. But instead of David, there are two cleaners in BioHazMat suits, spraying down the room with what he assumes is disinfectant. *Did David die? That cannot be, he was improving. So, was he released? Surely not; he is not well enough yet.* He taps on the glass pane frantically but it sounds like muffled thuds. He then remembers the microphone.

"Hello! Hello!" his voice is high-pitched from panic. The two women do not turn, the sound of the disinfectant spray drowning every other noise. "HELLO!" this time, Simeon shouts and one of the women turns. Seeing his pale face, she turns off the spray and flicks her chin up to ask what he wants.

"Where is the, the, uh, young man who was there?" he asks, lowering his voice in an attempt to exude confidence.

The two women look at each other and then turn to him. They both shake their heads and one of them raises her shoulders to tell him she does not know.

"Ok, ok, thank you," Simeon stammers, his voice quavering again. He runs out of the experiment laboratory towards his office, his laboratory coat flapping behind him like a cape. His office is down the hall and then one level below and to save time, he gallops down the stairwell.

"Where is David?" he asks in a breathless voice as soon as he steps into his office. His assistants all turn to look at him but none replies. "Where is the volunteer?" Simeon repeats, a little louder.

"I don't know," one of them, the short, thin girl with a permanent scowl on her face, replies. She turns back to the samples she is examining under her microscope. The other two assistants shake their heads in unison and return to what they are doing. Simeon is breathing hard now as his heart starts to race. David needs more time to recover and releasing him early is not safe for the general population. Simeon has not had the opportunity to run full tests to ensure that the virus is completed eradicated from David's body.

Simeon tries desperately to think where else the young man can go. His thin body trembles with the rush of adrenaline. *Maybe David is at the building exit?* he thinks. That seems logical. Simeon turns and starts to head out of his laboratory when he freezes in his tracks. The Tall Man is walking towards him in large, leisurely, confident strides.

"Going somewhere, Doctor Olsen?" the Tall Man smiles.

"Uhm, David, s, sir," Simeon begins, "I, I can't find h, him."

"And … ?" the Tall Man's eyebrow raises.

"He, he hasn't been cleared of, of the virus, sir," Simeon says, there is a knot in his stomach and he feels nauseous. The Tall Man's friendly gaze is even more terrifying than his angry one.

"And … ?" he says, this time shaking his head as if not understanding what Simeon is talking about.

Simeon is at a loss for words. Does he not know the dangers of releasing a person who is still not cleared of carrying a dangerous virus? Simeon stands there, mouth slightly agape, not knowing what else to say.

"So where are we with the production of the virus? You are using the new formula?" the Tall Man asks, seating himself down on one of the laboratory high stools.

"Uhm, yes, yes," Simeon begins, confused that he has changed the subject. "We, we will have them this afternoon, sir."

"Good! My assistant will collect them. Thank you, Doctor Olsen," he says smoothly. Then, he stands up and strides off, whistling.

Simeon watches him disappear into the lift at the end of the corridor. He suddenly understands why they let David go. They *are* going to infect the general population and what better way to do it than through a human carrier. David still has enough of the virus in his body to infect anyone he comes into contact with. And as it is airborne, all David has to do is sneeze. He begins to wonder if they have changed the formulation of his vaccine to allow David to heal just enough but not completely eradicate the virus. Simeon's heart tightens with fear and panic. What has he done!

April 4848
"Ladies and gentlemen. We have confirmed that there is flu-like virus that has claimed at least forty-four people since its start about two weeks ago. The origin of this new virus is from the giant Red-Winged Blackbird, and bear some similarities to the strain of 3246. But this new virus, the E3 virus, is far more powerful. After the first symptoms appear, demise usually follows in about seven days. If you have come into contact with any animals or if you experience any flu symptoms, please go immediately to the nearest hospital. In the meantime, we advise the public to wear medical masks and be extra vigilant about hygiene. We have distributed the masks in all community centres and hospitals and THEY ARE FREE. Please make sure you collect one for yourself or for your families. The Federation Research Laboratories are working day and night to find a vaccine and we will let you know once it is found. Thank you."

The attractive young woman in a black pant suit with her light brown hair pulled tightly into a neat bun is the spokesperson for Sector Nineteen's Mayor's office. She steps off the podium as she finishes her announcement. The members of the press starts firing questions at her, but she quickly disappears into a waiting

Samuelson, which drives off as soon as the door slides closed. The Mayor has instructed his staff that they are not to entertain any questions.

The virus that sweeps through the South Zone is vicious and powerful. The doctors in the hospital has mistakenly diagnosed the first cases as bio-food poisoning because no one suspects a virus as the cause. A virus such as this is supposed to be extinct years ago. Its reappearance baffles all the doctors and they have no known vaccine in supply anywhere.

The Mayor enlists the help of all the top Federation virologists and scientists to find a cure, but the results are slow. They tell him that animals, mostly birds, caused the virus, which is curious because Sector Nineteen, like all other sectors in the FSA are closed off from the wilderness and forests. But he does not argue with scientists of the Federation; they know best. They tell him that the highest authority on virology, Doctor Simeon Olsen, has unfortunately committed suicide due to mental instability following the accidental deaths of his parents. But the Federation Research Laboratories has other virologists working on the vaccine.

What the Mayor fears most is that the virus has spread to other parts of the population. He is getting reports in the Central and North Zones of similar cases. His colleagues, the Mayors of Sector Fifteen and Nine has also communicated with him on having found the same virus-related deaths in their Sectors. This is a nightmare situation. If the spread of the virus continues, they will have to quarantine the whole country. That is an outcome they want to avoid; it will cost the country a lot of Digits from trade loss.

The President of FSA has been informed of the situation. They move him and his cabinet to a secure, virus-free location and the threat is elevated to a country-wide red alert. The World Health Organisation is sending their scientists into the country to assess the problem. This is because similar virus-related deaths have been found in the COE, brought in by a business traveller from the FSA who did not know that the illness was incubating in his body. The

WPO, the world governing body that the WHO is attached to, raises a worldwide alert.

In early July, the Federation virologists discovers a vaccine that appears to eliminate the virus. The WPO issues a worldwide production of the vaccine and all doctors breathe a sigh of relief. During its three-month reign, approximately 360,000 lives around the globe are lost.

September 4848 – News report

A five-year-old boy in Sector Fifteen is rushed to the hospital with flu-like symptoms and dies in five days. A young woman in Sector Nineteen also dies of the same symptoms. The doctors believe the cases are related and there is a new virus threatening the population. The Centre for Disease Control is now in charge of the situation, working closely with the WHO.

CHAPTER 16

"Man has responsibility, not power"
– Tuscarora

In the room that Kate has prepared for me in her habitation, the walls look recently painted, like clean sheets of white linen. The bed, large enough for two, sits against the back wall, smothered by a thick, sky-blue duvet and matching plumped-up pillows. A small armoire waits at a corner, like a silent observer. The room smells of lavender and clean laundry and is bathed in pale light from the large curtained window on the right wall. The soft glow gives the area an almost sacred feel.

On a shelf that lines the length of the wall to the left of the bed, is a row of digital photographs I recognise as having once belonged in the house where I grew up. My father's sable fedora, what he used to call his adventure hat, lies like a memento of that life, on the white writing table that is under the window. Kate obviously wants this to be my room and has filled it with all things familiar to me, as act that in its kindness and thoughtfulness makes my heart ache with gratitude.

Memories of my past life illuminate like decoration lights, with every digital photograph I examine. At the end of the shelf, like a propitious Pandora box, is a small wooden, latch-less chest. Excitement crackles like lightning. This is the box of wooden animals that my father had carved for me. I lift the square chest carefully off its perch with tingling fingers, feeling the rattle of wooden creatures inside it, waiting to be released. Then, like a six-year-old,

I sit cross legged on the bed, open the box and empty its contents slowly all around me on the bed cover. My heart feels like a million butterfly wings flapping simultaneously. I begin arranging the animals in concentric circles around me, a game I used to play as a child. This little act brings me back to the days when small, simple pleasures were all that mattered. Each animal is so familiar and yet so alien. The years have separated us and I feel like a stranger in their presence, a prodigal daughter returned.

I recall my father making me promise to keep these 'animals' safe, telling me that I was the guardian of their souls, among other things. It was the night before my parents' accident and he had looked so serious that I stopped laughing as quickly as I started, upon the realisation that he was not joking. I see the Lioger he was holding that night when we had sealed our agreement with a hug. I call him Leon. He is a little darker than the others and his wooden body is polished shiny from years of having been held more often in my grubby, young hands. Leon is also a little bigger, about the size of a large grapefruit, because he is after all the mighty Lioger! I smile and caress the smooth wooden body and mane that my father has expertly fashioned with his pen knife. His wooden eyes stare at me with familiar candour, asking me where I have been all this time. Kate appears at the doorway of my room. She chuckles at my little animal display and I grin in return, unashamed of my descent into childhood.

"I hope you like your room," Kate says, her eyes twinkling with something akin to nostalgia.

"It's nice, thank you," I say. It is the first time in a long time that I have a room almost similar to what I used to have growing up and I cannot deny the warm glow I feel. But spying the thin wrinkle of concern on Kate's forehead, I guess that she is not here to check on the room nor me. It has been three days since she gave my blood to Liam Anders for examination.

"Has Liam been able to figure out my blood?" I ask quickly. This is a question that has plagued my thoughts since the day I realised that I may have Lioger genes.

Kate enters and sits carefully on the bed, trying not to disturb my ring of wooden animals. I am still holding Leon in my hand. Somehow, the feel of the little wooden body calms me.

"Liam has completed the tests on your blood. He is as excited as a little boy with a new toy," she smiles, but not in humour, "Your blood is hybrid and, you are right, there is some Lioger DNA in it. That is possibly what is helping you heal so quickly. Your blood contains antibodies non-existent in human blood, that are resistant to most viruses that would normally kill us and even most other animals. That makes you immune to many bad illnesses out there." I listen quietly to Kate's even breaths. "Did you know that your mother was the first person ever to have obtained a sample of Lioger blood?" she says, a faraway, wistful look in her eyes.

"From when she treated them those years ago?" I ask.

Kate nods. "We are the only organisation in the world that possesses vials of Lioger blood. When your mother was alive, she was conducting research of the blood and became somewhat of an expert in its biology. Sadly, with her gone, the research has some-how been forgotten and put aside." Kate sighs. "How the blood got into you and then mutated, I still don't know and we may never know …" Her disappointment is obvious in the tone of her voice.

Then, like a rubber band snapping back into place, Kate's commanding voice returns, "Liam compared your blood to that of the Lioger that we have on storage and noted the obvious major differences. It made him curious. He keeps asking me where it comes from," Kate says and sighs, her face a grim recollection.

I remain quiet and shift slightly away from her, toppling over some wooden creatures. The answer to the question of my blood does not surprise me, but hearing it out loud is a lot. It feels like part of my existence is unravelling and cannot be reassembled.

"I told him it's from a new hybrid Lioger," she says, sounding apologetic. Doubt colours her expression.

"It's probably better that he doesn't know too much," I say, mostly to allay Kate's guilt at having to lie to Liam. I know that lying to someone you are close to feels like betrayal. I had felt the same when I lied to my parents years ago when I skipped classes to hide out in the forest, and their disappointment at the deception was more heartbreaking than the lie itself.

"Does he believe you?" I ask.

"I'm not sure. He is not as easy to read as I thought. But he didn't press the issue. I think he's just fascinated that there are 'newly-mutated' Liogers." Kate air quotes with her fingers and then gets up to stand by the window, unconsciously playing with the brim of my father's fedora.

"It's the blood's human proteins that intrigue him the most. He nicknames it, Super Blood," Kate says and smiles, although the frown on her forehead remains unchanged.

I look down at Leon, clasped tightly in my hand, feeling the familiar ridges in my palm. I notice a scar on his right haunch, which I don't recall seeing before and cannot remember how it got there. Holding this small wooden creature soothes the unease building within me.

"Does Liam have a theory on how my blood became what is it, Kate?"

The air suddenly feels dense as thick smoke. "He thinks it may be a natural progression of evolution. Well," her lips curl almost unnoticeable, "I may have influenced that. I asked him the question and he agreed. Seeing how Neo-Earth's animals have mutated, it is not unusual for the change to continue. But he is intrigued about the human proteins. That, he is unable to explain and I did not and will not tell him about you, Marra."

"How did I get mixed up in evolution?" I say, the question mostly rhetorical, but the words weigh heavily in the space between us. Although my parents are not mentioned, I somehow think that Kate is wondering, as I am, about whether they had something to do with my condition. But saying it out loud would be to expose the unthinkable and neither one of us want to release the thought.

"What's important, Marra, is that you are healthy and that this does not affect you in any way. If anything, it has given you the ability to heal much faster. I mean look at you! You were battered and bruised and barely eleven days later, you are healthy again, your bruises healed, your bones set. It's a medical miracle!" Kate says, and pauses, "It's a useful ... quality to have, especially in today's environment." She searches my face for an agreement. Finding none, she continues, "Your unusual blood doesn't change who you are, Marra," she repeats, as if doing so will render it true. "I know you have questions as I do. I have asked Liam to thoroughly check the properties of your blood once more. If there is something, anything, he will tell me."

I sense that Kate is saying all this mostly to convince herself that all is well. How long can she, can we, keep this quiet? *Secrets tend to find their way towards the light like jungle vines,* I remember my father telling me once.

"I'll let you settle in your room. I have to return to the office. We can start our work in the afternoon," Kate says, referring to our planned discussion about my recent attack. I still have not mentioned to her my suspicion that the Liogers saved me, waiting for the right time, the right words. Then, Kate adds, "I'm glad you are staying with me, Marra. You know that this is your home?" Her question sounds more like an affirmation, and I nod. I watch her walk out of the room and down the corridor, listening to her heels clicking on the floor until silence returns.

The Lioger genes in my blood confirms my suspicion that they have saved me. Do they think that I am one of them? The best way to know for sure is to experiment. But how will I get close to a Lioger to find out? I doubt if Kate will let me return to Sector Five with Yon still in the hospital — or at all for that matter. I think back to the months before. Why have the Liogers chosen this moment to connect with me? Have they always been around me, watching from afar?

It feels like my quiet, familiar life has been hijacked. And I am getting these ... 'sensations', they sweep through my body like a mild vibration, not uncomfortable but I know that they signal events to come.

I sweep my hands over the duvet carefully and herd all the

wooden animals together to place them back into their box. I will not get answers lying around in this room. Leon is last and I hesitate. He looks at me with wondering eyes and in them I see my father, his last commission to me. I decide that Leon will remain free and place him on the nightstand, next to my digital pad. I have to visit my old home. Kate doesn't have to know, I think. This is a personal mission. There may be answers there that I have not seen because I was not looking.

I grab my jacket, gloves, scarf, and eyeing the fedora on the writing table, I grab it on a whim and head for the front door. I walk rapidly to the entrance before my determination fizzles. I strap on my boots, I think of Yon. Somehow, I wish that he could come with me.

A whiff of chilled air hits my face as the door slides open. Its sharpness wakes every molecule in my brain. Although we are not even in the middle of October, it feels like snow is about to fall soon. My father's 'adventure hat' feels strange on my head and yet reassuring. I feel slightly self-conscious, but wearing it makes me feel bold. I don't know if this is a look that suits me as it did him. I recall my father wearing this every time he was in the fields or out walking. I touch it, its weather-beaten brim is tough and yet pliable; it holds so many memories and moments with my father and his family before him; a piece of Stollen history, now mine.

I cross the road and turn left in the direction of the airfield, walking with brisk conviction,. The route takes me past several cadre habitations, each looking no different to the next, like digital copies, before arriving at my mother's placard that points to the unpaved trail leading to my old home. I stop at the signage, silently reading the words, touching the paint that is starting to fade. I see my mother, her dimpled smile that turned her eyes into sparkling, light blue slits.

The trail, I realise, has disappeared with disuse. There have not been any feet for years to mark the path, to trample down the undergrowth, and no one to keep it tidy. I feel a tightness rise from my chest to my throat and know that this venture into my past will not be easy. I take slow steps towards my old home, letting my instinct guide me. All the years of having taken this same trail home is etched into my muscle memory. The ground is thick with fallen leaves, a carpet of green, red and yellow patchwork. It is silent; I feel like I have entered nature's church.

Despite the gloom, I am feeling excited. I am not sure what I will find there, but I know that I have missed my old home. I have always missed it, like a chasm that cannot be filled or crossed. My pace quickens. Suddenly, I want to get there as fast as I can. I start to jog and then run, jumping over tree roots and going around blocked passages, feeling the thundering response in my chest, feeling my lungs clamour for oxygen as I go faster and faster. I blot everything out of my mind, concentrating only on my breathing, hearing it echo all through the trees. I am a wild animal, free at last to run in the wilderness unbridled. I allow my legs to find their own way, sanctioning their every move and direction. The habitation emerges into view through the trees and I stop, my breathing jagged, my heart searing from blood pumped through it at high velocity; a pain I welcome.

It looks smaller than I remember and I see that vines have crept up one side of the outer wall and claimed it for their territory. But it's beautiful. A dark green habitation, half consumed by vines and surrounded by trees. It looks like a home out of an ancient children's fairy-tale book I once read in the library many years ago.

I fill my lungs fully, feeling the icy air enter, stinging my nostrils. Then, I stand up and continue on into the house.

The solar panels appear to be functioning, even if minimally, and the front door slides open easily once I give it a little push. The living area illuminates in a ghostly, yellow glow as I enter. No one has claimed any of the furniture. The large sofa sits there watching me, like an old friend. A thick layer of dust coats everything and is everywhere, despite the closed windows. The once-cheerful, yellow curtains hang like disappointed, unfurled sails waiting for a wind that never comes. I stand at the entrance, soaking in every detail; the open kitchen to the left with the small, sun-coloured round table; the living area to the right with the large, beige sofa, now stained darker, the colour of wet sand; the empty shelf that lines the entire wall on the right, where digital photos used to stand. The room smells of decayed leaves, damp and lost dreams.

I walk towards the corridor that leads to the rooms and the back end of the habitation. My footprints are marked in the dust on the floor, intruders in a home that stood still in time. I push the button to my room. The door does not slide open as it should, an indication that the solar power connection in this section of the habitation has fried. I apply a little pressure and attempt to slide the door open manually. It moves inch by inch until I am able to see the edge of it. Then, placing my fingers there, I summon all the strength in my arms and pull it open. It yields with a protesting whine.

My room looks serene, tired, sad. I have forgotten how much I have loved this private space of mine. The bed, strangely, is neatly made, complete with pink duvet and pillows, and looks out of place in the bleakness of the room. Here too, dust has dominion. I half expect the wardrobe to be full of my clothes and then remember that I have given most away. It is empty and looks lonely and bereft of purpose. I sigh and exit the room; this is no time for sentiments. My point of coming to the house is to find clues about what my parents were doing in their laboratory.

I proceed in the direction of the laboratory, in the back of the house. The door is open and I enter. The light is not working here, but thankfully, there is enough daylight streaming in from the door, to cast a dim view of everything.

It is as I remember, rows of empty shelves and bare tables. I walk around the room and begin to look at every shelf, under the tables and corners, hoping that my parents have left something behind. Nothing. Nothing but dust. My parents were thorough. Everything that was there, no longer exists. I walk out, my spirit deflated. It appears that they may have taken the mystery of my hybrid blood to their graves.

I take another sweeping look around the habitation. Besides

loss and regret, nothing else remained. Yet, in spite of this, I feel strongly that my parents would have left something for me to find, or maybe it is just my mind wishing this to be true.

I cast a last look at the habitation before leaving, a deep hole where my heart is. Some things lost just cannot be found and there is nothing else to do but move forward.

The crunch of my boots on the ground bounces off the trees and echoes through their branches. The leaves are brittle from the cold and morning frost; It's like walking on corn flakes. I slow down and stop to check my wristband. I have a few hours before having to meet Kate in her office. I change direction and decide to explore the area close to the perimeter wall. It was forbidden territory when I was a child and now that I can, it seems a pity not to take the opportunity. The walk in the woods would help lighten the lead weights in my chest. The chill in the air is biting, but keeps my mind clear.

Seven's perimeter wall, I hear, is built with the ancient fortress in mind, minus the moat. Most of us arrive and leave by hovercraft and hence never get to use the large gates of the wall, situated on the northern perimeter close to the airfield. I hear it is a sight to behold, like ancient, colossal gates that slides open on both sides, as wide as a large building and just as high.

I remember my father telling me that the perimeter wall close to our old habitation is only about two kilometres away; an easy hike. I start off and before long, I see it even before I am anywhere near it. It looms large and forbidding over the trees, an alien-looking, ugly, dark grey block, breaking the natural beauty of the surrounding forest. I walk towards it, watching it expand as I get closer. At its feet, I cannot help but marvel at its construction. It rises so high above everything that the trees in the area look like saplings next to it. In the academy, we were told that the perimeter wall was built taller than the surrounding forest trees so that we could see danger from above the treeline. There is a walkway at the top that goes all around the wall. Defence Wall Unit Warriors perform a thermal scan of the surrounding forest outside the wall from every sentry point, every half hour, mostly for Liogers and Primes.

I see a large rectangular outline on the wall further down, which looks like a double doorway. There is a man-sized, white number '8' painted on one side of it, that covers the entire door. This, I know, indicates that it is the eighth entry point into the wall out of many others. I think that a lift within brings the Warriors to the top, where they will be posted on surveillance assignments. I suddenly wonder if Yon has ever been assigned on the wall and if he could take me up there. I remove the hat and tilt my head back. The view from above must be extraordinary, a sea of green against the sky.

The carphite-concrete feels cold to the touch. Seeing it up close, I cannot imagine any animal being able to penetrate it. I hear that the Wall Surveillance Unit Warriors have rooms to rest in when it is not their turn to keep watch. I think that I might enjoy a job as a part of a wall surveillance team; being posted at the top of the world to watch over the land below sounds wonderful.

As I move along slowly in the quiet, dim forest, my ears pick up a distant roar, barely audible but I am certain of it. I feel the tiny, invisible body hair on the back of my neck rise on cue, a gentle vibration sweeping over my body. I stop and listen, closing my eyes. Nothing. I refuse to move and continue straining my ears for the sound. Still nothing. I look up at the wall and wonder if anyone up there heard it too. No movement, no sirens. The silence is palpable like tar. Have I imagined it? My intuition tells me other-wise. I stand there, hesitating before I decide that there is not much that I can do. A roar that only I can hear is not a strong enough motivation for Seven to be on full alert. I could be wrong.

Walking up the road towards the square, I remove my father's hat again to examine the grey sky. A flake caresses my cheek. Then, more of them fall from the sky; they look like tiny, white feathers. I tilt my face completely upwards, watching their unhurried, zig zag trajectory towards the ground, settling on my face, on the pavement, staying still for a second before melting. I stick my tongue out to catch the next flake and giggle when I do. Snow has arrived, like a guest far too early for her appointment.

I put the hat back on and continue on the road. By the time I reach Kate's building, everything is starting to be coated in white. The flakes are coming down thicker and with more fervour and I see people hurrying by, eager to get indoors and away from the cold. I hear a snippet of a complaint directed at the weather, "… can't believe how early winter is this …" as two men walk briskly away in the direction of the science laboratories. Although I prefer warm weather, snow has a way of making everything look clean and unblemished. I stand outside the building and watch from under the brim of the hat how Seven is progressively turning powdery white.

Once inside, I find Kate's assistant. It looks almost as if he has not moved since I last saw him. Only his clothes, a brave and daring lemon-coloured suit, indicate that something has changed. My gaze is transfixed by the design on his head. His voluminous locks are brushed up and frozen in place, like a white-blond wave in mid curl before it reaches the beach. He barely looks at me as I approach her office. "She's expecting you," he says in his thick mid-European accent, his eyes glued to his screen. I am beginning to suspect that he hates his job and maybe even people in general.

Kate looks at me over the spectacles perched on her nose. She smiles and removes them. Then, she comes around, and points to the sofa.

"The hat looks good on you," she says, as I remove it and my outer layers, placing them in a neat pile in a corner of the seat. Without asking, she brings me a glass of water and settles herself opposite me.

"The snow is early this year," I say, feeling silly for indicating the obvious. Thankfully, Kate does not appear to mind my awkwardness and bad attempt at conversation. She takes her pad and puts her spectacles back on.

"I've read your report," she says, "twice, and you make no mention of how you end up in the cave."

"I, um," I make a split-second evaluation of whether to tell Kate of my suspicion and decide, "yes, I want that part to come from me verbally because it may sound a little strange ..." I trail off as I observe the line between Kate's eyebrows deepen. To her credit, she says nothing and I take the cue and continue.

"I think that a Lioger pulled me into that cave." This time, her eyes widen and she pulls off her spectacles.

"What?" she says, a little louder than usual, but I hear no mocking tone in her voice.

"When I woke up in the cave, before the rescuers arrived, I heard breathing around me. I couldn't see them, but I think that they were Liogers." Then, I add, "three of them," then, "I think," as if those two words can make what I say sound more plausible.

"How can you be sure of that, Marra?" Kate sounds incredulous and I cannot blame her. I sound crazy. Unfortunately, the bruising on my body has healed completely and I cannot show her what I showed Yon.

"Before I blacked out, I felt teeth clamp on my right shoulder and it dragged me backwards. I had the bruises on my right shoulder but they are all gone now."

"Why didn't you tell me this before the bruises healed?" Kate's voice is tinged with irritation.

"I'm sorry, Kate, I wasn't sure if I should then. I mean, I didn't think it was something anyone had to know."

"Marra," Kate says and pauses, a hint of despondency sweeps over her face. "I know that I can never replace your parents, but I hope you know that you can trust me. You are my god daughter and I take my role seriously. I will protect you, no matter what. Do you understand? So, you can tell me anything, ANYTHING, and I will believe you."

Kate's eyes glisten slightly and she lowers her gaze to her pad. "I'm sorry, Kate," I say, feeling a little ashamed for having hurt her. I forget how important it is to Kate to take care of me, something that sometimes feel strangely like her mission in life, as if she owes me that.

"I think," I begin, realising too late that I am repeating my 'thinking' a little too much, watching Kate raise her head to listen, "that the Liogers have been there all along to protect me. Even in the first incident."

Kate sits up. "How do you mean?"

"In the first incident, they knew the Primes were on their way and so the roars were their way to warn me to leave." I let the information sink in before continuing, "and when Yon and I were attacked, they suddenly appeared and came to our rescue. One pushed me out of the way of the Prime as it came at me. I think they also kept Yon safe while he was passed out, because he was with me."

Kate's mouth is slightly agape, her lilac eyes bright as she stares at me. "Because of your blood," she finally says. "Fu ..." she begins and then changes her mind, "This is incredible!" She looks like she wants to say more, but cannot find the words and stands. She paces the room as is her habit when she is nervous.

"Do you know what this means?" she says, her voice strangely calm.

"Actually, I don't," I reply. "It's my theory. We can't be absolutely sure unless we test it out," I say.

"What do you mean, 'test it out'? You mean get you in front of a Lioger? That's crazy and out of the question."

We fall silent, the air thick enough to slice through with a knife. Despite Kate's disagreement, I am still determined to test my theory. Maybe I can do this without Kate finding out.

"Don't think I don't know what you are thinking right now, Marra. Your mother used to have the same look. You are NOT to attempt any 'contact' with a Lioger, do you hear me?" Seeing that I still am refusing to acknowledge, she sits next to me, takes my hand and stares into my eyes, the lilac of her irises blazing. "Promise me," she says.

My chest feels tight, irritation mixed with a dose of indecisiveness. Although I don't really want to promise, I find myself acquiescing and nodding in agreement.

Kate lets go of my hands and head to her desk. "We will keep this all between you and I — the new hybrid Liogers, your blood work, your ... theory," Kate says. "I am keeping you here in Seven for now. I don't want you back in Five. We don't need to track those new hybrids at this time. They don't appear to be of any primary threat presently."

"So, we are going to forget all about them?" I cannot believe that Kate is willing to stop tracking the Liogers. Now that I know about my strange, mutant blood, my need to find them has grown more urgent.

"We won't forget about them, but they are not our primary concern at this time," Kate says.

"Why? I thought you said it was important we find them because they are undetectable on thermals." An unfamiliar sensation of heat is rising in my chest, and my voice sounds an octave higher.

"We have a far bigger threat to deal with at the moment," Kate says, and falls silent. Once she senses that I am calmer, she continues, "We have our first virus victim in the hospital, in isolation. He was admitted yesterday complaining of flu symptoms. The doctors didn't know it was the virus until he tested positive. The director has declared a medical quarantine. No one can leave or enter Seven for now."

My mouth falls slightly open. I have read about the virus fatalities in the human Sectors, which the Federation are blaming on the animals, but I thought that a cure was found in summer. A look of wonder must be etched on my face.

"This is a mutated strain of apparently the same virus, that spread early this year," Kate's voice is terse. She looks old and tired; the lines on her face appear more pronounced and the dark circles under her eyes are visible despite the powder she uses to disguise their existence. I don't know how she deals with the enormous pressures put upon her as Deputy Director of Mission Control.

Something melts in my heart and I suddenly feel sorry for Kate. I may be all alone in the world, but I am relatively free to do what I please. Kate is responsible for the close to seven thousand people living and working in Seven, not to mention those who are posted in remote Sectors, countries and ocean zones like the oceanographers and marine biologists at the North and South poles. We are a large organisation of various disciplines and keeping everyone safe is a monumental task.

"How did it get here?" I ask.

Kate shakes her head. "We don't know. We test everyone who arrives and no one is marked with the virus." She looks at me and for a split second, I see a wave of fear wash over her eyes. "We have to contain this and find a cure quickly or everyone in Seven will die."

CHAPTER 17

*"The greatness of a nation and its moral progress can be
judged by the way its animals are treated."*
– Mahatma Gandhi

The old Lioger sniffs the air. He looks around at his expanded pride. They have travelled far together. The journey is nearing its end. He can sense her presence now. They are bound by blood. He had saved her, but she had been frightened and so he had left her alone, preferring to guard her at a distance. Alas, she has forgotten him, forgotten their past together.

Despite this, he wants to see her again one last time before it is time for him to surrender his consciousness. He wants her to remember.

He leads his pride through the forest and snow that is thickening. There is danger coming, like a looming dark cloud; a danger that will change the world he knows, maybe permanently. The rest of the large pride feels it too. This is why they stay together. When the end comes, at least they will be in each other's company. They sense this great danger as a loud vibration in the pits of their stomach. Perhaps this is another reason why he has to find her, to look one last time into her eyes. Perhaps she is the key to the survival of his species.

His internal instincts are guiding him towards her. When they get there, he will try to contact her. There is not much time left.

CHAPTER 18

"When the well's dry, we know the worth of water."
– Benjamin Franklin

"Where is Doctor Anders!?" Kate's voice is like thunder in a storm.

The director has caught the virus and is in serious condition. She is now the acting head of the CAEP. Scientists and doctors in white, laboratory coats are running through the hospital corridors and two of them are following Kate. I hide and wait around the corner, allowing them to pass me.

The virus has erupted in full force and Seven is completely immobilised. More people are admitted to the hospital and everyone is now wearing medical masks for protection against the virus. Children are asked to stay home and habitations are sprayed with anti-bacterial compounds daily to help delay the reach of the virus.

In the hospital, there are sounds of crying everywhere and some people walk around with shocked and panicked looks. To add to the commotion, a snow storm is howling outside, blanketing everything in a thick sheet of powdery, white ice. It seems ironic that while the world looks clean and pure, chaos reigns.

I have been ordered to stay in Kate's habitation, but I want to see Yon and so I have sneaked into the hospital and into his room. In the confusion of doctors and people being brought in from the viral attack, no one notices me. I slip in quickly as soon as his door slides open. He is awake and in the midst of writing on his pad. He grins from ear to ear when he sees me.

Yon, like all patients in the hospital, is placed in a transparent tent, a square cocoon. It's a virus and bacteria-free zone. I head for a chair, the blue mask concealing my smile. I pull it up and sit just outside of his enclosure.

"Miss Stollen! I am impressed by your insubordination!"

He sports a full, sandy-coloured beard, a look I am not sure that I like, even if it makes his eyes appear even greener. He notices my gaze on his beard.

"What do you think? Do I look like a mountain man?" He turns his head left and right for me to have a better look at the thick hair covering his chin and mouth area.

"I'm not sure ... " I say, opting for diplomacy. "It's ... it's thick."

Yon's laugh is one of those that comes naturally from deep within, a beautiful, earthy sound that has the effect of drawing a smile.

"It's a no, then," he says. I am about to protest when he wags a forefinger at me. "Tut, tut, it's ok. You prefer my clean, good looks, that's fine."

I roll my eyes, but my heart is doing somersaults. Yon has the inexplicable ability to lighten my mood.

I start to remove my medical mask.

"Is that safe, you removing the mask?" Yon's eyes grow large with genuine concern.

"It's fine. I'm sure patient rooms have been sprayed and decontaminated," I say, not really knowing if it is true, but I feel strange talking to Yon through a mask.

"What's the latest news on the virus?" I know that nurses will tell him all about what is happening. I know he is the most popular patient among the female medical staff in the hospital, a fact I find irritating, even if it's helpful now.

"Not much I can tell you ... " he begins. "Patient Zero didn't make it. He died yesterday."

"Oh, that's not good." When I spoke to Kate in her office two days, I recall her saying that he was admitted the day before that. The problem, I hear, is that Patient Zero was already feeling ill even before being admitted to the hospital and along the way had been in contact with a dozen or more people, who in turn would have been in contact with others. "That means that the virus kills the host on the fourth or fifth day," I deduce.

Yon nods. "That's what Emma, I mean the nurse, tells me. But the problem is that they don't even know how he got sick and for how long, before the symptoms appeared."

Emma — so he is on first name basis with the nurses now. An uncomfortable sensation rises from my chest. I take a deep breath to force it down. Why am I feeling annoyed with this information?

"But I should be fine under this state-of-the-art, virus-free tent," Yon says, waving his hands around the tent, not noticing the irritated look on my face.

"You should be," I say, trying to sound casual. "I see the arm is better." I notice that he only has the rib cast on. Yon's smile is like sunshine. He pulls back his short sleeve and flexes his left arm and then turns his wrist around.

"Good as new, but I'm told to take it easy for another week or so." He looks at me with serious eyes, "I can't wait to get out of this hospital.".

"I was supposed to leave in two or three days and then the virus erupted and now all patients have to remain where they are,"

"At least you get to spend more time with Emma," the statement escapes me before I have time to reflect upon the impact of the words and immediately, my face feels warm. I stand up and walk towards the window, wishing I could go back in time to erase the sentence.

I take far too much interest in the shape of the snowflakes rushing down from the sky outside. I hear no humorous remark from Yon, which is unusual, but I am too afraid to look at the outcome my words have brought. The silence is thick and sticky like tar.

"It's uhm," I hear him begin to say, "it's a howler, the snow storm, I mean." Him changing the subject to be kind makes me cringe in embarrassment and all of a sudden, the room feels too hot and my clothes too tight.

I turn and peer at him so that he cannot see how red my face is, and manage a quick smile. "Yes, a big storm," I say, feeling stupid. Then I pull my medical mask back on and the hood of my jacket over my head, hiding the shame of my childish remark. "I had better go. You need to rest."

"No! No, don't go, Marra." his words surprise me and I stop. "Tell me what's happening with," he searches for an idea, "with Kate and the hybrid Liogers." He looks relieved to have found it. His enthusiasm settles my discomfort and I hesitate by the door.

"Come on, Marra, sit," Yon waves his hand towards the chair. Then, he adds on a quieter note, "please."

I move back and sit on the chair. My medical mask is still on. The warmth in my face is fading and I can breathe again. I peel the hood from my head, feeling the awkwardness of the situation permeate the air.

"So, what did she say?" Yon asks, his voice casual and light as if nothing has happened, and I feel grateful for his discretion.

I remove my mask. "The search for the hybrid Lioger is on hold. Seven is on total lockdown until they find the cure to the virus," I say.

Yon nods. He already knows this but is asking mostly to make conversation. "I wish I could get out of here," he sighs. "I miss our habitation."

Our habitation. I cannot deny the effect Yon has on me but I don't know what to do about it. I wish I could ask my mother. Asking Kate would feel somehow wrong, uncomfortable.

For a few seconds, we listen to the howling wind outside. I wonder if I should tell him about my hybrid blood. Then, good sense takes over and I dismiss the thought. Why would I tell someone I like that I am a hybrid? It would only drive a wedge in our friendship. He would start pretending that all is normal and I would hold it against him for treating me that way instead of acknowledging that I am different ... maybe I over-analyse situations, instead of just letting them play out and run their own course. In this instance, however, I am not ready to let Yon know the truth about me. I'm afraid that our friendship will change.

"I'm planning a hospital break," Yon suddenly says. I look at him and he is smiling like someone with a dark secret. "Will you help?"

"Help how?" I say this slowly. The idea of doing something illegal sounds delicious and appeals to the hidden rebel in me.

"Bring me my clothes, shoes, and a jacket with a hood would be great. With a medical mask, it will be easy to leave the hospital." The uniform he came in was probably cut away by the medics in order to treat his wounds.

"Won't you get into trouble?" I think of his position as Warrior. The very definition of their role is not to break any rules.

"They have bigger things to worry about. They won't miss me here. And, I am more useful out there."

I am about to ask him why not get Emma to help but stop myself in time.

"How will I get your clothes?" I ask instead.

"Call Assman at the base. He'll get you my clothes."

"I can't call the base and ask for an … Assman!" My eyes widen in horror. They would court-martial me for making a prank call.

Yon laughs, tilting his head back. "Ok, call for Corporal Asherman and if he needs verification, tell him I call him Assman and that he still owes me twenty Digits on a bet he lost."

"What do they call you at the base?" I wonder if Yon has a silly nickname too.

"Handsome, Gorgeous, Pretty Boy … " he stops when he sees my eyebrows shoot up, and breaks into laughter. "I'm kidding!" he says between chuckles. "I'm just Hunter, plain old Hunter."

"You had better be nice to me or I won't help you," I say, exasperated at his teasing.

"Don't make me escape this hospital in a lady's robe, Marra. I don't have the knees for it." He grins, tugging at his hospital gown.

I roll my eyes at him again. "Fine. I'll call your friend. I'll be back as soon as I have your things."

"Thank you," his dimpled smile does strange things to the rhythmic beat of my heart.

"I'd better return to the habitation before Kate finds me missing," I lie, suddenly feeling the need to return to the quiet of my room.

Yon looks disappointed, and a tiny jolt of elation move through my body.

"I'll come back and break you out," I smile.

Yon's grin fills his tent. "I'll hold you to that. My sanity is in your hands."

"I'll see you again," I smile, pulling up the medical mask over the bottom half of my face and the hood over my head.

"Hey, Marra!"

I turn.

"Glad you came." His smile makes up for all the discomfort I felt earlier, and there is a look in his eyes that makes my knees go slightly wobbly. I am happy my mask is back on because warmth is creeping up my neck to my face again.

A stream of people is rushing in, some limping, supported by relatives in medical masks while others are carried, unconscious. The virus is spreading with the ferocity of a forest fire. There is the sense of panic and despair in the air.

I head for the exit, thankful the snow storm has abated and thinned. It is a relief to be out of the hospital, away from the noise. I crunch through the thick blanket of snow as fast as I can in the direction of Kate's habitation.

Suddenly, Seven's emergency siren goes off. This means that there may be a perimeter breach or any other imminent danger, beyond the virus. Everything and everyone stop at the same time,. Then a second or two later, as if a restart button is pressed, everyone starts to move and rushes away towards their habitations, as required. My curiosity is piqued and instead of going where I am supposed to, I turn and run in the direction of Kate's office.

I take the stairs two steps at a time and then walk straight past her assistant, knock loudly once and enter her office. The same two scientists I saw in the hospital are there and all three heads turn to look at me across the room at the exact same time as I enter, the conversation left hanging in the air.

"Marra! What are you doing here?" Kate's voice is terse and annoyed.

"The siren … " Suddenly, I am not sure I have done the right thing, barging into her office.

Kate stares at me for a second or two, as if wondering whether to allow me into the conversation. Then, she turns to the two men, tells them to go back to the laboratories and keep her informed. She waits until they have left and the door slides close behind them.

"We have a situation," she says, heading for the sofa, massaging her forehead.

"What kind of situation?" I ask. The warning siren has stopped and now I hear a loud announcement for everyone to remain indoors.

Kate sits down on the sofa, still massaging her forehead. "Doctor Anders is missing."

"What? How can he be missing? How does anyone go missing in Seven?"

Kate shakes her head almost imperceptibly. "That's not all," Kate says, not hearing my questions. I wait for her to speak. She has her head tilted back, eyes closed, continually massaging a pain in her head that does not appear to subside.

"It seems we're missing three vials of Lioger blood we have on storage, all our research on the blood and …" she opens her eyes and looks at me with apologetic eyes. "Your blood samples."

I stare at Kate. "Do you think he took them?"

"Very possibly, because the logs show that it was his ID that removed them."

"Why would he take my blood samples? What use would that be to him?"

"Frankly I — we don't know. I am asking Cho and Patel to figure that out."

"How can he disappear, Kate? How can he leave Seven without anyone knowing?"

I hear a sigh. "I think that he had help, possibly from a Warrior on Surveillance duty. We are now checking who was on duty last night. The only feasible way to leave Seven would be from the top of the Southern wall where it is furthest from everything and everyone. He was probably picked up by a waiting hovercraft." Kate opens her eyes and looks at me, a deep shadow of disappointment and something more bitter written across her face.

"Seven is not built as a military base, Marra. We are a science and research facility and everything we do here we share with the WPO in order to help the world better understand the hybrids and ensure their safety. Our wall is to keep us safe from the animals outside, nothing more. We don't survey the skies for possible infiltration, much less for people escaping."

Kate's face pales a little and she looks down. "Of all the people working here, Liam is the last person I suspected. I vetted him personally, checked his professional and personal history thoroughly. He was clean; an impeccable record!" Then, on a more forceful tone, she says, "I don't even understand why he stole the blood and research. What use would they be to him unless," she looks up suddenly, "unless he plans to sell the information to a third party?" Kate sounds unsure.

"Could he have been working for the Federation all this time, Kate?" I ask, in slow, measured tones. I remember how she had looked at Liam, the glimmer of affection was real.

"That's possible. But the Federation has most of our research information, much like the WPO. It's part of our agreement," she says. Two silent seconds tick by and I see Kate's face transform; she has recalled something important. "They have all research findings except ... except for Lioger blood. We have never shared that with anyone. It didn't seem necessary because your mother didn't want that to be public knowledge and after she died, we filed the research away, to continue her work on it at a later date, which hasn't happened."

"But why would he want the blood ..." I say and stop abruptly as Kate's door slides open and a tall, trim man with dark hair peppered grey, walks in. He is in a Defence Unit uniform decorated with insignia I don't recognise. I am not familiar with military ranks, but he carries himself with the confidence of a high-ranking officer. He does not seem to notice my presence as he takes large strides towards Kate. I move to the window to give them space.

"Kate … Madam Deputy, sorry to interrupt," his voice is loud and thick, a voice that is used to giving commands.

"Cameron," Kate replies, her voice calm as a vast, windless ocean, but there is a sadness in her eyes. She stands to face him, sighing audibly.

"May we speak privately?" he asks, referring to my presence.

I make a move to leave the room.

"That's alright, Marra, you can stay. We're past formalities now, Colonel," Kate says and I stop in my tracks.

I look at him. His face does not betray surprise nor annoyance. I move back to my position at the window.

"I'm sad to announce that Director Vasiliev didn't survive, Kate, and you are now the Head of Seven. I'm here to make things official." He draws out a large pad. Kate stands there staring at the pad, appearing to hesitate for a second or two. Then, she offers her hands, imprinting both her palms onto it. The Colonel scans her irises and finally hands her a silver key on a chain, that she loops around her neck and then tucks into her shirt, rendering it invisible.

"Director," the Colonel holds out his hand to shake hers. I watch all this in muted awe. Kate is now Director of Seven. Understanding her, I don't think this is how she would have wanted to earn the position and title. I look at her from where I am standing by the window. Kate's face is a mask of serenity. I see no frown lines on her forehead. It is as if she already knew the news as soon as the Colonel walked in.

"Was his family present, Cameron?" Kate asks.

"His wife was."

Kate nods. I see regret. I know that she respected the Director. They worked many years together.

"I have other news," the Colonel continues tentatively, on a softer tone. Kate nods, giving him the signal to proceed. "I had this recorded for you."

He calls up the video screen and forwards the recording slightly.

The voice of President Monroe of the FSA fills the room.

"... working very hard to find the cure to this latest viral outbreak. In the meantime, it is important to stay indoors and wear your medical masks," President Monroe says, pausing for effect. He is mask-free, which means that he has been placed in a virus-free and secured location.

"This brings me to a matter that now appears of paramount importance ... the animals! Early this year, citizens of America and the world have been killed by viruses that we now know came from them. We found the cure for the first outbreak in summer ... but it seems that yet another virus has developed, the E4 virus. We can continue to fight these outbreaks, one cure at a time, but soon, we will run out of resources. These viruses will kill us faster than we can find the vaccines. Humanity's survival is at stake.

"These animals waged war on us and in the first wave, millions of us were killed and made homeless. And now, they are killing us again, this time with their diseases, their viruses ... " he pauses to let his words sink in. "If we don't do something about this, humans will become extinct. We will cease to exist." The President looks directly at the camera, nodding slightly, inviting everyone to agree with his assessment of the situation.

Then, he continues, "I have been working with top Federation scientists and virologists on this issue for some months now, to find a solution to this threat to humanity. And I'm happy to announce that we are at the threshold of a breakthrough. I am already in discussion with the WPO and all other country leaders to roll this out worldwide. This time tomorrow, I will make an announcement confirming the solution and a plan on how we will implement it. Thank you, stay safe and God Bless the Federal States of America!"

The Colonel shuts off the video and stands with his hands behind his back, feet slightly apart, gazing at Kate. His expression is placid and betrays no emotion, a trained reaction from years of leading men into dangerous situations. I stay where I am, almost afraid to breathe. I hope Kate will not ask me to leave. I want to hear everything.

She eyes me for a second or two and then turns to the Colonel. I know she trusts me, as I always hoped she did.

"Your assessment?" She asks.

After a moment, he replies, "We have located Liam Anders. He is there, with the president," the Colonel says, his voice calm and unmoving.

The shock on Kate's face is violent. She takes a step back and sits on the edge of her desk. This is confirmation, without a shadow of a doubt, that Liam is working with the Federation. The question is, for how long?

"Liam left this for you in his habitation," the Colonel continues to say. He hands her a small nano-drive, which Kate takes with a hesitant hand.

"You've seen it?" she asks.

"Standard procedure, Kate."

She nods and expects him to leave, but the Colonel stays where he is.

"Something else, Cameron?" Kate asks, her voice now uneven, something hot and menacing simmering underneath.

"Watchers at Sentry Point Ten picked up a large group of thermals, weak and almost invisible, but there. They are some five kilometres away during the last sweep, hence the warning siren," the Colonel says in his unchanging voice, unfazed by Kate's obvious annoyance.

"What does that mean, group of thermals? Do we know what animals?"

"I've sent drones to the area. We'll know soon."

"This day keeps getting better and better," Kate says, her sarcasm dripping like hot lava on the floor. "Will you contact me as soon as you know?"

"Will do," he says. He offers Kate an unexpected smile, which softens his hard features. Then, he turns and walks out, his heavy boots pounding on the floor.

Kate returns to the sofa and I follow. She looks at me, a strange expression on her face.

"Many years ago," she begins, "your parents and I were given a drive, much like this one," she holds the nano-drive up in the air and then continue, "from Kondo, who worked for the Federation as a staff sergeant, training all the cadets for battle. He did that to get close to them and spy on their activities. I went along with the idea and got him recruited." Kate's eyes are faraway, reliving the memory.

"He was killed. They said it was heart failure. We knew it was more, but without proof, there was nothing we could do. Kondo must have known that his cover as FSA Peacekeeper was compromised because he hid the drive in the hilt of a dagger he knew would pass to your father upon his death. It might have been a year too late when your father found the drive, but it was the first concrete, irrefutable evidence that the Federation was testing biological agents to kill animals." Kate looks at me. "The drive was nearly stolen the same year of your parents' accident by a Federation spy working with me as a biologist, Anthony Kilmer. I told him about the drive. If I had not, they would not have known that we had it."

"Had?" I ask.

"The drive was lost when your parents died. At least, I couldn't find it. I, I'm sorry, Marra. Your parents' death … was my fault. I should not have told Anthony about the drive. I think that the Federation went after your parents to get it when they didn't find it in their habitation." Kate is gazing at me. I see deep sorrow, pain and regret. I begin to understand her overt protectiveness of me; she is making amends for something that she thinks she caused years ago. I am her atonement.

"Kate," I say. "It's not your fault." And I let the words do their work. Her eyes start to water and she looks away quickly. I get up and go to her and this time, I'm the one who hugs her. I feel Kate's shoulders relax and we stay that way for a few seconds.

Drawing away, we smile at each other, words unnecessary. Kate looks better; years of guilt appear to have been lifted from her shoulders.

"I want you to return to the habitation, Marra," she says. "It's safe there."

"But I want to know what's on the nano-drive, Kate."

Kate ponders for a few seconds and then sighs. "Alright, but only because I trust you to keep this to yourself for now."

Kate goes to her desk and plugs the nano-drive into the system. A video emerges. Doctor Liam Anders is smiling into the camera. His handsome face fills the screen.

"Hello Kate," he says in his deep, velvet voice. "First of all, let me apologise for leaving so abruptly. There is nothing more I can do at the CAEP and the Federation needs me now. I think that I owe you an explanation for this cloak-and-dagger act. Allow me to start from the beginning. I was born, not in northern COE, as my biodata suggests. I had that ... amended. I was born in Old India. My adopted parents, God rest their souls, renamed me Liam Anders, but my birth name was Aarav, Aarav Kapoor. I was the only survivor in the town of Ajjipura from the first wave animal attacks in India ..."

CHAPTER 19

"In nature there are neither rewards or punishments —
there are consequences."
– Robert Green Ingersoll

Liam's voice fills the air in Kate's room. He tells us about how his whole village was killed by the Gajas, the hybrid of ancient elephants, and how he lived in a WPO Displacement Camp, north of Old India, alone with no one to take care of him for a year. He befriended a couple, who were camp administrators in charge of the displaced population of Old India. He became their helper, running errands all over the camp, to such an extent that when their term was up and they were returning to Northern COE, they adopted him and took him with them. There, Liam grew up and studied animal biology and genetics. He worked hard to become top of his field and to achieve the reputation he has.

All through his life, however, he tells us how the rage never left him, how everything he had planned and done since the day he landed at the camp was towards his ultimate goal of killing all animals in the world. They had robbed him of a home, a family and he wanted to do the same to them. He had waited for this day since he was found, trembling, hiding in a broken schoolroom in Old India.

Liam speaks in even tones, fury flowing deep like a tremor under his calm façade. This is not the man I met and spoke to a few weeks ago. I am mesmerised by his transformation and terrified by his true nature, by the cruel streak I hear lying just beneath his words, peeking through his eyes. He smiles throughout the video as if everything he is saying is normal, as if he is telling us a bedtime story.

"Tomorrow, the world will find out the culmination of my work. President Monroe will make the announcement and this world we live in will change. We will turn the tide of events and move them to humanity's advantage. We will win this war once and for all!" Liam's smile is magnificent, his teeth gleaming white and perfect. He looks almost like a preacher announcing the coming of the next saviour. "There will no more need of any surveillance, no more need of carphite walls nor any other protection. Humanity will be free, finally!" Then, like a flipped switch, his smile disappears and his tone changes. "Goodbye, Kate. Under other circumstances, we could be very good friends. You are a remarkable woman and I will not forget your help these two and a half years." The video ends in a snowstorm of static, leaving both Kate and I breathless with shock.

"What does he mean the world will change tomorrow with the announcement?" I ask. Kate is chewing on her lower lip, something I have never seen her do before.

"I don't know, Marra. But Liam is a talented geneticist specialising in genomics. He also has a degree in virology. So, I am guessing it will have something to do with viruses ..." Kate eyebrows shoot up all of a sudden. "Oh my god, I think that they have manufactured a biological agent to kill the animals, like what they tested on the Primes all those years ago. They must have perfected it in some way."

"Is that why he stole the blood samples? He thought that my blood is hybrid Lioger blood ..."

Kate looks at me with wide eyes.

"That's why he needed the Lioger blood! Liogers are immune to most of the bacteria and viruses that kills other animals. And your blood is even stronger than that! He needed the blood to perfect their formula. Oh my God! What have I done!?"

"Kate!" I raise my voice to stop her from descending into self-blame. "You didn't know and I was the one who suggested we give it to Liam to examine. No one could know."

Kate looks defeated. She had trusted Liam, I have no doubt; bore affection for him. I don't know how betrayal feels like, but it must be like the stabs of a thousand knives.

"The first patient …" Kate says slowly. "He was Liam's right-hand man. I wonder …" Kate gets on the communicator and a masked doctor appears on the holo-screen. "Susan, did you autopsy Dietmar's body? Were there any suspicious injection marks on him?" The doctor shakes her head.

"Kate, we had so many urgent cases that I ordered every deceased to be cremated immediately upon death. Why? Was that important?" I hear an exasperated groan coming from Kate.

"It was, but never mind. Thank you, Susan," she says and without waiting, switches the communicator off.

I look at Kate.

"Liam worked very closely with Dietmar. I can't know for sure, but the only way the virus could have arrived at Seven is if it was implanted here. I think somehow, Liam injected it into Dietmar and then made a hasty escape. This is why we couldn't find any traces of it entering our compound!" Kate says. Suddenly, she grabs her pad off the table and sends it flying across the room. It cracks, tiny fragments of it shooting everywhere like projectiles, and lands with a loud bang on the floor.

A frozen second or two later, "Francois!" Kate shouts. The man's white-blond head peers in cautiously from the doorway, a knowing look on his face. His hair is brushed standing straight up on his head, giving him the look of someone who has just received a jolt of electrical shock. He looks at the debris by the wall and nods as if it is nothing he has not seen before.

"I'll get you another, updated with all your documents," he says as casual as announcing the time, and then his head retreats and the door slides closed.

I wonder how many pads Kate has hurled against the wall.

The little outburst appears to have made her feel better. Her breathing is even. This is a side of Kate I have never before seen and it is impressive; frightening. I have seen her angry, but not like this. I remain silent, letting her stew in her thoughts.

I have never met anyone like Liam; a person capable of deceit and treachery; a person who pretended for two and a half years to be someone else. My universe is simpler, more direct. This is perhaps the reason why I am more comfortable away from people.

In the wilderness, animals avoid us. They don't pretend to like us so that they can devour our bodies. The boundaries are clear. We don't bother them and they don't kill us. I realise that we have misread the Primes all these years. Their aggression on the human population of the FSA is due to what the Federation did to them. Had they been left alone on their mountain to live in peace, I doubt they would attack just for the fun of it. The Federation has inadvertently created the monsters that they now seek to destroy.

Lioger genes run in my blood. Does that make me animal or human or both? Suddenly, a memory erupts abruptly in my mind. I have not thought it important at the time, but maybe … and I am struck by the desperate urge to leave.

"I'm going back to the habitation, Kate. There is nothing I can do here. I want to check on something," I say.

Kate nods while shouting for her assistant. He walks in, unhurried, the same tired and knowing look on his face.

"Get me Holt, Cho, Patel and Reyes. Emergency meeting NOW!" I hear her voice, loud and commanding as I leave her office.

I move as best as I can in the snow, which comes up to halfway up my shins. With all the events happening in Seven, the snow ploughs have not been deployed in areas deemed less important. It is then that I remember my promise to Yon. I will call his base when I get to the habitation. It will be useful to have Yon out of the hospital.

As I wade through the snow, I go over the memory came up when I was in Kate's office. It was sudden, like a lightning strike and now I cannot get rid of the thought. I see my father's face the last night I saw my parents. His words echo in my mind: "Promise me to keep all your animals safe. You are the guardian of their souls, especially Leon, because he is very important. He will keep you safe. He is the keeper of all your secrets." My father's words made me laugh at seventeen — they sounded melodramatic and out of place. I remember the hurt that had flashed for a split second across his face and my laughter ceased immediately. I didn't understand why he was being so serious then, for such an 'inconsequential' thing. My heart is racing now, both from excitement and from the gruelling task of wading through snow. I am sure now that his words were hints, like clues to a buried treasure.

The habitation is warm when I enter. I leave my boots in a pool of melting snow by the entrance, like an untidy child. I run towards my room in my socks, a trail of melted ice marking my path, dripping from my jacket. I see Leon in his frozen prowl on the bedside table. I grab him and examine him closely, turning him side to side, up and down. Then, I see it, the scar on his right haunch that I earlier found strange. It is more than just a scar, it looks like a small square piece has been removed and then patched back. I look around the room for something to use to pry open the square without damaging Leon permanently. Finding nothing, I take Leon to the kitchen and search for a small knife.

Finding one, I very carefully push its tip into a small section of the square and gently tilt the tip upwards, wriggling it carefully. I see the square piece coming loose and suddenly, it comes flying off and lands somewhere on the floor. I look all around my feet but cannot see it. I will have to look for it later, because what is important is embedded in Leon's haunch. A nano-drive.

My fingers tremble slightly from the rush of adrenaline. I must get this to Kate. As I make my way back to the door, I remember my promise to Yon. I stop and call the Defence Unit base on the holo-screen for a Corporal Asherman and ask him to bring Yon's clothes to the hospital. That completed, I make my way back to Kate's office.

"… no need to alarm the population, Cameron," I catch Kate's last words as I enter her office. The Colonel is there with four other persons in laboratory coats. They are all sitting around Kate's large desk. The Colonel must be bringing news of what the drones have found. I wonder what she means by not alarming the population. Everyone looks at me as I enter. I have clearly intruded on their discussion. But I see Kate nod, acknowledging me, which I take as a sign that she is allowing me to remain. I quietly move to the window area to allow them time to conclude their conversation.

"I will keep monitoring the situation, Kate. As soon as there is any danger, I will sound the siren again," the Colonel says and then, he strides out of the office, still ignoring my presence. I wonder if he is the same with women cadets in the Defence Unit.

"Keep working on the virus vaccine and update me the moment you find something," Kate tells the other four persons there. They leave in a single file out of her office, each looking more tired than the next. This is a grim time to be a virologist.

I walk to Kate, but before I hand her the nano-drive, I ask, intrigued, "did the drones find something?"

She nods. "They located the animals, but they scattered as soon as the drones drew close. The animals are at the base of the perimeter wall now. Mostly at the Eastern side. As the storm has stopped and we're able to see the prints quite clearly on the snow."

My heart skips a beat. "Prints?"

Kate looks long and hard at me. "Liogers. They are Liogers, and many of them. A large pride, judging from the multiple, giant paw prints," she says. I can hear her fatigue. This is one more problem to add to her long list of emergencies to handle. "It appears that they are grouped outside of Seven. The thermals are weak. I think these are the hybrid Liogers we were looking for. They've come to us instead. They are staying hidden so far and as long as they do nothing more than group, I am lowering the danger level for now. I don't see the point of letting the population know. We have more urgent things to take care of." I hear her heave a huge sigh, as if it helps with the stress on her shoulders. She leans back and massages her forehead; the ache is still bothering her.

Slowly, I extend my arm out to her and show her the nano-drive in my palm. Kate's eyes widen. "Is that ...?" she starts to say and stops. She takes the drive from me, handling it like it could potentially explode in her fingers. "Where ...?"

"Dad hid it in Leon, I mean the Lioger carving he made for me years ago. I just suddenly remember what he said to me that night before … you know, before their accident the next day," I say.

"Oh my God! All this time!" Kate slumps down on the sofa. She looks devastated.

"I didn't think to look into your things. Of course he would have hidden it with you!" Kate stares at the nano-drive in her hand like it is a magical object. Grief is written on her face is large, bold letters, and I can understand. To find a lost object that could have made a friend's sacrifice worthy, eight years too late must be painful.

"Are we going to watch it?" I ask her in a timid voice. She may have seen it, but I have not.

My words snap Kate out of her thoughts and she looks up at me, her eyes shimmering.

"Yes," her commanding voice returns.

The images that I see are horrible. I close my eyes when the video shows the dying animals, my heart unable to bear the pain. When I open them again, I realise that they are wet with tears. How anyone can do something so terrible to animals that only want to live in peace on a planet that is as much theirs as it is ours, I cannot fathom. The cruelty of the act is beyond anything I have ever witnessed. I had not realised the depth of the Federation government's hatred of the animals.

I realise that some people assume the importance of physical pain is limited only to humans, that animal agony is not as relevant. They will save a person from pain, but will not think twice about inflicting it upon an animal. They believe that we alone possess souls and consciousness to understand friendship and loss. But I have seen scrub jays gather around the body of their deceased friend as if honouring their fallen comrade in a forest funeral. I have also seen footage gathered by our animal behaviourist in Old India of a giant female Gaja mourning the loss of her calf by guarding it for a few days, touching it gently with her trunk, her grief obvious. Breathing the same air and created on the same planet, there is a link between animals and humans that is undeniable. It is arrogant to separate the two, giving the right of survival to one and not to the other.

The video ends and I breathe a silent sigh of relief, though my heart is aching. I look down to hide the tears that have gathered in my eyes. A second of silence goes by, then, suddenly, I hear my father's deep voice fill the room. My heart stops for a microsecond and I look up in confusion.

Kate's mouth is slightly agape. We stare at the screen in unison, wordless, watching my parents' smiles fill it. Kate moves back and sits at the edge of her desk for support. She is seeing ghosts.

"*Schatzi*, if you are watching this then, well … " my father sighs and smiles. That was what he used to call me, his 'little treasure.' He looks the same as the last day I saw him. I feel my heart tightening. "Then, your mother and I are no longer with you. And I am very sorry for that, my sweet girl." A lump rises to my throat and I am having trouble stopping the tears that now roll freely down my cheeks.

"Know that you are the light of our lives and we love you very much," my mother says, her light blue eyes shining. She turns and looks at my father. That simple act is so familiar, it brings an ache to my chest.

"We owe you an explanation of everything that we have been doing," she continues. "I know you are angry sometimes that I push you so hard and that we don't discuss our work with you. You asked me once, when you were eight (remember?), why you have such strange eyes? You told me you hated and wanted to change them."

My father chuckles slightly at the recollection.

"Remember what I told you?" she continues.

I remember. She told me that they were special, magical eyes that were given only to extraordinary little girls who possessed super powers.

"Well," my mother continues from where he left off, "you are extraordinary and you have special powers. You possess very special blood that makes you virtually immune to almost every disease and virus. I have been testing your blood for years. Remember how you hated that I had to draw a vial of blood every month? I am sorry I had to do that, my darling, but see, I was testing you to monitor your condition." Then, the light in my mother's eyes dimmed.

"Your eyes, they are the result of your special genetic makeup. It is time you know how you became ... you." She quietens and turns to my father, her expression unreadable.

My father clears his throat and begins, "Before you were born, when we were still living in Sector Two, your mother fell ill. We were in the fields and your mother, well you know how she is," he looks at her and chuckles, his eyes full of affection as they always were, while she rolls her eyes at him, her lips curled in a smile.

"We were in the fields," my mother takes over, "and silly me, I cut my hand on a jagged rock while tripping on a root and falling. You would have liked that fall, Marr darling," she giggled. "Imagine it in slow motion! Like ... splat!" She throws her arms out in a wave and feigns falling. Then laughs, a sound I have missed so much, a sound that personifies my mother.

"Except that it wasn't that funny," my father frowns. "She cut her hand very badly and Kondo and I rushed her home," he turns to smile briefly at her. "She was a terrible patient! She cleaned and dressed the wound and then went on her day like nothing happened!" He winks and my heart melts.

"A day later, I fell very ill," she continues. "An unusual bacterium in the rock entered my bloodstream and caused a high fever. My body was in agony. We had no known cure for it. I tried everything. Nothing worked," my mother says.

"She was dying and I was desperate. Then, I remember the Lioger blood we collected and frozen for research. We had been studying the blood to find out all about its genetic sequence and properties. I remember we discovered that it contained antibodies resistant to a wide range of bacteria and viruses. I extracted the specific protein responsible for this immunity factor and introduced it into your mother. You see, Lioger blood is quite similar to our blood and so compatibility issues are almost non-existent. And besides, we had already tested that before … " he stops, suddenly, hesitant to continue.

Kate already told me all about how you and mom saved the Liogers, dad! I want to tell him but can't. I deduce that my mother's illness must have been after that incident.

"By then, I was unconscious and near death. Your father saved me," she says, smiling with pride. My father drapes an arm around her and kisses her on her forehead.

"During all this time, we," my father says in measured tones, "we did not know that your mother was three weeks pregnant." My mother's eyes drop, a look of regret on her face. I have seen this before. I recall how my mother would sometimes look suddenly sad. I used to think it was me, that I disappointed her. I am realising now that it had nothing to do with me.

"My health improved rapidly but the Lioger genes became fused with my blood … which became your blood," my mother says. "The difference was that my immunity was temporary, but yours was organic. It became who you are. You are the first human with Lioger genes. Do you remember ever being ill? If you cannot, it's because you were … are never sick. Cuts would heal rapidly, bones would set in no time. The blood made you stronger." My mother's light blue eyes shimmer with regret. "I felt guilty for such a long time, my darling. I thought I had harmed you, made you into a hybrid. I tried reversing the condition, ran test after test to remove the Lioger elements. But with each test, the blood became stronger, as if attacking it made it bond even more unto itself. And when your eyes progressively turned into the colour you have now, my guilt grew." My mother looks down. My mother might have been a strong woman, but I know that she was highly sensitive and easily moved to tears. She used to cry not only when sad, but especially when happy.

"But we realised that we were worried for nothing," my father continues, a confident smile on his lips. "You are perfect. There is nothing wrong with you, *Schatzi*. On the contrary, not only is your immunity strong, the animals bonded with you naturally. Do you remember playing with Liogers, Schatzi? Imagine our shock when Liogers started appearing at the perimeter of our home a few weeks into your birth!"

"Your father and Kondo almost had heart attacks!" my mother's peals of laughter echo through the room. If I close my eyes, I can almost imagine her standing next to me. When the laughter subsides, she continues, "I, on the other hand, was fascinated! I have never before seen this kind of bonding in my life! Somehow, they sensed that you are one of them and chose to stay close, maybe as a protection," her eyes are wide and animated like a child discovering a new toy, the blue of her irises playing with the light.

"And we would have Lioger cubs playing around the perimeter of our home. It was magical! They never came close to the habitation but remained just outside the perimeter boundary. They would arrive in the morning and disappear in the afternoon," my mother continues. Her eyes crinkled and turn to slits, a look I remember so well. "When you grew bigger and started to walk, the Liogers would let you sit on them and even pull their fur. We would watch you from about five metres away because the Liogers were nervous around anyone but you."

"You didn't even realise that it was not normal to be playing with them. You grew up that way, Schatzi, with Lioger cubs as friends until you were five years old," my father's handsome face beamed with pride.

Their words are like keys to the vault inside my mind. With each detail, the doors are unlocking one by one. I have always thought that my dreams about playing with Liogers were just nightly wishes. I am getting confirmation that they are memories. My suspicion that the Liogers are protecting me is no longer conjecture. I wonder if they have been tracking me all these years. For the first time in my entire life, I feel settled, calm, the jigsaw pieces of my existence falling perfectly into place.

"We were so sorry we had to leave the habitation behind. You were inconsolable for months," my mother says. She pauses for a second. "I sometimes wonder if the Liogers also miss you as you did them." My parents look at each other, their eyes doing most of the communication.

"So there, my sweet girl. You now know all. I wish I was there to see you grow into the beautiful woman I know you will be. Maybe even to chase away some boyfriends, eh?" My father chuckles, but there is no mirth in his laughter.

"Know that we both love you very much, my darling," my mother continues. My father sniffles and looks down; this is how he hides his tears. "We will always be with you, even if we are not there," my mother finally bursts out crying. They look into the video for a second before my father's hand reaches out to stop it. The last image I see is my mother sobbing into my father's shoulder and him shutting off the video, eyes shimmering with tears.

The silence that follows is so loud, I can hear it. I go to the window and stare out at the dark afternoon sky. The wind has stopped but a slight snow is drifting down, taking a lazy zig-zag trajectory to earth. It looks like cotton blowing in the wind. Kate is still sitting on the edge of her desk, staring at a point in the far wall. What do you say after a revelation like that?

"So now we know how you got your unusual … biology. I can't believe they never told me," I hear Kate say behind me, a tinge of sadness colouring her voice. My heart is aching all over, similar to my body after it has gone through intensive exercise. Despite this, my mind is clear and calm. I have the sensation of sitting on top of a mountain looking out over the valley, over the wide expanse of land that Mother Nature created. I've found a family, unconventional though it is; a family that shares my blood.

"Kate, why did my parents leave our home in Sector Two? Mom said that I was inconsolable for months."

Kate sighs and comes to my side. She drapes an arm around my shoulder, both of us watching snow fall. Seven has activated the floodlights on the whole town, given the recent emergencies and they bathe the area in a glaring white-yellow light. The snow ploughs are back at work and this time, they seem to be clearing the snow everywhere, possibly preparing for evacuation.

"Come sit with me," There is a resigned tone to her voice. I look at her and in the glaring light coming from outside, I can see the lines of stress clearly on her face.

"From what your parents reported …" Kate says, "One morning, without warning, the Liogers appeared but not at the perimeter, at the door. Your father checked the satellite feed and perceived a group of thermals approaching the habitation at great speed. Since the Liogers were already there, he guessed that they would be Primes, and he activated the emergency evacuation protocol. Luckily for them, the beasts were still very far away and the Defence Unit hovercraft is faster than they are. The Liogers left as quickly as they appeared. Your mother thought they went to slow the Primes down. You and your parents had just enough time to run into the hovercraft as the Primes arrived. Your mother said that the group was not large but they were angry giants."

"Why did the Primes attack after so many years?"

"I asked the same question. Before they had you, your parents were already living there for seven long years," Kate pauses, idly scraping a phantom mark off the sofa seat. "We didn't know until we saw the video Kondo sneaked out of the Federation years ago. The massacre of the Primes must have prompted the attack. In fact, we checked records and realised that it was the first Prime attack in years."

"Were there other Prime attacks after that?" I ask.

"Yes, we had to pull our agents out of Sector Three as well, a month later I remember," Kate says.

There is a strange sensation in my body, like a low vibrational hum. It is actually quite pleasant; a sensation of unity, of knowing that something is close by. Then, as if answering to the call, a Lioger roar cuts through the darkness, and then one more and then another, over and over, again and again.

CHAPTER 20

"Whatever you do to the animals, you do to yourself."
– Ben Mikaelsen, Touching Spirit Bear

The emergency siren is so loud that it drowns out all other sounds, even the roars. The vibration in my body increases in intensity, and I feel like I am sitting in a hovercraft, the hum of the engine going through my bones. While pandemonium erupts outside, I feel calm. I don't know how, but I am certain that the Liogers do not want to harm us. If anything, they are there for protection.

"Kate!" I shout through the din. She does not hear me. I walk over to her and tap her shoulder. Kate turns to me, annoyance on her face. Normally, this would stop me talking, but now is not the time to lose courage.

"Kate!" I begin again. She holds up a finger to tell me to wait.

"Shut of that damn siren!" She screams at the Colonel on the holo-screen. A few seconds later, the siren shuts off. The sudden silence is shocking, like a world suddenly gone deaf. Even the Liogers stop roaring.

Kate turns to me, her face dark and menacing

"My blood, Kate," I say as calmly as I can.

"What do you mean?" she says.

"The anti-virus, it's in my blood," I say.

"This would mean exposing you, Marra," Kate says. I realise then that she has thought about this but has chosen not to use my blood because she still wants to keep me safe.

"I can't always remain a secret, Kate," I say. *Secrets tend to find their way towards the light like jungle vines,* my father's words remind me.

She looks at me quietly for a second or two. "Let's go to the labs," she finally says.

I visited my mother's workplace many years ago as a child. It was a quiet area with quiet people who talk in soft whispers, like a sterile church that smells of disinfectant.

The place I walk into with Kate is not the same. Laboratory coats are flying everywhere as scientists run from one room to the next. Kate walks with me in quick, long strides towards the end of the left hallway. She is taller than I am and for every two steps she makes, I have to make three. I am almost trotting next to her just to keep up. People are getting out of our way as soon as they see Kate's face, her scowl like a threat to violence.

As we enter, a young, dark-haired woman in a laboratory coat looks up, sees Kate, and walks in quick steps to us. Her hair is pinned up into a bun but loose strands have escaped and are falling down her face, which has a look of despair.

"Director!" she says in a voice that matches her age. She smooths back her hair and removes her medical mask, seeing that neither Kate nor I have them on.

"Linda, this is Marra. She's come to donate some blood," Kate says and seeing the confused look on the young woman's face, she signals to her to follow us into an office.

Once inside, she waits until the door slides closed. "Linda, Marra's blood is ... special. It may contain the anti-viral properties we need to counter the virus."

Linda opens her mouth to ask more but Kate holds up her hand and her mouth closes on cue.

"We don't have time to talk about this in detail, Linda. When this is all over, I will give you an explanation. For now, just take her blood and work with it, alright?" Kate says.

The young woman nods emphatically, "Come with me," she

tells me. If she is upset by Kate's brusque behaviour, she does not show it. She is young to be at the head of such an important job. I assume she must be the lead virologist.

She takes not one, but five vials. Years of donating my blood for my mother's research makes me immune to the fear of needles. I am always fascinated at how eagerly the vials fill with the dark, red liquid. When she is done, we head back to Kate, waiting at the door. "How long would you take to work out a vaccine?" she asks.

"I need possibly twenty-four hours for a first sample," Linda says.

"That's impressive!" Kate raises her eyebrows in appreciation.

Linda laughs lightly. "Yes, the advances in research equipment has improved timing tremendously. The process used to take much longer."

"That's excellent. We need that vaccine urgently. Let me know how you get on. Call me in an hour to check in," Kate says and finally produces a smile that Linda returns readily like a child eager to please.

We walk out in silence, but instead of heading back to her office, Kate directs me back to her habitation.

"I don't need you in the office now, Marra. You need food and rest. There is all you need in the kitchen. I still have work to do. I'll be back later," she says and gives me a quick hug, then, without waiting for an answer, she turns, leaving me at the crossroad and heads back to her office.

I stand there in the glaring light. Although it is early evening, it feels much later. It has been a very long day. Normally, stars can be seen abundantly but the floodlights have eclipsed them. The snow ploughs have done a good job and I can now walk easily without having to trudge through snow. The evening has returned to its quiet state. The vibration inside my body has also stopped.

Finally, I walk slowly back towards the habitation; the evening air is so sharp that I cover my nose and mouth with my scarf, but I welcome its sting and bite. I sit on an old bench, reluctant to return to the confines of walls. I wonder what the Liogers are doing. Where are they now? Then like a switch, a faint tingling within my body starts up again and I instinctively turn my head in the direction of my old home. It feels like that is where they are gathered, outside the east wall. I debate whether to go there. What can I do? I cannot climb over a fifty-metre wall and I am certain that I will be denied entry to the sentry point. I need Yon to help me get up there.

I decide to return to the habitation, my head heavy with questions. As I get closer to the habitation, I see someone pacing outside of the front door, jumping to keep warm.

"I don't want to go back to the base," Yon grins. I notice that like me, he has chosen not to put the medical mask on.

"When did you get out from the hospital?" He looks cold. He must have been waiting a while. How does he even know where to find me?

"An hour or so ago. Assman! He came as soon as you called. You must have impressed him," he says, every breath rising out of his mouth as condensation. It looks like he is talking while smoking. "Well? Can we get out of this cold?"

"Yes, yes, of course," I say. I don't think Kate will mind that I invite Yon into her home, at least I hope not. I am grateful for the warmth that greets us as we enter. I insist we leave our boots at the entrance and then take my jacket into my room, and throw it towards the bed. It misses and lands on the floor and I leave it there, eager to get back to Yon.

I return to the living area to find him walking around in his socked feet, peering at digitals of Kate. I realise, with a start, that he has shaved his beard off, but his hair is still unruly and a little too long, making him look boyish.

"Did you really escape or did they discharge you?" I ask.

"I was discharged," he laughs. "I told the doctor I was needed for duty when the siren went off. Thank God I have the clothes."

"Are you ok though? Your ribs?"

"No pain. I'm good." He pats his rib cage for effect, but gently, which makes me think that he may be lying.

"You must be hungry," I say, moving towards the kitchen. "I can make us dinner, and … "

"Nooo," Yon says, stepping ahead of me towards the kitchen. "I'm making dinner. You can sit and watch me. I've been eating hospital food and I want my next meal to be mouth-wateringly delicious." He opens Kate's fridge and rummages inside, removing vegetables.

"Are you implying that my food is not mouth-watering?" I smile, knowing full well that I am not a good cook. I climb up on a high stool by the kitchen counter, watching him busy himself with the meal preparation, offering no help.

Yon stops, cocks his head to one side and looks at me with one raised eyebrow.

I laugh and the sensation is freeing. It feels good to laugh out loud on a grim day like this, a relief, a needed reprieve.

"You do know that Kate may be home at any time?" I think it wise to warn him.

"Yeah. She was the one who told me to get here," he says.

"What? When did you speak to her?" I am surprised because she has not mentioned any of this to me.

"Well technically, it was Francois. Kate checked on me in the morning before you came. I told her I wanted out and she told me that she would speak to the doctor."

"And you didn't think to tell me that?" I am surprised that Kate would check on him. Then a thought dawns on me. "So you were lying to me about wanting to escape? Kate wants you to watch over me, doesn't she?" I am upset. I dislike people making decisions about my welfare without discussing it with me first. It somehow makes me feel I am being treated like a little girl.

Yon stops chopping, hearing the heat in my voice. "I'm sorry," he says, an apology on his face. "I did need the clothes and telling you that I am escaping just sounds like a cool thing to say to impress you," Seeing no change in my mood, he adds, "And yes, Kate wants me to stay close to you, not that you need help. Just so that I can help if you want it ... "

I am upset at Kate and Yon for conspiring, but I am also happy to have him here. My thoughts confuse me, making me even more upset.

"Can you get me up on the wall?" I ask after a few seconds. Maybe I can blackmail his emotions to my advantage.

Yon looks at me, eyes narrowed. "Why do you want to get up there?"

That is a good question. I don't really know why but it is more about seeing the Liogers and letting them see me. Can I say that? Does that sound sane?

"What did you and Kate talk about? I ask instead.

Yon concentrates on his chopping, trying to disguise his discomfort at the question.

"If she asked you to watch over me, then I have a right to know what she told you."

He places the knife down. "Just that with all the ... stuff going on, she wants me to make sure that you are safe."

"And why would I not be safe?"

"She told me that Doctor Liam Anders has disappeared since last night and was worried that he might try to hurt people close to her, which would be you."

I don't know if he is lying. He looks and sounds genuine, but so did Liam. Suddenly, I wonder if Kate has indeed sent him to the house. I look at the knife, it is close to his hand. My pulse quickens and slowly, I lower myself off the high chair and back away.

I am about to run out of the habitation when the door slides open.

"Oh good, someone is preparing food. I am starving," Kate says and throws her pad down on the sofa.

I stand there, embarrassed, under Yon's puzzled stare.

"What's happened?" Kate asks, sensing the awkward silence.

"Nothing," I say and head for my room, embarrassed. I have become paranoid. I actually thought Yon was an assassin. I roll my eyes at no one but myself.

I stay in my room until I hear a knock and Yon stands at the doorway.

"Hungry?" he asks like nothing happened.

Yon prepares a lavish meal. While I chew wordlessly, Kate and Yon debate the situation, I just listen with interest. Sometimes, standing outside of a conversation, we hear the most because we can see the full picture instead of just one side.

Watching Yon speak, I notice how his eyebrows knit together when he is thinking of something important. I cannot believe that for a few seconds, I actually thought he would hurt me. He throws me smiles and glances as he speaks and reminds me that my father used to do the same to keep me included in conversations, a kind and thoughtful gesture. Then, I remember that Liam did the same.

"And?" Kate asks.

I have no idea what the question is. I look at her blankly.

"Why do you think the Liogers are all grouped here?" Kate repeats. I look at both Yon and Kate slowly.

"They are here for me," I say, and watch as they both look at each other.

"Why would they do that?" Yon asks, his eyebrows knitted together.

Secrets tend to find their way towards the light like jungle vines, I hear my father say to me.

"To protect me, like they did the last two times," I say.

Yon's look tells me that Kate has not told him about my genetic makeup. I don't care anymore. Sooner or later, all this will be revealed, especially if they actually find a vaccine from my blood.

"I have Lioger genes in my blood, Yon," I say, the words sounding strange said out loud.

"Marra," Kate begins.

I shake my head. "This will, sooner or later, become news, Kate."

"How ..." Yon starts to ask and seeing Kate shake her head, he stops.

"I'll tell you about it one day," I say to him. We all sit in silence for a moment.

"Wait," Yon suddenly says. "If the solution the President is referring to is really a biological gas to kill the animals, and Liam stole the Lioger blood to perfect it, then wouldn't that also affect you, Marra?"

Kate's eyes widen, "Oh my God! You're right!" She thinks for a second. "Even if the agent is harmless for humans, it might kill you! With the winds at this time of year, the gas will affect every Sector and God knows how long it will stay in the atmosphere." Kate stops eating, the cogs of her mind turning at full speed. "Maybe Mr Sanderson is already aware of what exactly the solution is. I have to speak to him." Kate gets up and grabs her jacket.

"Where are you going? It's freezing out!" I ask. I can hear the winds howling again outside.

"I'm going back to the office. If it gets too cold, I'll stay there and see you in the morning," Kate says. As she is about to leave, she turns and gives Yon a frightening stare. "You sleep on the sofa!"

"Yes, ma'am," Yon replies, trying not to smile.

I clear up the dishes and wash them, while Yon makes himself comfortable on the sofa. I enjoy the warm water on my hands and the mechanical act of washing dishes allows me time to think.

The solution to be announced tomorrow by the President appears to imply the elimination of all animals in the world. I don't think that they have thought things through. A world where only humans exist is not going to work. We need the animals, every species, to live. Will the 'solution' also wipe out the already dying number of bees? How will crops survive after that?

The question of dying doesn't frighten me. I am more concerned at the thought of a world without animals. I hear music coming from the living area and Yon's terrible singing. If I have a regret, it would be not to have known love like my parents had.

I wonder what Linda has found. I wish I could be a fly on the wall of her office. How would she react seeing my blood under the microscope? Do they all know by now at the labs that Marra Stollen is a hybrid human? What will they do with me? Is my blood useful? Have they found something?

"If I knew you like washing dishes so much, I would have let you do all of them back at Sec Five!" Yon's baritone voice says behind me. I smile to myself. He is leaning on the counter, his cheeks in his hands.

"Well, finish up and come over and watch a video log with me," he says after realising that I have no response to his first sentence.

I practise bravery and sit next to Yon, still keeping a respectable distance. He has chosen some kind of strange, ancient film about talking and warring apes, which I have not seen. I wish I could live in the time where they still made films and read books and wrote on paper. In this century, we are just concerned about survival. There is no time for making beautiful movies or writing.

"Back before Kate arrived, did you think I was going to hurt you?" Yon says, his voice uncharacteristically sober; a hint of something in his tone.

I look at him surprised and also embarrassed that he brings this up. "I," what do I say? "I wasn't sure," I finally tell him.

Yon sits up and turns to face me. "Marra, I would never hurt you, ever," he looks a little hurt.

"I'm sorry," I say, "and embarrassed. So much is going on that I thought for a second … I mean, look at Liam. Who would've thought?"

Yon settles back on the sofa. "I agree, even if I have never met the guy. But I hear he worked here three years. Talk about the long game!"

I frown, "The long game?"

"A plan that took a long time to achieve."

"That's how no one suspected, I guess. It's smart. He was probably using the CAEP's biological data on all the animals to build his …" I search for the words, "his 'solution' for humanity."

"So … you're part Lioger?" Yon says, but I can see that he spots an opportunity to tease me.

I tell him about how, as my mother put it, I became me. Yon listens without interrupting, which is impressive. I have always thought that he had trouble listening. When I finish, he continues to say nothing, making me squirm in my seat with uneasiness.

"I've always thought you have amazing eyes. I didn't think they were Lioger ones. But I did think they were crazy beautiful."

I feel warmth rise from my chest and up my neck, colouring my face, and I look around for a reason to escape.

Yon laughs all of a sudden. I look at him, confused.

"You look terrified each time you blush. Marra, there is nothing to be afraid of. It's actually pretty."

"Pretty?" I snort. "You don't blush and so you don't know how terrible it is. It's like the weather forecast is written on my face."

"May I?" he says.

"May you what?"

He comes closer; I can feel his body heat emanating from his skin. My heart is off to the races. I am like a terrified child, not sure what I am supposed to do. Then he bends his head towards my face and kisses me lightly on my lips.

The contact sends a shudder through my body. My face is on fire. I hold my cheeks in my cold hands to cool them down. I can't look at Yon; I feel clumsy and inelegant.

"Hey," he says in a soft voice prompting me to peer at him. "I like you, gold eyes, blushes and all." His smile is not the one I normally see, the crazy, toothy grin with deep craters for dimples. Instead, it is a smile that is subtle and kind. I look up at him, less embarrassed, and this time, he doesn't ask me for permission.

His lips are gentle, and when we part, Yon smiles and takes me in his arms. I don't tell him that this is the first time I have been kissed; I think he knows.

I sit in the crook of Yon's arm, watching apes and men fighting, listening to the steady, hypnotic beat of his heart. This is strange and new to me, this close contact.

I find myself thinking if my parents will like him. I know that my mother would. They both share boldness and the courage to be themselves. My father would probably question him repeatedly to make sure that he was worthy. At least if I die from a biological agent released into the world, I would have died knowing how a kiss from a man feels like, and I'm ready for death now.

I don't know when and how, but when I open my eyes, I am in my bed and the timer on the table next to it reads six, zero, four. The sun will not make an appearance for another hour and

and a half. I am in the same clothes I wore at dinner. I must have fallen asleep and Yon brought me to my bed. I wonder if Kate has returned. I wonder how it will be with Yon today. What does a person do after a first kiss?

A tiny vibration is running up my spine and I sit up. The feeling is getting stronger and, in the distance, I hear roars. I walk to the window. The snow has stopped but not the wind. The combined sound of Lioger roars and howling wind is like a bizarre song, beckoning for me to find them.

I shower and then dress as warmly as I can. I will ask Yon to take me up the wall. I must see the Liogers for myself. The cubs I played with would have died of old age because Liogers normally live up to about eighteen years. But who knows? Maybe one of them is still alive. Otherwise, these must be their descendants. How else can I explain them continuing to look for me?

I walk past Kate's room. The door is open and the bed not slept in. She did not make it back last night. A flutter of unease passes through me. I hope she is alright.

Yon is sprawled out on the sofa in a T-shirt and shorts, his long limbs sticking out at the end. He is snoring a little. My face feels hot thinking about the kiss last night. I never knew a man's lips would be soft. I hesitate to wake him, he looks kilometres deep in sleep. But I cannot get up on the wall without his help. So, I nudge him, gently at first and then with more energy.

He moves a little and then, stretches out, holding both his arms up. His eyes are still closed and he opens one just enough to peek at me. His morning smile is enough to melt all the snow in Seven. My heart does somersaults like a baby Prime, just looking at him.

"Morning," he says. "I'd kiss you but maybe I'd spare you my morning breath." He slowly swivels and sits up on the sofa, producing at the same time, a large yawn. "But I can give you a hug. Come here," he opens his arms, waiting for me to slide into them.

Yon's body is always warm, but it is practically burning right now. I can hear his slow, steady heartbeat through his shirt.

Interesting that while mine often races in his presence, his appears to be calm. Do I not excite him as he does me?

"Why are you up so early?" he asks, his voice still hinting at sleep.

"I need you to take me up the wall, Yon. The Liogers are roaring again and I want to see them."

He cocks his head and listens. "Oh yeah! I hear them. But I don't know how I can get you up there, Marra," he says. "Even I don't have that kind of authorisation."

"Who does then? You must know someone. Assman?" The roars are sounding quite desperate to my ears.

"Let me take a shower. It will help me think," he kisses me on my forehead and then drags himself to the bathroom like a drugged man.

I prepare tea and sit waiting. The roars appear to have stopped but the wind has picked up. I pray that it will not snow. I want to be able to see the Liogers and a storm will not help. I wonder if Kate managed to speak to Mr Sanderson?

Yon appears in the same clothes he had on the day before, but he smells clean. He is awake now and strides over confidently. Before I have even time to react, he kisses me on my lips. This small gesture leaves me breathless and surprised. Is this what we are now? Two people who kiss each other in the morning? I flash him a brief smile and look down into my tea, sipping it with added concentration.

Yon appears oblivious to my anxiety.

"I may know a private who does wall duties," Yon says, chewing on a piece of bread. "But that means I need to return to the base and find him, and you can't come with me."

"And then you'll contact me? I can meet you at the eastern wall. That's where they are, the Liogers," I realise that I sound like an excited teenager. I hope Yon doesn't hear it too.

"Keep your wrist communicator on. I'll call you," he holds my hand. I marvel at how large his is next to mine. I have not held hands with anyone besides my parents and notice that the sensation is vastly different. Yon's hand is warm, like his body and the touch is electrifying. Every part of me is jumping to attention. It is an effort to keep myself level-headed.

"I'll get going," he says and takes me in his arms. He kisses me again before he disappears out the door, winking as he goes, leaving my heart feeling like it is having a bubble bath and singing a song. I can easily get used to the feeling of being special to someone. It is intoxicating.

I look around the habitation. I don't want to stay inside. I remember the tingle of unease when I think of Kate and decide to find her.

The sudden cold slams into my face like a slap. I wrap my scarf tighter around my nose and mouth. The air is freezing and I can feel it in my lungs like an unwanted guest. I run towards Kate's building, hoping that the activity will warm me.

Running up to her office, I am met with an open door. Her assistant has not yet arrived and the foyer is dark, light streaming in from Kate's office. She is speaking with someone. I don't know if I should enter, but I have come this far. I knock on the assistant's desk and see two heads turn.

The Colonel is there. He is in his uniform. Kate looks like she has not slept much. Her eyes speak of worry and fatigue. She looks at me but does not invite me in, and I sit on her assistant's desk and wait. The Colonel and her speak in quiet tones, preventing me from hearing anything. After a few minutes, he leaves, but this time, he nods at me; acknowledgement of my existence, and it feels like a small victory.

Kate is sitting on the sofa massaging the area between her eyes when I walk in. I take my seat across from her. She does not look well. She coughs and my intuition tells me that something is not right.

"Kate, I think you had better get yourself checked at the hospital," I say to her.

"I'm fine, Marra. Just a headache. And I have a lot to do," she coughs again. "Not every cough is an indication of sickness, Marra. I can 'hear' your mind thinking from where I am." She chuckles.

"How did it go with Mr Sanderson?" I ask. Kate is one person that I cannot influence in any way, and so I drop the subject.

"He is already in discussion with the WPO about this. The good news is that not all countries agree with President Monroe. Some will not roll out the solution that he is prescribing."

"And what is the solution?"

"It's as we feared. It's a lab-engineered biological agent in gaseous form that apparently is safe for all humans but not so much for the animals. The Federation guarantees it. They claim that if the animals are not eliminated, the virus outbreak will have no end. The Sandersons are fighting the order." Kate stops and takes a large breath in. I watch her with concern. "I'm fine!" she tells me before I ask.

"Will the announcement still be made?" I get up and fetch her some water.

Kate nods her thanks. "President Monroe is adamant on it for the FSA. He doesn't care if the rest of the world agrees or not." Then she takes a look gaze at me. "If we cannot stop him distributing the gas here, I will have you flown out of the FSA."

I think of all the animals he will kill. I think of the Liogers, whose blood I now share. "But what about the animals, Kate? Can we save them?"

Kate sighs. "IF the gas is released, I don't think we can save the animals, Marra. We lack time to organise an exodus."

"But Kate, this is wrong. They can't kill all the animals. I don't think the virus came from them."

"We can't prove that and the Federation knows it. They have been trying to find a reason to eliminate the animals for years." Kate squeezes her eyes shut. Her headache must be getting bad. She leans her head back on the sofa.

This time, I don't ask for permission. I call for the medical team on my wrist communicator to come and get Kate. I am surprised that I hear no protests and looking over, realise that Kate has fainted.

CHAPTER 21

*"The proper use of science is
not to conquer nature but to live in it."*
– Native American Proverb

Kate is still unconscious when we reach the hospital. They give me a mask and insist that I wear it. I don't tell them I am immune to the virus and don't need it. As she is the Director, all the senior doctors are there with her, and I am ushered out of the room.

From what I gather, Kate is in the beginning stages of the viral attack. I think of Yon and our dinner the night before. He will need to be tested too, and I send him an urgent message on my wristband communicator. The reality of this nightmare is sinking in; I cannot lose them both. I must find Linda. I leave the hospital and run to the laboratories, heading straight to her office. "Oh my God, I wanted to speak to you since yesterday!" Linda eyes glows as if I am the best thing she has seen all morning. She does not remove her mask this time, seeing that I have mine on. "Come!" she says and grabs my hand. I follow her to the office we were in with Kate the previous day.

"Your blood is amazing. I have never seen anything like it. It has properties we have never encountered before. Kate is right, you are the answer to counter the virus. But how? How did your blood become this …" Linda says all this in one quick breath, her eyes wide with wonder.

I look at her not knowing what to say, how to explain. I shake my head.

Linda takes it as a sign that I really have no idea. "Well, you are a medical miracle, Marra! I'd like to run further tests on you. Maybe we can determine how your blood evolved!" This is what I am afraid of, to be the object of medical studies. For a few seconds, my thoughts are frozen. Then, I remember Kate and the whole point of finding Linda.

"I don't have time for that now, Linda. Kate's been diagnosed with the virus. How close are you to a vaccine?" I ask her.

"Oh my God! Yes, of course! That's urgent. Uhm, we are close, but not quite there yet. We're isolating proteins and running tests. I'll try to speed things up." Linda's otherwise smooth forehead now lined with worry.

"Please hurry," I say. Then as I am leaving, I remember. "And get yourself tested too. You were in contact with Kate yesterday."

Linda makes three quick nods in succession.

I return to the hospital. There are more people than before, everyone in face masks. Some patients are lining the hallways, the rooms being full. It is chaos. I am not allowed anywhere near Kate. I cannot make anyone understand that I will be fine, that I am immune. I sit in the waiting area that has been sectioned off from the rest of the hospital. I am the only person sitting there. Most people avoid the hospital for fear of contracting the virus.

Doctor Odam walks past and I run after him. "Doctor! How is Kate?"

He turns and recognises me. I can see from his eyes that he is not smiling under his mask. He shakes his head. "She's not good. The virus is stronger now. She should have been wearing the mask! We are doing all we can to make sure that her condition doesn't worsen."

"Linda is working on an anti-virus with my blood," I tell him.

Doctor Odam's eyes widen a little. "I'll get in touch with her so that I know when it is ready. You should go back to the habitation. The hospital is not a safe place to be. Excuse me, Marra," and he walks away.

I'm at a loss of what to do. Kate is sick, Yon is away and I stand there not knowing what to do next. I look around at the chaos of nurses and doctors all around me. How many have died? And how many more?

I walk out of the hospital and into the freezing morning air. I am not sure if I want to go back to Kate's habitation. What would I do there? I've been thinking of the Liogers. Their survival is as much at stake as mine. I would like to meet them. I am wondering how this will be possible. If the Federation biological agent is really released, they will die. How do I save them?

If I find the Colonel, maybe I can somehow get him to give me authorisation to go up on the wall. I take off my mask, wrap my scarf tighter around the half of my face and begin my walk towards the base. There is still daylight, but it is fading and if I walk fast and maybe run, I can make it to the base before the light disappears.

My wristband is vibrating — an incoming message. I fish around in my pocket for the hearing piece, plug it to my ear and tap the wristband to answer the call. Most people have it continually on, but I dislike the sensation of something plugging my ear.

"Marra, are you alright? How's Kate?" Yon sounds concerned and from the breathlessness of his voice, he must be running.

"I don't know about Kate. They won't let me see her. They just said that they will take care of her and keep her condition stable," I tell him. "Have you got yourself tested?"

"No, not yet, but I'll get to it soon."

"I think you shouldn't wait to do that, Yon. The virus is getting stronger."

"I promise I'll do it this afternoon, after I meet you, ok?"

I frown and realise that he can't see me. "I'm on my way to you, Yon."

"What? I'm on my way back to town," Yon says, chuckling a little. "Let me come to you."

"Too cold to stop now," I continue walking.

"Then we'll meet somewhere in the middle, I guess, but I have a feeling I'll get to you sooner than you to me," Yon says and laughs.

"Did you get authorisation to take me up the East Wall?" I ask, unimpressed. The cold is not making me chatty or in a good humour.

"Not quite," he says.

I stop in my tracks. "What does that mean?" The freezing air starts seeping into my body and I have to move again.

"I'll let you know when I see you. Muah!" Yon says and the line cuts. He sounds like he is not running anymore and I am a little annoyed that he has cut me off.

I continue walking because if I don't, I will freeze. I have underestimated six kilometres. I feel like I have been walking without any end in sight. In the distance, I see a Humpt driving towards me. I slow down. The Humpt stops next to me and the window rolls down. Yon's familiar grin greets me.

"Need a lift, ma'am?" The deep craters of his dimples clearly are visible on his cheeks. The effect of his smile is contagious. He makes my heart flutter like butterflies.

The Humpt feels warm. Yon leans over and kisses me on the lips. I suppress a nervous giggle that rises up my throat. I am still not used to this new status I have. It feels strange, like I am in the skin of a different person. He caresses my frozen cheek, his hand warm, a look in his eyes, that I cannot define.

Yon turns the Humpt around. "Aren't we going towards the Eastern wall?" I ask, looking back the direction I thought we were going.

"Nope," Yon says. "I can't get into the Eastern sentry point, but I know someone at the main gate," he winks.

I have never been to the main gate before, have never seen it up close. Will the Liogers go there to meet me? As the Humpt speeds towards the north side of the compound, I watch feathery white flakes are float down. It is beautiful. For a moment, I forget about all that is happening around me.

The compound is not large and we arrive at the Defence Unit base in no time. I realise that Yon is popular. He manages to pass me through the check point leading to the main gate with a couple of winks and a display of manly humour. I resist a temptation to roll my eyes.

The main gate is even more impressive than the wall. It is the same height and the two gates that slide open from the middle are at least thirty metres wide combined.

"Impressive, isn't it?" Yon says. He reaches over and squeezes my hand.

I peer through the windscreen at the structure. I see sentry points at both ends of the gate.

Yon parks the Humpt on the side of the gate and we both walk up to the door of the sentry point. Yon communicates with someone on his wristband and a few seconds later, the door slides open and reveals a lift. Yon ushers me in. The space is small and the air is chilled. It starts to move upwards as soon as the door slides closed. I feel Yon's hand clasp mine and look up into his face. He smiles and winks.

When the lift door opens, a large, young man with dark hair, in winter uniform stands there, smiling as if he has a secret to tell. He has a face that tells me he enjoys good food and jokes, and his eyes are a surprising clear blue. He takes a look at me, nods and then gives Yon a quick hug, the two men patting each other noisily on the shoulder.

"Welcome to Sentry Point Zero, bro!" he says to Yon. Where we are appears to be a small resting room and it is warm and cosy. I spy a bed in a corner and a small table and two chairs in another. It smells of men in the room and I cannot wait to get out onto the view point outside.

"Thanks for doing this Biggs," Yon says. "This is Marra," he motions to me.

I smile and take the hand extended out to me. "Thank you for allowing me here," I say.

"Anything for Hunt! I owe him many favours," Biggs chuckles. "Right this way and hang on to the side tightly, you look tiny enough to be blown away!" I hear Yon laugh.

We leave the room and enter a tight corridor that appears to branch off unendingly to the left. A few paces from the door, Biggs presses a button and the full force of the wind hits us. I grab Yon without thinking and he steadies me. The air is so cold, my teeth start to chatter. I put my hands into my coat. Yon is right behind me and holds me close, so that I don't 'fly away.'

Despite the biting cold, the view is magnificent. I can see for kilometres. I look down and notice that the area around the wall is cleared of trees, forming a ring around the outer wall. This makes it easy to spot any animals directly below the wall. Right now, I don't see any. I close my eyes and think of the Liogers. A tiny tingle starts at the base of my spine and then a faint vibration begins all over my body. I hope they hear my 'call.'

I wish that I could stay longer at the parapet, but the wind is strong and bitterly cold. I turn back and head inside the corridor. The vibration in my body is steadily getting stronger and as Yon and Biggs enter, I hear a roar from a male Lioger and then more from others in his pride.

I turn and make my way out again, squeezing past the two men. Over the parapet, I see only snow. Then, suddenly slowly, an enormous Lioger appears, first tentatively and then with more confidence. It looks old, but walks with the gait of the leader of the pride. It sits and it looks straight up at me. Something in me stirs. I feel like I know him and he knows me. We stare at each other for a few seconds. A very strong vibration is going through my body, as if the Lioger is purring and I can feel it.

An arm goes around my shoulder and I look over. Yon and Biggs are both peering down now. Bigg's eyes are large as dinner plates, his mouth slightly agape.

"Woah! Look at 'im! He's huge!" Biggs say, excited as a little boy.

"I want to go down to them, Yon," I say.

"I don't think that's a good idea, Marra," Yon says, shaking his head.

I push past him to get to the corridor. I don't have time to argue.

"Wait, Marra," I hear Yon say. I stop and look at him. "We can't open the gates. Only the Colonel can authorise that."

My heart sinks. The Liogers are starting to roar again, calling out to me. I want to find a way to get outside. Without Kate, it seems hopeless. I stand there in the biting cold and think. I don't have a choice, I have to ask the Colonel.

"Let's go find the Colonel then," I say.

The Colonel is already on his way to the main gate when Yon and I descend back to the ground. Biggs remains at his post up on the wall. By the look on his face, the Colonel is not too happy to have a non-military person on the base. Yon's eyes widen at the sight of the Colonel, knowing that he is in trouble.

"Who let you in here?" the Colonel barks as soon as he sees me. He is in his winter uniform accompanied by two Defence Warriors.

I don't want to get Yon into trouble. "Kate said I could come and take a look at the Liogers," I lie.

"Well, she can't authorise that!" the Colonel frowns. I can tell he is a man who is used to his rules not being broken.

"I'm sorry. With her in the hospital, I thought I'd come here and take a look myself." More lies. I am getting comfortable with this.

The Colonel's face remains unchanged. "Well, you can't stay here," he says. He looks at Yon, "Escort her out."

"Wait!" I say. "The Liogers. I would like to see them," I say, and add, "please."

"What do you mean, you want to see them? Did you not already see them from up there?"

"I mean, from up close, sir," I say. I wish I know how to explain more clearly. What I am asking sounds illogical and insane. No one wants to meet Liogers. Normally, people would run the other way. "Colonel, please. I will explain everything later, but please let me go outside the gate to meet the Liogers."

The Colonel looks at me like I am a person escaped from an asylum. To give him credit, however, he does not have me thrown out immediately. On the contrary, I can see the wheels of his mind clicking and turning, trying to determine whether I am mad.

"That's not good enough. Give me a good reason. It's ludicrous to want to meet Liogers!" The Colonel stands there with his arms crossed over his body.

I stand there listening to the growling and roaring outside, the vibrating in my body strong and relentless. Without Kate, I don't see how I can leave the compound. Yon is standing there, saying nothing because as a Warrior, the Colonel is his superior, and he cannot disobey. I am at a loss of what to do.

A beeping sound goes off and all heads start to look around. The Colonel looks at his wristband and turns and starts to leave.

"Wait!" I shout.

"Can't. The President's announcement is coming on in fifteen minutes." He walks with large, strides with his two Warriors on each side. They enter a Humpt and drives off.

"Nothing we can do here, Marra," Yon says. "Come on. We can catch the announcement at the habitation." He holds me lightly on my arm.

I look towards the gate. I am so close and yet am not able to get any closer. I follow Yon into the Humpt, my heart weighed down by disappointment. I feel like I am letting them down by leaving.

I can feel Yon's eyes on me once or twice but I don't feel like talking. I concentrate instead on the snow outside. It is interesting that it is the only constant in a world that is now out of control. I long for the quiet, placid life I had before. Nothing will ever be the same again. My fall into this abyss of the unknown is still ongoing. I don't know where the bottom is. Yon's hand is warm around mine. He squeezes it lightly and I turn to meet his eyes.

"You ok?" he asks in a voice laced with genuine concern.

I nod; words feel like useless sounds and I don't actually know what to say. I think of Kate, fighting for her life, one that she has given to the CAEP. Is it worth it? I think of my parents' sacrifice too. Will I do the same? Can I really change the world?

"We should check on Kate," I say. I observe Yon's beautiful profile. My parents would be pleased that at the end of my existence, I am not totally alone.

"Yes, we'll do that from the habitation. We can call the hospital."

"You still need to get yourself tested, Yon," I suddenly remember.

"There are more important things right now. I promise I'll do it after the announcement," he says. I am not convinced he will, but am too tired to argue.

The habitation feels warm and I settle myself at the sofa while Yon prepares tea. I realise that almost everyone at Seven is probably doing what we are doing and the thought stuns me for a split second. The video screen is up and I can see a backdrop of navy blue, the flag colour of the FSA, with the large white stars symbolic of the three remaining human-populated sectors we have.

The President saunters in, a look of authority and calm on his face, looking like he has just had a good night's rest and a perfect breakfast. He smiles as he sits down for his address, looking around, I assume, at his cabinet members, who must be all in the same room.

Yon arrives with the tea and sits next to me, his arm around my shoulder. I turn and lean into his body, resting my head on his shoulder.

As if on cue, the President turns his gaze into the camera and smiles like he has won a universal lottery.

"My fellow Americans of the Federal States. I promised you yesterday that I have a solution to the animal threat facing our great nation and, the world. I have concluded my discussion with my colleagues, heads of states across the globe, and I am happy to announce that this solution has been accepted. This solution will not only eradicate the threat that has loomed over our planet for decades now, but it will bring greater unity and peace every-where. It is humanity's salvation. Without deploying this solution, our people will perish from the assault of viruses unleashed by the animals. While I cherish every living being on this planet, I think of my family. And when it comes down to it, I choose to save humanity and my wife and children, as would every person on Neo-Earth.

"What is this solution, you ask? In forty-eight hours, we will release canisters in all the forest areas of the FSA via drones. These canisters are on a timer and will release an odourless agent into the air, which will infiltrate every area the animals are living. This agent is totally harmless to humans. It has been engineered and subjected to rigorous testing by our scientists and virologists. Humans are safe from its effects. It will only eliminate the animals, and in a humane, painless way. They will simply sleep and not wake up.

"We will allow twenty-four hours for the agent to totally immerse into the wilderness and then, Peacekeepers will be deployed, together with our scientists to assess the success of our mission. We will clean up the forests areas, incinerate all carcasses to ensure that we are safe and declare the FSA an animal-free zone, habitable once more for humans.

"Our allies across the oceans will launch the canisters at the same time as the FSA. It will be a global effort. All countries united in the common cause. Our freedom is at hand! This day will go down in history as man's triumph over the animals and the day we take back what is rightfully ours — our land, our heritage and our future!

"God Bless the Federal States of America!"

The video ends with the flag of the FSA and the national anthem of the country playing. It was obviously recorded earlier and not a live feed. The President is in an undisclosed location, probably because he does not want to be anywhere near the biological agent when it launches.

Yon voice-commands the video off and we sit there, speechless. I assume that the WPO is on the side of the FSA. If that is the case, then there is not much anyone can do from here on.

"We have to get you to safety," Yon says. I look up at him and there is fire in his eyes. He is angry. "Even if I have to steal a hovercraft, we are flying you out of the FSA before the canisters are deployed." I have not seen him upset before and there is a certain charm to his fervent determination to save my life.

Contrary to him, I feel a deep disappointment, like I have finally opened a treasure chest only to find it empty. The thought of my possible demise does not scare me. If anything, I am sadder that the Liogers will be killed. It has taken me this long to reconnect with them and in forty-eight hours, they will be eradicated. It is not fair. My whole life journey, the secrets, the heartbreak, all culminated in this, my last forty-eight hours on Neo-Earth. There is a cosmic joke somewhere, but I am not laughing.

"Do you hear me, Marra?" Yon's voice drags me back to the present. "I'll make sure that you are safe, I promise." It is strange that Yon wants to keep me safe. Two months ago, we were two people with two separate lives, destined not to meet again if not for the Liogers.

I sit up. "We must save the Liogers, Yon," I tell him. He takes me in his arms.

"Right after we save you," he says.

My wrist communicator beeps. It is the hospital. A simple message scrolls, "Hospital, now."

"Oh my God, Kate!" I say and jump off the sofa. Yon and I run to the hospital. There is still some daylight, but not for long.

We put on our masks and walk straight past the nurses, heading for Kate's room. Then, as we reach it, I turn to Yon and say, "You get yourself tested now. Then, you can come in." Yon's eyes widen with surprise but he does not protest. He nods.

I watch him walk away towards a nurse's station and then press for the door to slide open. My heart tightens with the sight of Kate. She looks pale and weak, not the person I normally see. I can feel wetness gather in my eyes.

Doctor Odam looks up at me as I enter. "Good, you're here. The virus has gained tremendous strength since its initial discovery here in Seven. I think that Kate's general stress has weakened her immune system and this virus moved in even faster. She must have felt ill at least a day ago but did not check herself into the hospital. Her condition has taken a turn for the worse. I want you to know this because …" his eyes meet mine. "just in case." He finishes his thought. Then, he continues in a low tone, "We have already lost five people in the last hour. This is a nightmare."

"What about the vaccine that Linda is making from my blood?"

Doctor Odam shakes his head. "She tells me it is not ready."

"What? Not ready how?" I remember Linda saying that it takes twenty-four hours and about that much time has elapsed. I push the communicator and call her.

"Yes, Doctor Reyes here," she answers after a few seconds.

"Linda, it's Marra," I say. "Is the vaccine ready?"

I hear sounds as if she is hesitating. "We have a first sample, but we have not been able to test it yet and I want to be sure," she says.

"We don't have time for that. Kate's condition has worsened," I say.

"But it hasn't been tested!" I don't have to see her face to know that her eyebrows have shot upwards.

"I'll take full responsibility. Please test it on Kate now. We don't have time," I say. I stare at Doctor Odam, willing him to agree. The way I see it, there is a fifty percent chance that it may work.

"Bring the vaccine over, Linda," he tells her.

"I'll," I hear more hesitation sounds. "I'll bring it over now," she finally says.

When I terminated the communication, Doctor Odam cocks his head to one side. "You are definitely Eva's daughter!" his eyes crinkle and he shakes his head.

Linda arrives ten long minutes later, carrying a case like it contained the world's most precious jewels. Dark circles under her eyes tell me that she has not been sleeping. She nods at me and Doctor Odam when she enters and sets the case down on the bedside table. Opening it, she removes a small vial of an amber, clear liquid and gives it to Doctor Odam.

With a syringe, he removes the liquid content of the vial and then carefully injects it into Kate.

"How long?" I ask, touching Kate lightly. She looks like she could break if I hug her.

"I don't really know," Linda says. "Maybe in the next twenty-four hours or less?" She looks at Doctor Odam for guidance.

I feel suddenly guilty for pushing her. She is young and is probably terrified at such a big responsibility.

"I'm sorry for being ... pushy," I say to her.

Her eyes indicate that she is smiling under her medical mask,

"No need to apologise. I understand. She is special to you. I would have done the same had it been my mother." Linda does not realise the impact her words have on me. Kate is special to me, like a mother.

Doctor Odam and Linda leave me to sit by Kate's side, watching her, noting how thin and fragile she looks. She did not even get to hear the President's announcement. What would she do? Break another pad? I smile at the recollection of that. It must be freeing to take something and just smash it against a wall. I did not know that Kate had that much passion in her.

Her hands feel cold. It breaks my heart to see her like this. "Wake up, Kate," I whisper to her. "So much I need to tell you."

I am interrupted in my thoughts by the door sliding open. Yon walks in quietly and standing behind me, his hand on my shoulder. I take one last, long look at Kate, stand up and look at Yon. His eyes look grim. I nod and we both leave Kate to her quiet slumber.

"Are you alright?" he asks me as we walk out. We both remove our masks at almost the same time.

I nod. Then, remembering, I ask him, "Did you get yourself tested?"

He nods. "We won't know until at least an hour later. Let's go back to the habitation. I'm starving and you must be too."

Back at the habitation, I help Yon prepare the food. We have grown comfortable in each other's company and he appears to have mastered the knowledge of when to speak to me and when to let me be inside my thoughts.

We eat in silence and then watch a video in each other's arms. The feel of his warm body has the effect of gently easing my doubts. It is late afternoon and the sky is dark. Seven is still bright with floodlights. I don't hear the Liogers but know that they are still there, waiting for me.

There is a calmness in the realisation that there is not much that can anyone can do to alter the fate of the world. This is how

I feel. No one can stop the President from killing all the animals and in that moment when the announcement was made, the realisation dropped like a heavy anchor to the bottom of a deep ocean. I wish I could jump on a hovercraft and tell him how wrong he is, or even prevent each canister from falling from the skies into the forests and jungles worldwide. But the reality of life is what my father used to tell me: "You can't save everything and everyone. Sometimes the best you can do is choose who to save and what."

"I've arranged with a friend to fly you out of Seven tomorrow night," Yon tells me.

I look at him blankly.

"I can pilot, Marra and I'll fly you myself out and away from the FSA."

"But to go where, Yon? You heard the President. They are dropping the canisters worldwide. There is nowhere I can go," I say. Hearing it out loud drives home the final nail in my coffin. I cannot outrun this deadly biological agent. This moment may be my one the last on Neo-Earth.

"Damn it! There must be somewhere we can go. I will not have you die because of this, Marra! We'll get you a mask and you can remain in a containment until ..." Yon stands up and paces. He doesn't even know until when.

"Until?" I ask him in a gentle tone. I give him a smile to tell him that I'm alright with whatever that happens. "I like that you are trying to save me."

He gazes into my eyes, an unfamiliar look on his face. "I wish we had more time. We can figure this out. I know we can."

I remember telling my father that I will know when it is time for me to die. He had laughed and told me that no one could know that. I was adamant. I told him I could. I don't know why I said it, but I believed and still do that I will know when death comes knocking at my door. And despite the odds against me now, I don't feel death calling.

"Maybe I'll survive it," I say to Yon. "We don't know," I tell him. I can tell he doesn't believe me.

A two-tone beep sounds, indicating the arrival of a hologram communication. Yon and I look at each other. It is probably for Kate but the person probably doesn't know that. "Answer," I say to it.

Standing in front of us, dressed in a perfectly-tailored white suit, is a gentleman with silver hair, slicked fashionably back. He sports a tan that can only come from living in the tropics. He looks to be a little older than Kate. He stands there smiling, hands behind his back, a friendly twinkle in his deep, grey eyes.

I have never seen him before, but he looks vaguely familiar. Where have I seen him before?

"You're shitting me ..." I hear Yon whisper beneath his breath. I am about to ask him who he is when the older gentleman speaks.

"Hello, Marra! Kate has told me all about you! How are you this evening?" His voice is raspy, as if he has been smoking all his life, a privilege nowadays reserved exclusively for the well-to-do.

The realisation drops with a loud thud, like a heavy object hitting the ground. He looks familiar because I have seen a younger photograph of him some time ago in an article circulated in the CAEP; an article written about the life of our founder's son and current leader of the CAEP, Mr Rupert Sanderson!

CHAPTER 22

"The best time to plant a tree was twenty years ago.
The second-best time is now."
– Chinese Proverb

Yon and I quickly get to our feet. No one, with the exception of the Director of the CAEP, ever sees or speaks with the founding family of our organisation. The Sanderson family has been on the assassination list of pro-human organisations for decades, and they have always kept themselves hidden from public view for their own protection. I hear that even their negotiations with the WPO is done through proxy by their legal representatives.

I am in awe that he knows my name. I stare at the hologram, unable to say a word.

Rupert Sanderson possesses a face that engenders trust, and I can almost imagine that he is a person who smiles at the world as he walks by, hands behind his back. I notice that he has Doctor Odam's thick eyebrows, but tamed and properly groomed. A group of crow's feet gather at the outer edges of his eyes when he smiles as he does now.

"You are even more lovely than I imagined!" he continues to speak in his raspy voice. "You must be wondering why I am calling you."

"Oh!" I finally find my vocal chords. "I thought you are looking for Kate," I say.

"No, no, I know she is indisposed in the hospital. Doctor Odam has been giving me updates every hour. And who is this handsome young gentleman?" he looks at Yon, who has been standing quietly behind me. I have forgotten all about him.

"Yon Hunter, sir," Yon says.

"Ah, the Defence Warrior. Yes, Kate told me about you too. I need to speak to Marra." He turns to me, "Is it ok that Mr Hunter stays here while we have our conversation?" There is a politeness to Rupert Sanderson that can only come from years of private schooling and classes on decorum and etiquette. He feels like a character out of an ancient book.

I nod a little too enthusiastically. "Yes, sir. I have no secrets from Yon," I tell him.

"Alright then," he says. "Marra, Kate told me about your special biology and the vaccine." He pauses, appears to think and then relaunches, "In fact, before I go into all of that, maybe I need to tell you about your father."

I am taken a little aback by this. What would Rupert Sanderson know about my father? He sees my eyebrows shoot up and laughs.

"I didn't think that Rolf told many people about how we knew each other, the old bastard," Rupert Sanderson says, still laughing to himself. I am intrigued. My father who died leaving behind only three shirts and two pairs of trousers was friends with a multi-billionaire?

"Rolf Stollen and I went to school together on the islands. We were both born in Neo-Afrika before the animals took over the continent. He was six years older than I was and his parents, God rest their souls, made him my 'guardian', a big brother of sorts. His parents were close friends of my parents back when they were alive. We grew up together, except that Rolf was never quite the city boy. He preferred running around in the bushes with the Ukuu tribe boys in his 'adventure hat', that dirty old thing handed down to him from his grandfather. Kondo was his best friend. And I guess I was just this annoying child he had to watch out for." Rupert smiles as he recalls his past with my father. He is now seated comfortably in an oversized armchair that seem to make him look small.

"But he was always a kind soul, your father. He took his role as guardian very seriously. Took care of me, made sure I was safe. I never forgot that." I smile. I can easily believe it. My father was the kindest man I knew. His generosity knew no bounds.

"When his parents were killed in the first wave animal attacks, my parents took him in. He was like a brother to me." He is silent for a second, and looks a little sad. "I was devastated when I was told of his death." I feel a pull in my heart, and almost something shared between us.

"I have been following you, my dear. Like he watched over me as a boy, I feel it my duty to watch over his only child." Rupert smiles at me, his eyes shining.

"As you know, everyone at the CAEP is tagged so that we can keep track of your whereabouts in case of ..." he looks up and thinks. "Well, anything really, emergencies, kidnapping, accidents ... you have a tag too, but it can be removed when you leave the CAEP." He pauses and gazes at me. "Now, you know that everyone's identity is linked to iris biometrics." He grins for effect. "YOUR iris biometrics have not been made public. Your father has requested this of me when you were born. Only I have your biometrics. What does this mean? This means that you can go anywhere without anyone knowing. Your current biometrics were constructed to give you an identity, but they are not you. Only your name is correct. Everything else is a construction. It is a safeguard normally reserved for members of my family. We hide in plain sight. No one can find us." He pauses and drinks some water.

I am barely following what he is saying — does this mean that I can disappear?

"I am telling you all this because I would like to bring you to safety. I am unable to convince the WPO to stop this nonsense of releasing the bio agent on the animals. But the good news is that not all countries agree with the solution. That idiot, Gaja bafoon, President Monroe, prefers not to mention that little fact, because he loses credibility when people know that not everyone agrees with him." I notice how his eyes shine brighter when he is upset. I am beginning to like Rupert Sanderson. I see a little of my mother's passion in the man.

He stops talking and looks at me, smiling, as if waiting for a reaction.

"So," I begin. "You're saying that you want to take me out of the FSA?" I ask.

"Precisely. You can stay with us here," Rupert talks as if it is perfectly normal that I am uprooted to go live with him and his family, just like that.

"I'm," I search for the politest way to say it. "I'm grateful, but what about the animals, sir? What about the Liogers and some of the other animals here in the FSA? We can't let them die."

Rupert Sanderson looks at me and frowns, but not unkindly. He appears to be thinking or maybe sizing me up.

"What do you propose, young lady? You know we can't save them all. We do the best we can, but at the end of the day, if the country's government is as stupid as President Monroe, then we cannot do much more."

"I have a connection to the Liogers. We could take them to safety. They are a special hybrid. We cannot let them die." I know now that a little of my parents are in them and I am not willing to sever that connection.

Rupert purses his lips. "Connection how? You mean that you can 'speak' to the Liogers?"

"Not so much speak, sir. But they have saved my life twice. I don't think that they will harm me. I need you to tell the Colonel to allow me access to them through the main gate. I can get them into cages to transport them to safety." I say, a plan forming in my mind as I speak.

"I know your intentions are good, Marra. But I don't know if we even have cages that big for those Liogers …" Rupert says. I have not thought of that. He is right. I have not considered the logistics of transporting giant beasts across the ocean. How will they be able to find anything large enough to contain them? I feel my heart fall into the depths of my stomach.

"We'll see what we can do," Rupert says, probably seeing my face fall. "The issue of course is that we can't take all of them,

Marra. Considering their sizes, I think you must choose." He pauses for a second. "I'll speak to Colonel MacLaren about letting you see the Liogers. I look forward to meeting you in person, Marra. Be ready tomorrow at twenty-one hundred hours. I will send my private aircraft for you." And with that, the hologram blinks out.

I turn to Yon. He is unusually quiet, a preoccupied look on his face.

"Are you alright?" I ask as he turns off his wrist communicator.

He smiles. "I have to get to the hospital."

My eyes widen. "The virus?"

He nods. "But hey, we caught it early, so I'll be fine," except that he does not sound like he believes it.

I take two steps and hug him with a tenacity that I don't normally show. The sudden move must have surprised him because it takes him a split second to hug me back. We stand there in each other's arms for a while. I can hear his heart beat faster than usual through his shirt.

"But I want to help you do this, Marra," Yon says. "At least before you leave." There is an unmistakable tone of regret in his voice. He knows that he cannot follow me where I am going. I hug him a little tighter.

A two-tone beep goes off again, signalling the arrival of another hologram communication.

I stand away from Yon and answer the call.

"So, I get a call from Sanderson telling me to open the gates for you," says the Colonel, his voice hanging somewhere between resentful and curious. "Also to get some very large cargo containers or cages ready? Someone has made quite an impression on the big man."

I sigh. There is nothing that I can say that could make him dislike me less.

"Sir, it's important, yes, sir," Yon says in his Warrior voice, and I feel grateful because I am speechless.

"Hm," the Colonel's eyes narrow. "When would you like to have the gates opened for you?"

I clear my throat. "If it is not an inconvenience, in about half an hour, sir? I want to see them first. We can get the cages ready for tomorrow evening?"

Even Yon looks at me with surprise. It is early evening, but it is bitterly cold outside and the snow has thickened.

I hear an impatient grunt from the Colonel. "Fine! Be here in half an hour. You still have the Humpt, son?"

"Yes sir!" Yon says.

"Right then. See you both later." The Colonel does not wait for us and cuts the communication, something Kate used to do.

"I don't think he likes me very much," I laugh, more out of nervousness than anything else.

"Nah," Yon says as he starts to gather his jacket, gloves and hat. "He's like that with a lot of people. That's just who he is. He is actually alright. You can't always judge a person from their behaviour alone."

I stop and look at him; it's a profound statement that takes me by surprise.

"How do you think Kate is doing?" Yon asks. It has been at least three hours since she received the vaccine.

"Well, no news means good news?" I say, but I am curious to know if the immunity proteins of my blood have made a positive impact on Kate's condition. "We'll check on her later."

"Let's get moving then. The snow is going to slow us down and the Colonel doesn't like to be kept waiting," Yon says.

I turn to step away, then impulsively swing back and plant a kiss on Yon's lips. He looks at me with worry.

"I'm immune, Yon," I tell him and smile. He grabs me and kisses me longer. Then, he gazes into my eyes without a word.

"Yon, I can drive myself to the base. You need to get to the hospital," I say, lying because I hate driving the Humpt and can do it if forced, but badly.

Yon shakes his head. "I promise I'll get to the hospital later. Now, I have to get you to the base. Besides, I want to see you with the Liogers. It will be a first time any human attempts this." That drew a boyish grin from him.

We wrap ourselves as warmly as possible and head out. The air has dropped below zero and the snowflakes look much heavier as they fall in quick succession. Despite this, we arrive at the base with a few minutes to spare. The vibration in my body starts up as soon as we draw close to the gates and my heart begins to race.

The Colonel is already there, looking grim. He is not wearing a mask, which is odd. I thought management or at least people in his position would be obligated to wear the mask to show good example. But then again, the Colonel is not a man who is used to doing what everyone does. I give him a weak nod as I walk towards him.

"Right, let's get you to the Liogers," he says, a tinge of sarcasm in his voice. "But we will have snipers on the wall trained on the Liogers, just in case."

I did not expect that. "Is that necessary?" I ask.

"Hell yeah! What you are asking me to do is ludicrous! If it were anyone but Mr Sanderson, I would ask the person to go take a literal hike in Sector Two!" he snorts. "And if anything were to go south, I want to be prepared, young lady!" The Colonel's voice rises a note higher. "Let's go," he barks.

Yon is hanging back a little and the Colonel turns and looks at him. "You afraid of the Liogers, Warrior?"

"No sir," Yon answers. "I have the virus, sir. I don't want to get too close to you."

"Hell, son," the Colonel laughs. "We've all caught the virus. We have already lost a fifth of the population of Seven and I think that many more will die. But until the virus knocks us down physically, we just have to keep going. Come on, keep up!"

With that, Yon takes his mask off and grins like a man released from stress. I can see why he likes the Colonel. Underneath all that 'bark' is a decent human being.

We stand at the fifty-metre high gates, small and insignificant, looking up at the entire structure. The floodlights are bright and intrusive, too bright in the snow. I don't know how I will be allowed outside. Will they be sliding the gates just large enough for me to step out? Now that I am there, the vibration within my body is mixed with a gripping anxiety. What if I am wrong and I get devoured as I meet the Liogers? What if all this vibration inside me is a ruse created by the giant beasts to lure me to them — or something worse? This is insane.

The hammering inside my chest is increasing. But I cannot change my mind now that I have come this far. Instinctively, I grab Yon's gloved hand.

"Well?" the Colonel looks at me. There is an air of uncertainty written across his face. He doesn't think this is a good idea at all.

"I'm ready," I say, even if I am not.

"The gates are not made to let just one person out. So, this is going to be tricky," the Colonel says, standing with his hands behind his back as if briefing his troop of warriors. "We will slide it open to about a metre wide at which point you will step out. Normally, at one metre width, the Liogers won't be able to get in, too narrow for them." Then he comes close to me, so close I can see his bright blue irises clearly. "I'm only giving you fifteen minutes and then you have to get back in, understand?"

I nod. The Colonel turns and walks away, screaming at everyone to *clear the area*. Before Yon leaves, he hugs me and kisses me, promising that he will be close by watching.

I stand alone in the snow like a spot on a white sheet. The gates loom large and foreboding in front of me, a dark grey tower. It is a daunting thought that soon, those gates that have been protecting the population of Seven for so many years will finally open for the sake of one individual. I hope that I am doing the right thing.

Suddenly, I hear the sound of heavy metal whining, moving for the first time after many years of slumber, dislodging themselves from the ground. The sound is momentary and then the gates slide quietly and slowly. The silence falls heavily over the whole area. All I hear is my beating heart and low growls coming from the other side of the thick gates, almost like group purring.

I don't see any Liogers as the gates part. All I see is a patch of snow and trees in the back that are not illuminated. I walk closer to the gates as they open wider. I can hear the pounding of my heart.

Then suddenly, the gates stop moving, surprising me a little. I take tentative steps forward and out. Then I stand there, not venturing any further, the carphite metal gate right behind me, giving me some comfort and providing some security. My heart is hammering so hard that my breaths are coming out in short spurts, anxiety mixed with excitement.

I don't see them, but I can feel and hear them. They are in the shadows among the trees, where the lights cannot reach. Then, my eyes catch a movement, and slowly, I see a giant, milky white Lioger emerge from the shadows. He saunters in quietly, his head down. I can almost hear the gasps of the Warriors above me on the parapet of the wall. Quite unexpectedly, my heart rate starts to slow down. Something about the Lioger triggers a feeling of calm.

It walks towards me, head lowered, purring. Despite this, he still towers overs me. I estimate the Lioger to be about easily five to six metres tall from the ground to its head, a magnificent beast, all muscles, in a thick, winter coat. He stops about a metre from where I stand and sits heavily on the ground, looking almost as if it is made of snow.

The Lioger is not young. His huge mane has turned silver as has most of its fur. I recognise him as the same animal that looked up at me when I was on the parapet. Despite his age, the Lioger's eyes are still bright and proud. I take small, slow steps towards it. If it hasn't attacked or eaten me by now, then I can safely assume that it will not. My heart rhythm has returned to normal and I inch closer and closer to the enormous creature.

When I am close enough to touch, he suddenly nudges me with his nose, in a movement so affectionate that all fear leaves me. I confidently take the next step and without any warning, the Lioger nuzzles me, with eyes closed. Instinctively, I open my arms and hug its head with the soft mane. It is as if a switch, long forgotten, is flipped on and bits of memory return of a cub I used to play with when I was very young and still living in our forest habitation, a joyful creature I had rolled around on the ground with, played tag and fallen asleep next to each other on the grass.

"Leon!" I whisper. I feel wetness in my eyes. He must be at least eighteen or even close to twenty human years, a very old man, by Lioger standards. Given his age, he will probably not live much longer. I wish I could take back all the years so that I can spend more with him. I feel certain now that it was him who has been tracking and saving me. An old friend, my first in this world.

Then like magic, other Liogers appear out of the shadows, black and white beasts of all ages. They mill around us, cubs and adults. This is his family and from the number of Liogers I see, this is his extended clan. I estimate about fifty of them, all around me like black and white chess pieces, majestic, gigantic, calm. All the adult Liogers are purring and the sound produced is surreal. It seems to envelope me in a cocoon and transport me to another plane, somewhere where is there is nothing but a unified existence.

Some give me a quick nuzzle before moving away, the same way Leon did, as if this is how they acknowledge my presence and acceptance into their group. I can't stop crying. I feel like I finally belong, a feeling that has eluded me for the longest time. I have fleeting images of running around the forest with Leon as a cub and his siblings and riding Leon's mother. All these Liogers carry with them some tiny bit of my parents and through some cosmic accident, I carry part of their blood. We were all created by a cosmic coincidence, which some people would like to call fate.

I count seven cubs in all, three males and four females, and although still very young, they are already as big as I am. With their size, it's hard to imagine that they were born too long ago.

I settle myself on Leon's paw and lean against his mane. I can feel his purring go right through my body into my bones and into my soul, drowning out the vibration I feel within my own body. We are connected this way.

He looks tired and I sense that he is content, maybe from finally seeing me face to face after two decades of being apart. I wish I could hear his thoughts, see where he has been all these years and what he has done. I wish he had come and found me earlier. The list of wishes in my head is long, but I know that none of them can be granted.

"Time to go," I hear the Colonel shout over the parapet. I have totally forgotten that there are HELs trained on the Liogers from up there.

I don't want to leave but know that I must. I stand up and hug Leon again with all the affection I can muster. I can still hear him purring. He nuzzles me playfully as I turn to leave and I turn and hug him a second time. Reluctantly, I walk back towards the gate, looking back at Leon, still seated like a mighty, white Sphinx. As I enter the gates, he gets up slowly, elegantly and saunters back with all the other Liogers into the shadows in the trees. My heart clenches and a lump rises to my throat.

The gates start closing as soon as I am on the inside. I turn and stand watching until I can no longer see the other side. I feel Yon's arm come around my shoulders and turn and hug him.

"Well!" the Colonel's loud voice says next to me. He is standing with his hands on his hips, a smile on his face. "NOW, I have seen everything! I didn't think anything could surprise me, but you did — you did!"

"Can we have the cages ready soon?" I ask him.

"I have already started to have them made. I will make it my mission to get them ready for tomorrow evening! That was impressive!" He walks away muttering and before he is out of earshot, he repeats, "Impressive!"

"Let's go back to the habitation," Yon says. "I'll go to the hospital tomorrow." His smile tells me that he too is impressed.

I wake in Yon's arms. I remember falling asleep quickly. I have not slept this deep and well in a very long time. It feels like every muscle and cell in my body have relaxed in unison and taken a real rest. I look out the window and although it is early morning, it looks like night. I have never had a man in my bed before and the sensation is both good and strange. The good thing is that Yon is a natural bed warmer; his body is like a furnace and in winter, it is ideal. The strangeness thing is that I am not used to sharing my space and it feels like an intrusion, sleeping in an area that used to be all mine.

I look at his sleeping face, the long, upturned eyelashes are still and he is a wonder to behold. I still ask myself what he sees in me, a quiet, awkward girl who is uncomfortable with people, who cannot hold conversations and say witty, funny things, a girl who prefers to walk alone and watch the sun rise and fall from a quiet place. We are so different. He is light and I am dark, he is noise and I am silence.

I very carefully take his arm off my body and put it back on the bed, and then very quietly slip off the bed. I look back and notice that he has not moved except for his chest going up and down in perfect rhythm.

President Monroe's forty-eight-hour deadline ends in a little less than thirty-six hours and I don't want to waste the time I have left. And then there is Rupert Sanderson's promise to take me this night. I take a quick shower and emerge to find Yon staring at me from the bed, smiling.

"Where are you off to so early?" he asks, stretching his body out. Then, he flips back the blanket next to him, pats the empty area next to him and moves his eyebrows up and down twice in quick succession, making me laugh.

I go to him and he wraps me in his arms, smelling my body.

"I want to see how Kate is doing," I say. "And you too have to get to the hospital."

"Oh yes, the hospital," he says with simulated enthusiasm. "I'll prepare us breakfast like a good ... house guest." He kisses me on my shoulder before I get out from his embrace and get dressed.

At the dining table, I look at Yon.

"You are going to the hospital, right?" I ask. He does not look too eager to go.

He nods. "Yeah, I'll go," he says. "But later. You need alone time with Kate."

We have not spoken about what happens when I leave. I don't want to think about it at this moment. I am very fond of Yon and am trying to avoid the pain for as long as I can. It seems that whatever I choose, pain will follow, wherever I go, I will leave a life behind. I cannot bear the thought and so I put it out of my mind for now. I need to concentrate on saving the Liogers.

Kate is still is still in critical condition but I see a smile from Doctor Susan Chao, as I enter the room. She is the chief physician of the hospital. Doctor Odam is not there. It is early in the morning and perhaps he will arrive later.

"Linda's vaccine is working!" she beams. "Kate is getting better, although it will still be another few hours, I think, before she will regain consciousness. I've told Linda. The girl has been working here at the hospital just to monitor Kate's condition."

"Thank you! That's wonderful," I say, beaming. "Will Linda need to take more of my blood?"

"Perhaps. She has been reproducing the vaccine ever since Kate's condition improved. I'll have her call you."

"Will Doctor Odam be coming in later?" I ask.

Susan looks a little surprised. "Oh my God, of course you don't know! Doctor Odam is in intensive care. He collapsed late last night. He has not yet regained consciousness. But the good news is that we have given him the vaccine." She pauses and smiles at me. "In fact, we will be injecting everyone at Seven with the cure starting today. And we will share the formulation of the vaccine with the WPO so that they can roll this out to the general population."

This means that Yon will be vaccinated and will be safe from the virus. This is good news.

"The only thing is that the key protein is in your blood and we can't pump you dry," the doctor continues and sighs.

The notion of being pumped dry of blood does not appeal to me either. But I am happy to give as much as humanly possible. If only there are others like me, but then I remember them.

"The Liogers," I say, my eyes wide with the sudden realisation. This is how I can save the new hybrids. They have the same immunity as me!

"What do you mean?" Susan says, her eyebrows knitting together.

"This is how we save them!" My heart is racing with the thought. The WPO cannot allow the canisters to fall because they will kill the only animals capable of saving humanity! "I have to make a call," I say to her while running out of the room. With Kate still incapacitated, only Colonel MacLaren has access to Rupert Sanderson.

I hear her call out to me as I run down the corridor, "Save who?"

CHAPTER 23

"We stand somewhere between the mountain and the ant."
   – Native American (Onondaga) Proverb

The biologist standing next to me is shaking. He is a middle-aged man with a paunch and thinning hair, and he keeps pushing up the glasses that are already well placed on his nose, a nervous tick, no doubt.

"Tell me again," he asks, his voice unsure and tentative. "You step forward first and when it's safe, I step forward. And then I take a vial of your blood and then you will let me know when I can start taking blood from the Liogers?"

I nod. "You have the special needles for their thick hides?"

"Uhm, yes, yes," and nervously, he looks down and pats the bag he is holding in his left hand. "It will do the trick of taking the blood from Liogers."

"OK then, we're good to go," I turn and smile at him, hoping that it will give him some courage. He looks even more terrified.

The gates are slowly parting. Out of the corner of my eyes, I see him still fidgeting. He is shaking his body, perhaps something he does to help him relax. I hear him exhale and inhale a few times, like a runner getting ready for a long race. I can understand his fear. He will be only the fourth human in decades, after my parents and I, to come face to face with a Lioger. It is enough to terrify anyone.

When the gates are a metre apart, they stop. I turn and smile at the biologist before stepping out. This time, there is no hesitation, Leon comes out from the shadows of the trees and gives me a short roar. I walk towards him and he nuzzles me while I hold him in a hug. I feel happiness swell like a giant balloon, so large that I'm afraid it will burst. Then I turn and walk back to the gates and signal for the biologist to come out.

The other Liogers are starting to exit out of the shadows as well, but half appear content to stay under the trees. They know that the trees hide them. The Warriors cannot target them unless they send in the drones.

The biologist walks out very slowly, clutching his bag to his chest, as if it will protect him. I place him behind me.

"Take my blood now," I tell the biologist. Leon sits on his haunches and makes no move to interfere. It is as I suspected. He will not harm anyone who is with me. My plan is that if he sees me giving blood safely, then it would easier for the biologist to take blood from Leon. The hybrids possess higher cognitive intellect and I am counting on this for Leon to understand what I am asking of him.

I roll up my sleeve, feeling the cold attack my skin straight away. The biologist works quickly and despite his nervousness manages to draw a vial of my blood. I take the vial, roll down my sleeve and walk towards Leon. I bring the vial to his nose and let him smell that it is my blood. He looks at me, his gaze steady.

Then I turn to the biologist and ask him to come close. "Where would you draw the blood from?" I ask.

"The tail," he says. "The skin is thinnest on these hybrids there and it will be less painful." He pushes his glasses up his nose.

I look around Leon and notice that he has his tail curled around him. I reach down and stroke his tail. All of a sudden, he put his whole body down, as if he knows that I want to better reach his tail. I touch his tail lightly and then hold up the tip, which is about as thick as a man's bicep. Leon gazes at me with unflinching eyes. I can feel his mood and he is calm. I stand and look at him, show him the blood, let him smell it and then again touch his tail. I ask the biologist to touch the tail with me and show me where he will be plunging his needle.

I am gauging Leon's temperament. He looks as peaceful as a Blacktail deer. He seems to understand what I want and does not even react when the biologist starts feeling the tail for a vein. When he has found it, he looks at me, his pupils completed dilated from fear.

"This is the place. What do I do?" he asks.

I am down on my knees and start massaging the area of the tail where the needle will be introduced. Then I look at him and say, "Go ahead. Do it."

I can see his hands are shaking. "You must calm down. They can feel your heart beat. Breathe and calm down," I tell him.

He inhales and exhales with exaggeration and then inserts the needle into the area I have been massaging hard with my fingers. I expect Leon to jump, but instead, he turns his head and looks at the others and starts to purr. I don't know how, but I think this is his way of telling the others that he is fine and not to worry.

After the first vial, the biologist's confidence is boosted and he proceeded to quickly draw five more. He packs them all in his bag and smiles at me, relief written on his face.

I ask him to wait. I stand and hug Leon's mane. The vibration in my body is strong as his purring. "Thank you," I whisper.

Then we walk back to the gates and enter. Again, I stand there until the gates close. The biologist has left, running back towards the Humpt. He wants to get the blood as quickly as possible to be analysed for use in the vaccine. We need to make sure that it is the same as mine and compatible with human use.

"Young lady, I can die today and be content that I lived to see THAT!" the Colonel says to me. He has his hands behind his back. "Outstanding!"

"Have you spoken to Mr. Sanderson?" I ask.

"I have and he will request a holo-screen conference with the President of the WPO once we ascertain that the hybrid Lioger blood contains the same anti-viral properties as your blood and can be used," he says. He adds, "By the way, Kate is awake, I've just spoken to her."

I look around for Yon. When I spoke to him earlier, he told me that he will meet me here. Strange that he is not around now. The Colonel notices. "I asked Hunter to get to the hospital. He was coughing quite a bit."

My eyes widen. "But …" I begin to say. I thought that Yon had received his vaccine earlier in the day.

"I have a Humpt ready for you and Denver here," he points his thumb backwards at a young cadet with a face like a twelve-year-old, standing at attention by his side, "will drive you to the hospital," he says.

I nod and follow Denver to the Humpt, saying a quick thanks to the Colonel.

At the hospital, it is not difficult to find Yon. I just follow the sound of laughter. He is sitting in an examination room, surrounded by three pretty nurses, all giggling underneath their medical masks. He does not look too ill to me. Heat rises from the depths of my chest. I stop at the open doorway before they see me, and turn around and walk away. I don't quite understand why I am feeling angry. I decide to look for Kate instead.

She is seated on her bed when I enter. Her hair is tied back but the lines on her face are accentuated in the lighting of the room. A ripple of sadness passes through me. She doesn't look like Kate, the Director of Seven. She looks fragile and vulnerable. I walk up to her and give her a hug.

"Kate!" I smile. "The Colonel told me that you are awake. Are you feeling better?"

"If you mean if I am conscious, then yes, I am better," she tries to laugh and coughs instead. "I heard I was a 'test subject' for the vaccine?" she air-quotes and chuckles. "I'm glad I didn't die. Far too busy to die." And this draws another laugh from her. She takes my hands. "I'm getting all the updates from Cameron, the Colonel, I mean, and I am proud of you, Marra! I wish I was there to see that. Cameron cannot stop talking about it!"

I smile. "I wish my parents were here to see it," I grin at Kate. "I have never felt more alive."

Kate smiles. "Let's hope the WPO listens to Mr Sanderson and cancels the dropping of the canisters. That would be a huge victory for us all."

I suddenly remember that Kate does not know of what happened the night before. "Mr Sanderson spoke to me last night, Kate," I say to her.

A deep furrow forms on her brow. "He called YOU?"

I nod and tell her everything he told me, about how he was like a brother to my father and how I am 'invisible' to the world because my iris biometrics have been kept secret by him at the behest of my father; how this will allow me to disappear from 'the world'; how he has asked me to go and stay with him for protection and that he is sending his private aircraft to pick me up that night.

Kate is listening to all of this intently, the frown not leaving her face.

"What's wrong?" I ask.

"He told you that your father requested that your biometrics be hidden and that only he has your biometrics?"

"Yes," I am starting to worry. Kate appears very serious now.

"And you are sure he said that I told him about your special blood and the vaccine?"

"Yes." My heart rate is starting to increase. Something is definitely wrong.

"It's not safe for you here, Marra. We have to get you out."

"But Mr Sanderson said he will do that, Kate."

"I never told Rupert about you. And only I have your bio-metrics. It was something your father asked of ME, not him. Yes, they grew up together, but your father was never close to him."

My heart feels like it is being squeezed by a vice. I stare at Kate.

"Since I was unconscious, he could, of course obtain infor-mation from someone else about the use of your blood for the vaccine, but the point is that I never told him anything." She purses her lips, "This is now all out in the open. They will want to examine you, not just your blood." She says this mostly to herself, as if thinking out loud.

I remember Linda wanting to *run further tests* on me. I know that Kate is right, but how can I not let them use my blood if it can save people? I have not thought of future implications.

"What about the Liogers then?" I ask. "If I'm not safe then they are not too?" Have I just condemned them to a life of research as well?

Kate looks up at me, realisation in her eyes. She reaches for her communicator and keys something in.

"Director?" Linda sounds surprised.

"Linda, communicate the results of the hybrid Lioger blood compatibility ONLY to me, do you understand? I will handle the rest. Is that crystal clear?" Kate is using the voice normally reserved to scare everyone into doing what she wants them to do.

I hear Linda stammer her agreement at the other end. And Kate cuts the line. I can imagine Linda's frail self-esteem taking a beating from that abrupt end to the conversation. I sigh silently, Kate is back to being the Director again.

Then, Kate looks at me, her eyes look like how my mother's used to appear just before she told me something important, something I was meant to remember.

"Sometimes," she says, "noble intentions are remembered only as long as it serves a purpose. Humanity has a short memory, Marra. Look at the state of our world today. We continually make mistakes, even after we supposedly learn not to make them. It is not enough to give a hand, they will want the whole body."

She holds my hand. "The reason I loved your parents so much was because they were unique in the way they saw the world. They were the most optimistic people I have ever met. They believed in the system, in the collective consciousness. They reminded me that there were still good and kind individuals out there. But people like them often gave their lives to a world of politicians who do not care whether or not Neo-Earth is a better place.

"When they died, I think my faith in humanity was also lost until I saw how you grew up. You remind me that kindness and goodness exist, and it is my job not only to keep you safe but also to open your perception to people who are not like you. I don't want you to be disappointed in the world."

Kate looks out at the window, her thoughts faraway. "Look at Liam. Like millions of people on Neo-Earth, he lost his home and family. He was given a great opportunity to study and gather the accolades he did, and instead of using his opportunity to do good, he used it to plan a worldwide revenge on the animals, on all animals regardless of whether they were responsible for his family's deaths. He took the deaths personally, as if he was the only person hurt." I hear Kate sigh, as if doing it relieves her a little of the heaviness weighing her down. She turns back her gaze to me and this time, it is not sorrow I see but something more ferocious. "I want you to leave, Marra. The CAEP is no longer safe for you. I want you to go somewhere where you cannot be found, not even by Rupert Sanderson."

I stare at Kate, shocked. Where will I go? I thought that if the canisters don't fall, I can stay in the FSA. I think of Yon. He will be here.

"Trust me, Marra," Kate says, her eyes shining with determination. "I will make some calls. Now go. Get ready." Then, she pulls me into her embrace and hugs me as strongly as she can.

I leave the hospital, my heart heavy and head for the habitation. She wants me to get ready. I don't know if I want to.

The habitation is empty and I am thankful. I collapse on the sofa. I need the silence to recharge and to think. Not too long ago, all I wanted was to leave the FSA and see the world. Now, nothing would make me happier than to stay, to have a life with Yon. With the exception of Kate and Yon, I no longer know who to trust.

If Kate had not caught Sanderson's lie, what would have happened had I gone with him? What would he have done to me?

And if I brought him the new hybrid Liogers, would I have condemned them to a life of needles and tests? Kate may be right, if people knew that their blood has super healing properties, they will be hunted for it. Animals in the centuries before had become extinct after being hunted for 'medicinal' properties they possessed.

What will Kate do with the information about the new hybrid's blood? Will she tell Sanderson? Whether or not the deployment of the canisters happens, the situation for the Liogers is bleak. And if I cannot save them all, I would like to save Leon. And if the cages are big enough, maybe more of them.

I grab my jacket and head back to the hospital. While walking, I see Yon approaching in the opposite direction. He has just left the hospital, no doubt. I can feel his grin even before I see his face. He grabs me and swings me around in his exuberance.

"Where are running to?" he asks, planting a wet kiss on my nose.

"To the hospital to see Kate," I say.

"I was just there! I got my shot," he says.

"Yes, I know," I say and continue walking towards the hospital. Standing around when it is freezing cold is not a good idea. Yon walks next to me.

"You were there?" he asks.

"Yep."

"And you didn't come and find me?"

"You were busy and I went to see Kate instead."

Yon starts laughing and grabs my waist to stop me from walking.

"What?" I say, trying to seem like nothing is wrong. I can still hear the giggles of the nurses with Yon.

"Stop," he says, still laughing while I find nothing amusing. Then, very gently, he holds my face in his gloved hands, and kisses my lips for a few seconds. "There is no one I care more about than you, Marra Stollen. Not even the nurses of all of Seven can make me change my mind."

I continue to look at him while he holds my face prisoner. I am forced to look into his eyes, green like spring leaves. I feel an aching in my chest. How can I leave him?

"What's wrong?" he sees that his words have no effect on me.

"Come on, let's get out of the cold," I tell him and grab his hand as I continue on to the hospital.

We find a tiny, empty utility room and cram ourselves into it, standing facing each other.

"I almost made a mistake. Kate caught it before it got worse," I say.

"What mistake?"

"Taking Leon's blood. I should not have done that." I tell him.

"I don't get it," Yon says. "Tell me what you mean."

"Even if the canisters don't fall, they will be hunted for their blood. I thought I could save them ... but I might have condemned them to a life of testing and experimentation."

"You didn't do anything wrong. You did what you thought was right. And besides, 'might have' ... Kate caught it, right?"

"Also ..." I say, "Sanderson was lying. Kate never told him about me or my blood or the use of it for the vaccine. Why would he lie?"

Yon's eyes widen a little and then his brows knit together as he reflects on the question. "Maybe because he can. I don't know. Maybe he wants you all to himself with your special blood. He thought that Kate was unconscious and he could easily take you away. He just didn't count on the vaccine working so quickly."

"But why not just ask Kate?"

At this, Yon smiles. "Marra, have you seen how Kate is with you? You're like her daughter. She would never let anyone take you, not even Sanderson."

"What do you think he wants with me?"

He thinks for a moment. "Your blood is special, Marra. A vaccine for the world's viruses can be sold very expensively," Yon says.

My eyes grow large with disbelief. "He won't kill me!"

"No, he won't," he pauses, his voice cautious. After a second or two, he continues, "You're more valuable alive. Maybe that's why he wants to bring you to him."

I look at Yon, not quite understanding.

"If you are there and he gains your trust, it will be easier to have you contribute your blood. And maybe even use your connections to the Liogers to get their blood."

We stand there silently for a second or two. I feel my resolve solidifying and strengthening as I ponder the situation in my head.

"Yon, I have to take the Liogers away from here. Away from here to someplace where they can be free and safe."

Yon does not say anything. I know he is thinking that it is impossible to save all fifty of the Liogers.

"Is that why you are going to see Kate?" he asks instead.

I nod. "Kate wants me to leave the FSA. Go somewhere no one can find me, not even Sanderson. She doesn't trust him anymore."

We both know what my departure would imply and so we just let the silence embrace us.

"Well," Yon finally says, his voice laced with something akin to disappointment. "Kate loves you and wants what's best for you. If she thinks you're not safe here, then she has good reason to think that way."

"I want to speak to her again. Come with me," I say. "I want you to know everything."

CHAPTER 24

"The best way to predict the future is to create it"
– Abraham Lincoln

Kate has made her hospital room an office in the short time since I last saw her, which I find impressive. She has even summoned Francois, who is sitting in a corner. I assume that he has been vaccinated, but he still has his mask on. With him, it is probably a fashion statement. He has brought his pad with him and is busy typing something. Kate's head is bent over her own pad, reading a report, her spectacles dangling at the end of her nose. She has combed and tied back her hair and looks a little better than earlier, almost the old Kate I know. She looks up and smiles when Yon and I walk in hand-in-hand.

"I was wondering when that would happen," she says, waving her finger over the general area of our hands and then smiling to herself. I consciously let go of Yon's hand, feeling badly right after for having done so. If he is upset at me for doing that, he does not show it at all.

"I'm glad you are here, Marra. I was about to call you. Francois," Kate looks over at the young man. He looks up, expressionless. "Take a break. I'll call you in later."

"I want to take some of the Liogers away from here, Kate," I say as soon as the door closes. Yon goes and stands by the window, listening.

Kate takes off her spectacles. Her gaze is steady and unchanging.

"I will leave if I can take some Liogers with me," I say. "It was what we planned before. I am sure that the Colonel would have the large cages by now.

"We cannot use Mr Sanderson's cargo carrier, Marra. The whole point is to get you out somewhere no one can find you," Kate says. "I've contacted old friends of your parents and mine. They are a powerful family and discreet. They have all the resources necessary to take you to safety."

I frown. "And you trust them?"

"With my life," she says. "They are family to your father."

"But I thought dad went and lived with the Sandersons?"

"He did, but his best friend's family were the people he was really close to. They were not powerful back then, but they are today and they are one of the most respected ancient families on Neo-Earth." Looking at my blank face, Kate adds, "Kondo's family."

"Kondo? What can they do?"

"They have volunteered to help take you out of the FSA."

"Can they also take the Liogers?"

Kate purses her lips and reflects silently. "Why is it that important to you to take the Liogers?" she asks, not unkindly.

"They …" I begin and hesitate, "We have the same blood. We are hybrids, them and me. And they are my last connection to my parents," I reply.

This must have moved Kate because she sighs and types something into her pad. "There, I have messaged them to get here in a super cargo carrier. Even if they can take the Liogers, they cannot take all of them. So you must make a choice, Marra. And this will not be easy."

"Where will they take me?"

"I don't know and for now, it is better that I don't. But once you are safe and the situation is calm, they will tell me."

I hear Yon shift and look over to him. He is looking out the window, his brows knitted together and a shadow of sadness on his face.

"He can't go with you," Kate says, reading my thoughts. As she gets stronger, her old habits are returning, especially her inability to be tactful.

Yon shifts again, looking down at his shoes. I go and stand next to him by the window and hold the hand that I released before. Kate watches us and I understand her enough to know that the cogs of her mind are turning. I grip Yon's hand even tighter. I want him to know that I care about him as much as he does about me.

"At least not at this time," Kate says. "Yon can join you later, when things have calmed down."

"Would she not need protection, Ma'am?" Yon says, a note of hope in his voice.

Kate smiles. "She will be protected when she gets there."

There is a buzz and door slides open. Colonel Cameron MacLaren strides in, smiling like he has just had a good meal.

"We having a party?" he grins.

"What's the situation, Cameron?" Kate smiles, ignoring his quip.

"Well, I have the cages made for the Liogers, but I guess we won't be needing them where Marra is going?"

I look quizzically at Kate. Does the Colonel know?

Kate catches my gaze. "Cameron is an old friend of mine as well as your parents and one of a handful of people I do trust," she says, answering the question I was thinking of.

"We will be using the cages. I have transmitted a text message for them to come in a cargo carrier."

"And what's the situation with Sanderson? You still not letting him know that you are awake?" the Colonel asks Kate.

Kate shakes her head. "The doctors are under strict orders not to say anything. This will give us more time if he thinks that Marra does not know about his lies," she says. "He's still waiting on the result of the hybrid Lioger blood. We'll let him wait but eventually tell him that it is not compatible for the vaccine. My priority is to get Marra away from here."

There is a faint buzzing sound and Kate checks her pad. "The cargo carrier for Marra will arrive in about four hours."

"What's going to happen when he finds out that you've whisked Marra away?" the Colonel asks.

"He can fire me. I don't care," Kate sighs. "I'm done with all this."

"Oh no, you're not done!" the Colonel says. "Who's going to run this human zoo with me? Don't you think about leaving just yet."

As they laugh quietly. I realise how little I know Kate, who her friends are and the people she trusts. Then, I remember she said the carrier is arriving in four hours. That is very little time in which to prepare to leave my life behind.

"Best you start packing, Marra. Get to the gates and Cameron … the Colonel will help," Kate tells me. "I'm going to get out of this hospital and meet you at the airfield later. But before leaving the hospital, go and see Doctor Chao, she will remove your locator chip."

Yon and I walk hand-in-hand out into the bleak afternoon. The snow has stopped, but the wind is bone-chilling. Life is returning to Seven as people are making their way to the hospital for their vaccination. People are starting to smile again.

I don't even know where I will be taken to. If I had not met Yon, all this could have been an adventure, but Yon changed everything.

I pack what little I have, including my box of animals, some digitals and my father's hat. Yon sits on the bed watching me.

"I'll find you, you know," Yon says.

I look at him. I have never seen him sad and it makes my heart ache. "I will send you word on where I am. I'll make it cryptic, like a riddle," I say and smile. "We can communicate that way." I go and sit on the bed next to him.

"Where do you think they'll take you?" Yon asks, trying to sound like we are having just another normal conversation, but failing miserably.

"I have no idea. I have never met Kondo's family. I don't even know if they will really come with the cargo carrier." I am trying to put to memory every detail of his face.

"But you'll be safe and that's the most important." He kisses me on the forehead and then gets up and pulls me off the bed. "No time to mope, Stollen. You've got some Liogers to save." He smiles. My heart swells and I pull him in for a final kiss, just to be the brave one for a change.

I am impressed with the Colonel's efficiency. He has somehow managed to have constructed three giant cages and each is loaded onto an enormous cargo land vehicle. Even as I look, I know that that there will not be room to save them all. Leon alone will fill one cage on his own. My heart sinks. A hard choice awaits me.

The vehicles are lined up side by side with their back end towards the gates, and the cages ready to receive the Liogers. The idea is to open the gates to the exact width of the three vehicles so that the Liogers can hop onto the cages from the back of the vehicles.

When the gates open, I step out onto the snow and look around. My body is vibrating wildly and I know that they are close.

Then I see Leon emerge. I run to him and he lowers his head so that he can nuzzle me. It has become our greeting. The other Liogers, on cue, start to come out. I look all around me. How can I decide which to save?

I don't have a lot of time and so I go to a cage and start to bang on it, crying out to Leon at the same time. He just sits there and stares at me with his cool, steady look.

"Come on, Leon," I say. "Come to the cage. Let's go away together."

Nothing happens for a few minutes and I am not sure what to do next. I go up to him and start to try to push him up, but it is a futile effort because it is like trying to move a mountain with your hands. If anything, it appears to amuse him and he lies down on the ground.

"This is not a good time to sleep, Leon! Come on, let's go!" I tug at his paw. He looks at me and blinks lazily. I must look comical from the viewpoint of those up on the parapet, like a little girl trying to move a giant cat.

I stand and look at him. He eyes me with complete indolence, purring. Exasperated, I make a last attempt. "Leon! Cage!" I shout, pointing to the cages. That may have triggered something because he raises his body, stretches his head upwards as if about to howl and emits a light cough roar.

Then, slowly, I see Liogresses nudge their young cubs forward. And then I understand. They don't want to save themselves, but they want their cubs safe. The cubs mewl in protest but the adults keep nudging them forward and one by one, they climbed up onto the cages. It makes sense. The cages are too small for giant Liogers but can easily fit all seven cubs. There is one last cage empty and I want Leon to take it. I pull at him without any success. He refuses to move.

I sit with him, hearing him purr and knowing that he has accepted his fate. He is an old man and likely wants to die on the land he was born. We both watch the cubs jump up and down the cages, playing with each other. I wonder if they realise that they will never see their families again. It feels wrong to take them, but it seems like this is a sacrifice the Liogers are willing to make.

Then, quietly, still purring, Leon gets up. I stand up too and watch him towering over me, and he lowers his head so that I can touch his forehead and nuzzles me. I feel his purr reverberate through my body; it is in my bones, in my muscles, in my head and heart all the way into my soul. I close my eyes and hold on with my outstretched arms as much as I can, his giant head. Then, he moves. I look up and know that he is leaving, his eyes tell me that.

Panic grips me all of a sudden. I don't want him to leave. "No, not yet," I tell him, but he is already turning and the others are following.

"Leon!" I cry out. He turns his head around to look at me, as if saying good bye and then turns back to the direction of the dark forest and continues on his way. I hear a loud bang and look back. A jet black, adult Liogress has climbed up on the remaining empty cage. She is probably there to ensure the safety of the cubs, a sacrificial gesture for the pride.

I stand there and watch them disappear into the darkness of the forest until I can no longer see any movement. My eyes are wet and my heart feels like it has been cut into a million pieces. I know that I will never see Leon again.

I feel a gentle hand on my shoulder and turn to see Yon's face, sombre, full of kindness. I am confused. How is he out here? I look back and see that the cages are closed and the trucks have started to move away and the gates are closing.

"Come with me," I hear Yon tell me. My mind is still in a whirl. He gently guides me back to within the wall. I look back one last time, hopeful that I will see Leon staring at me from the trees. I see only darkness. The pain in my heart is almost as deep as when my parents died, a cutting, sharp sensation that makes it difficult for me to breathe.

Inside the wall, Yon takes me in his arms, but I feel no comfort. Then my mind gathers itself and I remember that I am now responsible for the cubs and the Liogress that have voluntarily put their lives in my hands.

"I have to be with the Liogers," I say.

His eyes tell me that he is concerned, but he nods and says nothing. We walk towards his Humpt. I see the Colonel standing some distance away. His empathy and thoughtfulness surprise me. He has allowed me the space to grieve and for that, has won some points of respect from me. I nod at him and he nods back.

Yon drives me, throwing me concerned glances, while I stare out the side window in silence. The aching in my heart has morphed into a kind of numbness. I concentrate on the darkness outside, on clearing my mind of thoughts, on breathing.

It's a short drive to the airfield. I did not hear the giant cargo carrier arrive while with the Liogers. It is parked there, a massive, dark, metallic bird with the back of it gaping open to receive the enormous cages. It is a wonder that something that huge can fly. Yon parks close to the aircraft as the cages are being gently trolleyed into the space provided and then locked in. I hear the cubs mewling and the Liogress panting. She sounds stressed.

I leave him behind by the Humpt and walk to the cages where she is. She is circling inside the cage, and I can sense her fear. I push my body right next to the bars and she stops and comes over, head down. We nuzzle through the cold carphite steel and I can feel her heartbeat slowing down. I understand her fear because I too am worried about the unknown future that awaits us both.

"That is incredible!" I hear a female voice say behind me.

I turn and am greeted by the sight of a dark-skinned, stunning young woman with high cheek bones and light-brown eyes. I can't see her hair through the cap she is wearing to protect her from the cold, but I am guessing that it would be black. She looks to be from the Neo-Afrikan continent. I hear that the tribes now live in different parts of the COE.

"I am Amani," she holds out her hand to shake mine. Her voice is tinged with an accent that I cannot place; she rolls her r's distinctly. I notice that her teeth stand out dazzling white against her perfect, flawless dark-brown face.

"Marra," I say.

"I know! I am your captain!" She is impressing me more and more. I have never met a female, Neo-Afrikan captain.

I see Yon walking towards us. "And that is Yon," I say.

"Yes, we have met just now," she says, still smiling that full-face toothy smile of hers.

"How far are we going?" I ask when Yon comes and puts his arm around my shoulders, and then adds, "Where are you going?"

Her smile does not leave her face as she shakes her head. "Let's say that it is a seven-hour flight. Can you imagine that long, long ago, this would have taken over fifteen hours?" She makes a strange lip-smacking sound that I am not even sure how to produce. "That's what I like about technology and innovations, when they actually improve our lives!"

A man arrives and stands next to Amani. "Hi!" he says brightly. He is not as tall as Yon, but looks fit and tanned. He is not sporting a military haircut and so I assume that he is not a Warrior. "I'm Olaf!" he says.

"My very capable co-pilot whom I am sure will take my captain seat from me soon," Amani says and then adds, "IF I let him!" They both burst out laughing like it is the best joke in the world while I look on.

He whispers something to Amani's ear while she nods. Then, she turns to me, all smiles again. "The animals are secure. We have provided them food and water. We must be off." Her smile suddenly switches off like a light. "You may want to say your goodbyes, Marra," she tells me kindly squeezing my arm lightly before walking away, giving Yon a quick nod.

A stab of panic hits me. I don't want to say goodbye. I look around and, in the distance, I see a Samuelson approaching us at top speed. That must be Kate. I look up at Yon and see that sorrow is written in his face.

"I don't want to leave you," I say to him and hug him. The ache in my heart is starting to throb.

I feel Yon kiss the top of my head and then rest his head on mine. We stand there in each other's arms until Kate arrives and stands next to us.

"Marra," she says. I turn and see that her eyes are brimming with tears, which is an uncommon look for Kate. I step away from Yon and go towards her. We hold each other like how I used to hug my mother.

"Kate, it's too early," I say. "I need more time."

"Oh, my sweetheart," this is the first time that Kate has ever used a term of endearment with me. "We have to get you going earlier because the situation has changed."

"What do you mean?" I ask, the vibration in my body is starting up again and I can feel the Liogress behind me, pacing in her cage. She feels it too, the dread, the darkness.

"Since we lied to Sanderson that the Lioger blood is not compatible, they will deploy the canisters as planned tomorrow. Sanderson is not happy. Said we wasted his time. But the biggest problem is that someone leaked to him that I am awake and he is sending his men over to retrieve you now. I think that they are getting ready to leave his location this minute," Kate looks at me, the usual fire in her eyes is replaced by something softer, more vulnerable. "We have to get you airborne."

"What's going to happen to all of you here?" I ask. The longer I can delay this, the longer I can stay.

"I'm ordering gas masks for everyone at Seven and we will be in complete lock-down tomorrow; all windows and doors shut. We will begin our evacuation to the COE where the European CAEP Centre is located, as soon as we can, depending on how much time it takes for the gas to dissipate to a safe level."

I listen to all of this in horror. Leon and his pride are in Sector Seven and probably heading back to Sector Three. They will be killed!

Kate appears to read my thoughts. "There is nothing we can do for the other Liogers, Marra, but there is something you can do for the cubs and the female you saved. You have to get yourself and them out of here now before Sanderson's men arrive."

I look at Yon and he is subtly wiping away his tears at the realisation that my departure is close at hand.

"Kate," I begin.

"Get on that carrier, Marra Stollen!" she orders me, but I hear a crack in her voice.

I hug her and this time, my tears fall as do hers. "I love you, Kate," I say to her for the first time.

"I love you too, dear girl," she tells me. Then she holds me at arm's length. "This is not goodbye. I will see you again, alright? We will see each other again." She hugs me one last time and Kate-like, she turns and walks slowly away, not looking back, supported by the Colonel who has also arrived in the meantime.

I turn and look at Yon who is trying to look brave, but I can see that his eyes are moist.

"I wish I could come with you," he tells me. I nod. I wish I could be with him for a long time. He takes me in his arms and holds me tightly and whispers in my ear, "I love you, you know. I think it started a long time ago when I first met you. I wish I'd told you sooner."

I kiss him. I don't know exactly how love is defined, but I know that I can see a future with Yon, living together, listening to his terrible jokes, laughing together, and then just like that, I suddenly know. "I love you too." I tell him and I can feel him hug me tighter.

"I will find you, Marra," he reminds me.

"Not before I find you," I tell him.

I look out the window for as long as I can until Seven has dissolved into the surrounding trees. I say a silent goodbye to Leon, somewhere down there, my friend who has been tracking me faithfully all these years. The cargo carrier is faster than it looks as we are soon above the clouds gliding smoothly over the stratosphere. I look over at my charges, the Liogress is asleep while one or two of the cubs are still playing but the others are all taking a nap. Some cubs are lying on their backs, their four legs up in the air, which makes me smile.

I walk around the cages looking at the sleeping faces. Like me, they are now exiled from the land they were born. The two cubs in one of the cages that are still playing comes to me and stares at me with the liquid gold eyes that look like mine, licking the bars and then my hand. I put my head close to where they are and instinctively, one of them places its forehead against my face. I feel their questions and the bewilderment over their predicament. I reach in and tickle each under their jaws. My heart is still aching from the thought of those I have left behind. I don't know when I will see them again. I think of Yon. Our time together was so short.

Tomorrow the canisters will fall and that will be end of all the animals in the FSA. I don't want to think of how they will die. I don't believe a word of what President Monroe said about it being a painless death. I would like to see him inhale a lungful of the biological agent.

I go to my seat and close my eyes, thinking of all the things that could have been, which brings out such sorrow that I think my heart will break into two. Therefore, I close my eyes and beg for sleep to claim me for a while, to numb my pain. I am exhausted.

I open my eyes when I hear Amina's cheerful voice over inter-communication line.

"Marra," she beckons me, in a playful sing-song voice. "You may want to look out the window."

Have seven hours already passed? I must have fallen asleep. The Liogers are up and I can feel their excitement. What is out there? I see bright sunshine. When we left Seven, it was late afternoon and the sky was dark. I wonder where we are and what time it is here. I look out the window as Amina suggests and involuntarily suck my breath in shock.

Wherever I am, the sun has already risen but not too long ago because it is still not high in the sky, and the land is bathed in the orange tinge of early morning. The land below is a vast expanse of brown and green plains as far as the eye can see. There are oases of trees here and there and bodies of water. I see a large group of animals, a monstrous group, grazing. What are they? From this distance, they are still indistinguishable, but then, I see another large group of animals, majestic giants and visible due to the enormous sizes — Gajas!

I remember seeing this place in my father's old geography video logs, a land in which both my parents wanted to live. My father told me once that it was where he grew up — the place I was named after.

Oh my God!

"Welcome to Neo-Afrika, my friend!" Amina's voice echoes throughout the space in the aircraft.

I stare in wonder.

EPILOGUE

"New beginnings are disguised as painful endings."
– Lao Tzu

15 September 4849

I am late and running as fast as I can manage. Bahati is running alongside me, or mostly in front of me. He is much faster and he knows it, but he looks back, slows down for me once in a while to help me catch up.

He has grown in the last months and I think he may be even bigger than his father.

"Go, go!" I urge him on. He is happiest when running, I can tell. He has returned late last night from weeks away and I am always happy to see that he is still playful. Neo-Afrika can be a dangerous place for a young Lioger still getting used to the lay of the land. The others are more independent but somehow, Bahati has bonded more closely with me. He reminds me of Leon.

The Lions of Neo-Afrika are magnificent creatures. They are unlike the hybrids we had in the FSA, even if here too, Mother Nature has made them enormous. From my observations, there have not been interspecies mating that have produced the hybrids we saw in the FSA. For this reason, I have chosen to use their ancient name. I think my parents would agree. The Lions here have retained their natural, genetic coat, the colour of wheat.

The new hybrid Liogers that I brought over are much larger than they are. The cubs and the female hybrids were the first black and white Liogers on the continent and hunting has not been easy for them because they cannot blend into the surroundings. But after many months of bonding with the local Lions, many have gone off to live their own lives with the local prides. It would appear that the Lions have also evolved with higher cognitive functions similar to the Liogers and the two species seem to understand the advantages of their combined strengths. I am curious what other hybrids will be produced from their mating.

Only Bahati refuses to leave me. He disappears sometimes for weeks on his hunts but he always returns. He seems to have luck on his side, or maybe it is because I named him that way.

"Do you hear it?" I ask him while he looks at me with uncomprehending eyes. I have reached the location I was told to wait at. "Do you see it?" I scan the skies for a sign. Nothing yet. People may think me crazy for talking to a Lioger, but I think he can understand me.

I live on a hill, surrounded by beautiful trees overlooking the savannah grassland of the Eastern part of Neo-Afrika. I live in the ancient home once belonging to my father's family, before he was moved to the city to live with the Sandersons. The Ukuu tribe has prepared it for me. They live about five kilometres away in their own little village. We visit each other sometimes and especially at special occasions, like the anniversary of the deaths of Kondo and my parents.

The canisters did not fall here because Neo-Afrika is supposed to be devoid of humans and therefore spared by the WPO. The rest of the world thinks that it is uninhabitable given all the giant animals that have overtaken the continent. It has been declared off-limits to humans a long time ago. So, no one will look for me here.

Some of the Ukuu, however, returned in secret decades ago and continue their lives among the animals. They believe and have proven right that the animals tolerate humans who are respectful of their territory. As long as we don't threaten them needlessly, they leave us alone.

I live on my own but once a month, Amina arrives on a small

hovercraft and brings me food, although I have less and less need of that now that my vegetable garden is growing well. She lives in the COE and spends a night here with me in my house when she visits. She teaches me Swahili. We have become very close, like sisters.

She brings me news of the world; how the FSA is now plagued with another virus and this time, they cannot blame it on the animals because they have killed them all. My heart still hurts every time I think that no animal and insects have survived the deadly biological agent unleashed by the canisters. Without any creatures to pollinate, the FSA is now experiencing famine and has declared a state of emergency. The WPO is now helping them cope with the food shortages.

She tells me how the COE decided at the last minute against releasing the agent and has now implemented a strict virus check at all their borders. In fact, viral body checks are now standard everywhere.

The CAEP has moved permanently out of the FSA and now only the COE division is left. Mr Sanderson was furious with Kate for going against his orders and forced her to resign from her post. They apparently tried to find out where I am and since Kate herself doesn't know, there was nothing they could get out of her. The Colonel has also resigned and Amina tells me with a wink that she thinks Kate and the Colonel are more than friends.

I look at the skies again. And then I see it, a tiny dark spot growing larger and larger. I feel a bump on my side and turn to see that Bahati is seated on his haunches next to me. He now towers above me, a giant, milky-white Lioger, still in his teenage years. He looks up at the sky with me, a look of puzzlement on his face.

"You'll see," I tell him and give him a quick hug. He is not only my sole friend here; he has also taken it upon himself to become my protector as well.

Suddenly, I hear it, the thwop, thwop, thwop of an approaching hovercraft. My heart starts pounding. I am nervous and yet deliriously happy all at once.

The hovercraft lands a few hundred metres away and I start running towards it, asking Bahati to stay where he is because he is too large and may be hit by the hovercraft blades. As I run, I see the cabin door slide open and a tall, dark-blond man, whose eyes I know are the colour of forest leaves in spring, jumps out and starts running towards me.

The End

ABOUT THE AUTHOR

"A fiction novel is a creation of the author's imagination, moulded by held beliefs."

Michelle Tanmizi is Chinese-Indonesian and has lived in various countries. She currently resides in Singapore. Besides being an Author, she is a leadership coach and trainer, and a motivational speaker.

Michelle's first literary work was a self-published poetry book in 2002, *Truth*. In 2007, she was a freelance writer for the former *Isalsa* magazine. In 2013, she was a contributing author of *Conscious Business*, part of the bestselling *Adventures in Manifesting* series of books, available at select book distributors. In 2014, she spoke at TedxTalks of the Hong Kong University of Science and Technology.

In her personal blog, https://mymohio.wordpress.com, Michelle writes about her beliefs and philosophy of life, hoping her articles will influence people positively. It is philosophy according to her experience and work with clients, from asylum seekers and trauma victims to executive leaders. She is an advocate of human resilience, impressed with how a person can rise from the brink of despair to achieve goals previously thought unattainable.

Environment and conservation issues also interest Michelle and she reflects her thoughts about them in her writing. She loves nature and animals and her eighteen months of voluntary work in East Africa has positively influenced how she sees the world today.

As an Author, she wants her stories not only to be exciting but also thought-provoking and to leave a positive, lasting impression on the reader; maybe even move people to improve the planet.

Late Dawn is her first speculative science fiction novel inspired by the conservation crisis we face today. She is now writing her second novel and a series of short stories.

MORE FROM THE AUTHOR

Michelle is available for speaking engagements and creative writing workshops. Please write to enquire.

If you are a member of the media and would like to request an interview with Michelle Tanmizi, please contact her at:

E-mail: MichelleTanmizi.Author@gmail.com

Mobile Telephones: +65 9193 7849 (Singapore)
+852 9616 8983 (Hong Kong)

Giving a Voice to Creativity!

Wouldn't you love to help the physically, spiritually, and mentally challenged?

Would you like to make a difference in a child's life?

Imagine giving them:
confidence; self-esteem; pride; and self-respect.
Perhaps a legacy that lives on.

You see, that's what we do.
We give a voice to the creativity in their hearts,
for those who would otherwise not be heard.

Join us by going to

HeartstobeHeard.com

Help us, help others.